BOSS GIRL

EMMA TALLON

bookouture

Published by Bookouture in 2019

An imprint of StoryFire Ltd.

Carmelite House
50 Victoria Embankment
London EC4Y 0DZ

www.bookouture.com

ISBN: 978-1-78681-590-3
eBook ISBN: 978-1-78681-589-7

As always, this book is dedicated to the love of my life.
My centre of gravity, my son – Christian.

PROLOGUE

She groaned and put her hands up to her head. *Why does it hurt so much? When did I fall asleep?* She opened her eyes groggily and pulled herself upright. She blinked and frowned as she looked around. She was in a room that could have almost been her own bedroom at home. Except it wasn't. *Where on earth am I?*

Trying to shake off the thick fuzz still swirling in her brain, she stood up, staggering. She squeezed her eyes shut for a moment as the throbbing intensified, but shook it off. She needed to focus. Why couldn't she remember how she got here? She tried to think back. They had been in a car. Someone had given her something to drink, said it would make her feel better… She froze. That was the last thing she could remember. It must have been drugged. *Why would anyone try to drug me?*

Her eyes darted around the room and widened as they settled on a camera in the top corner of one wall. She was being watched. Her heart thudded against her chest.

Panic set in and she raced to the door and tried to open it. It was locked. She put both hands on the handle and used all her strength to try to force it open, but it was no use. The door held fast. Ice speared through her stomach as the realization of how bad the situation was dawned on her. Her eyes flew around the room, looking for something, anything, that she could use to get herself out of here.

Rushing to the window, she grappled with the slatted wooden blinds, trying impatiently to move them out of her way. Grasping the rope pulley to the side she yanked it, pulling the blinds up.

She opened her mouth to shout, ready to fight for her freedom. But before a sound could escape, she paused in shock. She was not confronted by the tall buildings and busy streets of London that she had been expecting. Outside the window, there was nothing but miles and miles of untouched, wild countryside.

She backed away from the window as horror and fear washed over her. There was no point even trying. Nobody would hear her.

She jumped and screamed as an eerie voice came from the camera in the corner of the room. The gravelly whisper echoed loudly around the small space.

'Oh, there's no way out; I wouldn't waste your time. You won't be going anywhere.'

CHAPTER ONE

'This is it. This is the night we've been working towards for the last six months,' Tanya said heavily, her eyes gleaming with excitement. She squeezed Anna's hands, her smile stretching from ear to ear. 'And' – she took a deep breath – 'this time you can enjoy it just as much as me.'

They stood in a small hallway leading out to the back of their new comedy club. Tanya and Anna had been running a successful gentlemen's club in the busy West End for the last four and a half years and had decided to expand. Wanting to branch out into new ground, but also wanting to stay in entertainment, they had decided on a comedy club. Six months of research and hard work had gone into their plans, and now they were about to open the doors.

Anna grinned and felt the butterflies flit around in her stomach. Tanya was right. She could fully enjoy this opening in a way that she had not been able to when they had opened Club Anya. Back then she had been on the run from a psychotic, brutal ex who wouldn't let her go. She had been forced to stay in the shadows for her own safety, always watching her back. But she had come a long way since then, and there had not been any reason for her to look over her shoulder for a long while. This time she could enjoy herself and bask in the light of what would hopefully be a successful first night.

Tickets had sold out for the opening and it was going to be quite the party. If there was something Anna and Tanya knew well, it was how to throw a party. The house would be full, the comedy would be on point and there was a small army of staff who would make sure everyone was well fed and watered. All they had to do now was walk through the doors and cut the ceremonial ribbon. The local press were waiting outside to get their shots.

Anna squeezed Tanya's hands back and took a deep breath. 'Let's do this,' she said.

They entered through the main room of the club. The staff stood at the ready and clapped as they walked past. Anna smiled to them and nodded as they made their way to the front. They took one last look at each other and then opened the doors, smiling and waving as the cameras flashed from all angles and the waiting customers cheered. Tanya handed Anna the large pair of scissors and stepped back, letting her cut the ribbon.

'Welcome, everyone to the biggest, baddest, best new comedy club in town – The Last Laugh!' Tanya cried, raising her hands up to welcome everyone in. The ribbon fell and the first customers made their way inside, ready to be entertained. Anna and Tanya stepped aside, welcoming people as they passed. As she filled one of the journalists in about their plans for the next few weeks, Anna felt as though she was walking on air.

*

Freddie popped the cork on the bottle of Dom Pérignon, then poured it into the seven glasses that were standing ready on the bar, next to him. He was thrilled that it had been such a brilliant opening night for the girls. He knew how much Anna had been looking forward to this day. She had been chomping at the bit for a new challenge for the last couple of years.

Anna loved their first club, Club Anya – it meant the world to her. She and Tanya had opened it up together, risking everything they had. They'd built up its reputation and kept it fresh and modern together for years. It would always be their first and most precious 'work baby'. But since Carl had taken on a management position, there wasn't as much for her and Tanya to do and she had time on her hands. She couldn't sit about and do nothing with that time – she wasn't built that way. Anna needed something to consume her, something to really sink her teeth into. Her drive was one of the things Freddie loved most about her.

They had been together for four years now, and to say they had been through a lot together would be an understatement. Little had they known when they first met, but the man Anna had been running from had been the same man who was trying to usurp Freddie's well-earned position as one of the heads of central London's underground. When Freddie had killed Tony, he had not only kept his firm safe but had freed Anna from the dangers of her past.

They had lived in peaceful bliss for three years, before another threat had reared its ugly head. Ben Hargreaves, the Secretary of State for Justice had come at them with a vengeance. His daughter had been kidnapped outside Freddie's club and Ben had threatened Freddie's freedom and Anna's life if Freddie did not find her and get her back to him. It had almost cost Freddie everything. And even though they had found her, it had still cost him a brother.

Michael, the youngest Tyler sibling, had been unmasked as the kidnapper, and a very disturbed young man indeed. Freddie had managed to save his life by faking his death and smuggling him out of the country with false papers, but even so, they would never see him again. Michael would never be able to return to England; it was too risky. Instead, Freddie kept occasional tabs on him where he now resided in Rio, and sent money over from time to time through his business contacts, to ensure Michael never went without. He missed his little brother, though, and the guilt of not recognising his dark mental state sooner still ate him up inside.

Despite these dark times, Freddie and Anna were still as strong a couple as they could be. And today especially, Freddie was full of pride for his partner. He handed out the champagne to the small group around him and held up his glass.

'To the two most fierce and amazing businesswomen in all of London. Congratulations on another resounding success and the continuation of it, as time goes on. To Anna and Tanya!'

'To Anna and Tanya!' they all chanted, before chinking their glasses together.

He sipped at the cold, crisp champagne and watched as Anna chattered animatedly to his younger sister Thea. Next to her stood Paul, his other brother and second in command. He looked troubled and Freddie shot him a questioning glance. Paul gave him a subtle hand signal that told him something was up, but they couldn't discuss it here. He nodded, almost imperceptibly and picked up his jacket. He placed a hand on Anna's back and kissed her cheek.

'Something's come up – I've got to go.'

'OK, I'll see you at home later,' she replied with a warm smile.

'Paul?' Freddie said.

'Go, go. I'll stay with the girls,' Paul's partner James replied, 'and Tom, of course.' He indicated towards Tanya's boyfriend. James was enjoying himself immensely and didn't mind that Paul had to go. Like Anna, he understood how things were if you were with a Tyler. They had been together for nearly two years now, publicly for one of those. It was nothing new.

'OK,' Paul replied to James with a nod. 'Right, see you later, everyone.' He picked up his jacket and the pair left the building. They walked around the corner to where Freddie's new black Mercedes was parked. They jumped in and Paul began talking as they drove away.

'Stanley failed the drug test.'

'Fuck sake!' Freddie hit the steering wheel in frustration. 'Are you serious?'

'I wish I wasn't,' Paul replied heavily. 'He had coke in his system. Been thrown out of the competition.'

Freddie groaned. This was the last thing he needed. Stanley Wright was a boxer on their payroll. He was one of the best and had a stronger love for money than he did for the sport. They had fixed several competitions and made increasing amounts of money each time. This one was their seventh and would have been the biggest haul yet. All the bets were set up; their bookies were at the ready to cash in when he fell in the fourth round. This outcome was going to cost Freddie a lot of money, and that was something he did not take kindly to.

'Where is he?'

'Done a runner. Sent Dean to bring him in, but appears he'd cleared out of his flat before Dean got there. Looked like he left in a hurry,' Paul said.

'Well, he's not completely stupid then,' Freddie replied. He sighed loudly. He was fuming. What he really wanted to do right now was find Stanley and teach the stupid twat a lesson he wouldn't forget. He knew he had to be clean, he knew there would be a standard blood test. What on earth had he been thinking, doing cocaine?

'What's the chat?' Freddie asked.

'That we have no backup. Which is true. With the bookies, about sixty per cent of the bets are now invalid. We'll have a lot of pissed-off punters, but that will pass. The rest are still fair game and we're set to lose a lot of money if we can't find someone to go down in the fourth.'

'Right.' Freddie tried to think as he drove, but he already knew there were no other decent options. 'We'll have to substitute a straight shooter and let the chips fall where they fall,' he said, shaking his head. 'Fuck sake,' he swore again. He was livid. It was a good thing Stanley had the sense to scarper because if he was still around right now Freddie would have ripped him a new one.

He took a deep breath and tried to calm down. 'I've had someone on my radar for a while. It won't help us on this one, but I think he could be a long runner. Ring Irish Craig. Tell him I need a meeting soon. And tell him I want to meet his son.'

CHAPTER TWO

Tanya heard the doorbell ring as she turned off the shower and stepped out onto the mat. She quickly wrapped a towel around her hair and another around her body and then stepped out into the hall. Tom had already opened the door and was welcoming Freddie into her flat.

'Oh, what are you doing here?' she asked, surprised to see him. 'Is Anna with you?' She moved her head to look behind him, but Freddie was alone.

'Not this time, Tan – just me,' Freddie replied.

'Oh. Well what do *you* want?' She smiled, her banter friendly.

'Actually, I'm here to see Tom,' he replied.

'Oh. OK then.' Tanya was surprised. She had been seeing Tom for about a year now, and although he got on well enough with Freddie and Anna, they only ever really hung out as a group. She hadn't realised that he and Freddie were on one-to-one terms.

'Well, don't misbehave too much!' She smiled at her boyfriend and walked back to the bedroom as the pair turned into the lounge.

She closed the door and frowned. What did Freddie want with Tom? She knew Freddie Tyler too well and would bet her last penny that this wasn't just a social call. Aside from when it came to Anna and family, all Freddie's time and energy was poured into his work. The man ate, slept and breathed 'the life'. He wouldn't take time out of his busy day just to hang out with Tom if there was nothing in it for him. She narrowed her eyes. She would find out what it was when he was gone.

*

Tom welcomed Freddie in and poured him a coffee.

'Thanks for coming over,' he said.

'No problem, mate, what's up?' Freddie asked. He'd been surprised to get the text from Tom asking if he was free for a chat.

'Well, I have a proposition for you.' Tom took a deep breath. He appeared nervous and excited. Freddie wondered if he'd finally worked up the guts to ask him for a job.

'Look, I heard on the grapevine that you got the go-ahead for that big building project,' Tom said. 'So I know you'll be looking for a foreman. I want to ask you for the job. I'm good at what I do, I've been running projects on-site for years, but I just haven't had the title. I also have the right contacts to put together a good crew for the build – I know who works hard and who's worth having. That's valuable to have on a big build like this.'

'It is,' Freddie conceded.

'And more than that' – Tom licked his lips nervously – 'I want to work for *you.*' He gave Freddie a meaningful look. 'I want in, Freddie. I'll be as loyal and hard-working as they come. I don't mind doing some dirty work, as long as I'm finally in a position where I'm respected, you know? Respected and earning something decent for my future.'

Freddie breathed out heavily. Tom had been angling for a while but having considered it, Freddie wasn't convinced he was cut out for life in the underworld. Tom seemed like a good guy, but he wasn't hard. He was big and muscular and could no doubt hold his own in a bar fight should he ever need to, but he lacked the type of hardness you needed in this line of work.

The dark side of their world was a bleak, unforgiving place and the mentality required to survive it was something not many people possessed. Most of the people who lived this life had come from harsh backgrounds or suffered difficulties that would break the majority of men. They had come through it and risen like the phoenix does from the flames. Those people had been born of fire, as Anna liked to say.

Tom wasn't one of those people. He had never suffered real hardship or risen above difficult beginnings. He had grown up in a secure family who had normal jobs and his life so far had been an uneventful journey of his own making.

Freddie knew that what attracted Tom was the outside image. Tom saw the money, the power, the suits, the cars, but he didn't see the blood and sweat and grit that lay beneath the surface.

Would he be able to stomach the things that Freddie dealt with? Freddie was fairly sure he would break under the pressure of the first real challenge he was faced with and that wasn't someone Freddie could afford to have around. When the shit hit the fan, he needed men who would turn up, clean up and carry on as if nothing had happened.

'Tom, I don't think you fully understand what I do,' Freddie said eventually. 'I know it might look appealing, but it ain't all sunshine and roses.'

'I know that, Freddie,' Tom burst out, 'and I do understand what you do. I know the decisions you make aren't easy and aren't above board. I know there'll be things I don't agree with,' he said honestly, 'but that doesn't matter. If I work for you, *that's* all that matters. You're the boss.'

Freddie studied him. His gut told him that hiring Tom was a bad idea. He wasn't strong enough and although he liked him, Freddie always asked himself one question when he took a new man on – *would I trust him with my life?* Freddie didn't know if he could put that level of trust in Tom. He felt torn though. If Tom was going to be part of all their lives now that he was with Tanya, he couldn't ignore him forever.

'Please, Freddie,' Tom continued. He shot a look towards the hallway. 'I need to do something more with my life. Tanya has the club and now this second one… I feel useless. I'm nowhere near her level,' he said unhappily. 'How can I expect her to look at me with respect and pride when I spend the rest of my days earning a pittance by breaking my back under someone else's command? Christ, I wouldn't. I don't want to be the loser boyfriend forever.'

Freddie frowned and shook his head. 'Firstly, you aren't a loser and I know Tanya has *never* seen you that way. You forget, people like her and me, we came from humble backgrounds and that's not something we ever forget. Tanya will always have respect for someone who's working hard in life, no matter what level they're at.'

'Well, that's OK for you to say,' Tom replied. 'You don't have to sit like a twat in a swanky restaurant that your girlfriend picked, waiting while she pays the bill. Do you know how that feels?'

Freddie tilted his head in acknowledgement. No, he didn't know how that felt and he wouldn't want to either. 'Alright, look,' he sighed. 'I'll give you the job. You'll be on probation and you'll have to prove your worth like anybody else. There are no free rides, got it?'

'Got it. Thank you, Freddie,' Tom replied gratefully. 'And um, the other part?'

'I'm not going to put you on my payroll. You aren't what I'm looking for.' Freddie watched the disappointment appear on the other man's face. 'But here's what I will do. If I need an extra set of hands on something, or something requiring your set of skills comes up, I'll give you a shot.' Tom's eyes lit up in hope. 'I'm promising nothing. But we'll see. If that happens and you prove to be an asset, we'll talk.'

'OK, thank you, Freddie. I really appreciate that,' Tom said with a big smile. He held up his mug. 'Cheers. To possibilities and opportunities,' he said.

Freddie clinked his coffee to Tom's and smiled. He hoped he had made the right decision.

*

Twenty minutes later, as she finished applying her liquid eyeliner, Tanya heard Freddie shout out a goodbye to her. She shouted one back and placed her make-up back in its bag. Rubbing her glossy lips together in the mirror and checking herself over one more time, Tanya nodded in approval and went to find Tom.

'There you are,' she purred, giving him a winning smile. He was in the kitchen, tidying up the cups he had just used. Tom was meticulously tidy, all the time. It was something Tanya found she really liked about him. She didn't like clutter or mess either. 'Good guy chat?' she asked.

'Yeah, hope you don't mind me inviting him over here?' Tom said.

'No, not at all.'

Although they were pretty serious and Tom spent almost every night there, Tanya had not invited him to live with her. The flat was still completely hers and despite the love and trust she felt towards Tom, she liked to keep that last line of defence up. Just in case.

'So, what did you guys talk about?' she asked casually.

'Freddie offered me a job, actually. I was pretty surprised,' Tom lied. He didn't want to tell Tanya that he had begged Freddie for the position.

'But you have a job,' Tanya replied. A feeling of worry began to curl up through her stomach. Tanya had been part of the shady underworld of London once, and understood the game well. She had no problem with it; it was just part of life in this city and Freddie was underworld royalty. But Tom was just a nice, normal guy. He wasn't whiter than white, of course, but he also wasn't part of Freddie's world and Tanya liked that. She liked that their relationship was uncomplicated by all the issues that way of life could bring.

'Yeah, I wasn't exactly looking, of course, but what he's offering would be a huge step up for me and the money is a lot better too. It's too juicy to turn down.' Tom smiled.

Yeah, I'll bet... thought Tanya darkly. She paused before answering, working out the best approach.

'What is the job?' she asked eventually.

'Foreman,' he answered. 'He has a friend who runs a building company; they work together on a few projects. He just said the job's mine if I want it.'

'How neatly tied up,' Tanya answered.

Tom's eager smile faltered. 'You're not happy – is it because it's Freddie? I know people say working with friends don't always work out, but you and Anna manage OK. And I wouldn't mess it up. I never let anyone down – I'm not like that.' He frowned, upset.

'No...' Tanya shook her head and laid her hand on his muscular forearm. 'It's not you I'm worried about. You're amazing at your job; you should have been promoted years ago. It's just... how much do you know about what Freddie does? Really?' she asked.

Tom shrugged and looked away. He knew plenty, and he wanted a piece of the pie. He knew Tanya wouldn't like this though, so tried to answer casually. 'I know he owns a few clubs, has some property. And that he's involved with some big building projects.' He paused and then exhaled through his nose. 'Look, I know Freddie ain't all kosher, alright? I know he does a few shady deals, I've heard the talk, but come on, who doesn't at his level?'

Tanya licked her lips nervously. Tom didn't understand who Freddie was. No civilians did really. It was all just rumour and gossip, if you weren't in the know. She needed to explain it so that Tom understood what he would be stepping into, but without outright telling him the details. It wasn't done. She spoke carefully.

'Freddie... has fingers in a lot of pies. Most of which are a bit more than just shady. He's done things...' She struggled to find the right way to phrase it. 'He just ain't quite who you think he is.

It's a dangerous thing, to get too close to Freddie. Professionally speaking. You are your own person and this is your decision, but I just want you to understand the situation fully. If you take this job, you're in Freddie's pocket. And it won't come without a price.' Tanya bit her lip. She had said enough. Probably too much, if she was honest.

'You think he's just trying to use me?' he asked, feigning concern.

'No, I don't,' Tanya answered honestly. 'He wouldn't offer you any job if he didn't think you were the right person and if he didn't trust you. But he will ask things of you, Tom. And I can guarantee you they won't be above board and they'll probably be things you aren't OK with. And at that stage you won't have a choice. *This* is the last point at which you'll have a real choice,' Tanya stressed. She fiddled anxiously with a button on her shirt.

She wouldn't ask him not to take it, though she desperately wanted to. It was his life. Tanya didn't believe in treating Tom any differently to the way she expected to be treated by him. And she would never have accepted being told what to do, if the situation was reversed.

Tom stepped forward and held her gently at the tops of her tightly crossed arms. He looked down at her with love in his eyes.

'You don't need to worry about me. I'm a big boy,' he said, his warm smile creeping into his tone. 'And I'm OK with having to do a few things for Freddie in return for getting me such a good position. I wanna take it, Tan. It's exactly what I need to move up in my career and you know what, I could do with the extra money.'

'I have enough for both of us—'

'Yes, but, Tanya, you pay for almost everything we do. And I hate it,' he said honestly, his eyes beseeching her to understand. 'I love how generous and big-hearted you are, I really do. You're amazing. But as a man, it gets to me sometimes that I can't be the one to treat you to the more expensive things.' He looked down at his feet, embarrassed.

Tanya's heart reached out to him, this big, handsome man that she loved so much. She hadn't realised how he felt. She had never really thought about it, because the difference in their financial states had never bothered her.

'You know I don't care about all that,' she said softly.

'I know you don't. But I do. I want to feel like I rule the world one day, Tan, and I can't do it sitting still.'

She nodded. That was that then. Tom would accept this new position and Freddie would have a new recruit for the firm. She could have happily punched Freddie if he had still been there, but of course she never would. She would never say anything. It was done. The decision was made and now she would just have to hope for the best.

CHAPTER THREE

Freddie and Paul strode into the warehouse. It was a large space filled with gym equipment on one side, and a social seating area and full-sized boxing ring on the other. Most of the floor around the ring had been covered by interlocking rubber tiles. Freddie preferred them to mats – they stayed in place rather than sliding around when the boxers jumped down.

A few large men were pumping weights on the gym side, music booming from a sound system held on the wall by a bracket. They all paused and nodded their respect to Freddie when he walked in. Everyone knew who owned this gym. A few years before, Freddie had bought the warehouse in one of the more rundown areas of the East End, on the estate he himself had come from, and transformed it almost overnight. It was his way of giving something back to the community. Anyone who lived in the area was allowed membership for free. Anyone outside of it had to pay. Not that there were many people outside of the estate who would want to venture in.

He looked around and felt the same nostalgia as always whenever he walked in. It wasn't the gym their dad had taken them to when they were kids, of course, but it was very similar. It had the same smell of rubber and sweat when you walked through the doors. It held the same promise to the young fighters of today as it did back then, the air filled with an almost tangible current of determination and purpose.

Freddie had been just ten when his father had died, leaving them alone and without male guidance in this world. Boxing had been his dad's passion and he'd passed it on to his sons. Keeping it alive somehow felt to Freddie like he was keeping a part of his father alive too.

Freddie and Paul turned towards the boxing ring and, taking a seat in the social area, watched two young men spar with one another. An older man with a weathered face sat down next to Freddie.

'How ya keeping, Craig?' Freddie asked, without taking his eyes off the boys in the ring. Craig had been a good friend of their father's, sharing the same passion for the sport. He had since passed this onto his own son, these days too old to get into the ring himself.

'Ahh, I'm stickin' out, lad, stickin' out.' Craig's thick Irish accent crackled out as he spoke, his voice hoarse from years of chain-smoking. 'What de'ya think to ma boy?' He motioned up towards the ring and glanced at Freddie. 'He hasn't been beaten in six counties, bareknuckle or gloved. He's quick and he never tires.'

'So you say,' Freddie replied. 'He's certainly got skill. What does he want out of life?'

Craig wasn't surprised by the question. 'Not much really. He ain't all that clever with the books – his schooling didn't go so well. This is all he knows. But he does it well and he's a good boy too. Doesn't ask questions, does as he's bid.' Craig nodded to himself, proud of the son he was discussing.

'Mm,' Freddie murmured. 'This won't last forever though. Bring him over.'

'Seamus,' Craig called. The broader of the two boys looked over. 'Get ye'self over here, lad. Come and meet the Tylers.'

The boy jumped down, taking off the boxing gloves and throwing them back into the ring. He wiped his hands on his black knee-length shorts and straightened his back. He reached them and paused.

'I would offer you my hand, Mr Tyler, but I don't want to get you all sweaty,' he said apologetically. He looked at his father anxiously, as if worried he had said the wrong thing.

'No worries, mate.' Freddie chuckled. 'I'm Freddie – this is Paul.'

'Nice to meet you both.' Though still very clearly evident, the lilting Irish accent was not so thick in Seamus's voice.

'And you, son. How old are ya?' Paul asked.

'Just turned eighteen.'

'And how long have you been competing in the backroom leagues?'

'Three years.'

'Why do you think you always win, Seamus?' Freddie interjected, his voice carefully flat.

Seamus blinked and considered this for a moment. 'I don't know. I'd say it's part skill, part luck and a touch of the good Lord's grace.'

'And,' Craig interrupted, 'because he's the best.'

Freddie turned his attention to Craig. 'You would think that, you're his dad. And he may well be. But if *he* thought that, I wouldn't be interested. Believing you're the best only makes you sloppy.'

Craig acknowledged this with a tilt of the head. 'Fair point.'

Seamus looked from one to the other, waiting for further questions. His breathing was still heavy from the fight, his bare chest rising and falling. He had the look of a typical young Irish man; pale skin, dark hair and blue eyes fringed by long, dark lashes. His lips were full and his face flushed from the exertion.

Freddie looked the boy up and down as Seamus continued to answer Paul's questions. He had potential and he came from good stock. Craig had grafted in their world all his life – he knew what was what. The boy seemed pretty straight so far.

'You ever broken an arm, Seamus?' Freddie asked casually. Seamus didn't flinch.

'Twice. Once by accident,' he replied earnestly.

Freddie saw Paul turn his head away to hide a grin and Craig rolled his eyes.

'OK. Did it bother you?'

'No. Well, the accidental one did – he was me best friend – but the other one had it coming.'

'You work? Other than your boxing, I mean.'

'Yes, I work shifts down the packing factory. Not great money but it's steady.'

Freddie took a cigarette out and lit it, offering the packet to Craig and Paul who each took one. He offered it to Seamus who declined, shaking his head.

'No thank you. I don't smoke.'

'Good.' Freddie blew out a long puff of smoke. 'Don't start either. I'm going to offer you a job, Seamus. A trial period at first, to make sure you have what it takes. On the boxing side, I'll have you here training every morning with Robbie from seven till ten, got it?' Seamus nodded eagerly, his eyes shining. 'You'll train until Robbie tells me you're ready, then we'll get you on the circuit. When that day comes' – he put weight behind his words – 'there will be games I expect you to throw and rounds I expect you to finish in. Are you OK with that? It's fine if you're not, but you tell me now.'

'I understand, Mr Tyler. This is a business.' Seamus already knew that this would be asked of him and had come to terms with it. He knew that his father had put a good word in to get him this opportunity, and another like it was unlikely to come along again.

'Good. On top of that, once your morning training is over each day, you'll work directly for me. You'd resign from the factory today. Every afternoon, every evening, seven days a week you'll need to be available to do jobs for me, as and when I require you to. It could be anything from picking up a package to breaking another arm. Some jobs are dirty and not much fun. But I need someone to do them. Someone who is one hundred per cent loyal to me, and who I can trust to keep his mouth shut in any circumstance.' Freddie searched Seamus's expression for any doubt, but all he saw was excitement and focus. 'In return you will be well paid and – not that it looks like you need it – you'll be under my protection. I'll start you on a monkey a week, plus a bit extra if I throw any particularly dirty jobs your way. You'll start at the bottom of the ladder but there's plenty of room for you to work your way up if you graft hard and do well. That's my offer. Have a think about it and let me know.'

'I don't need to think about it, Mr Tyler,' Seamus answered quickly. 'I want to accept and I just want to say that I'll make ye pleased that you took me on. I'll be more useful than any other fella ye can think of.'

Seamus was ecstatic. He couldn't believe his luck. Five hundred pounds a week sounded like a fortune to him after the crappy wage he'd been getting at the factory. And a job working directly for Freddie Tyler himself! It was like all his Christmases had come at once. He knew he hadn't much to offer the legal business world. This was the best opportunity he could have dreamed of.

'Alright, well, let's not get ahead of ourselves yet. It's a trial. I'll see how you go,' Freddie replied to the eager young lad. 'Be here tomorrow to meet Robbie, seven sharp.' He stood up and held his hand out to Craig. Craig took it and shook it.

'Thanks, Freddie.'

'No thanks needed – he's going to have to work hard for it. I'll see ya, Craig.'

'Sees ye later, Freddie, Paul.'

Freddie walked away, happy with the outcome. Seamus was exactly the kind of person he'd been looking for. Aside from the boxing, he would do nicely as someone to train up in the other businesses. Seamus wasn't like Tom. He was from their world; he'd grown up in it.

Paul pulled a wedge of fifty-pound notes out of his pocket and counted out five hundred. He handed it to Seamus. 'There's this week's wage. Someone will drop it off to you here every Friday morning. Enjoy.'

Paul chuckled to himself as he walked away. The boy had stared at the pile of notes as though he had just won the lottery. He tried to remember back to the days where five hundred quid had seemed like a lot of money. That was a long time ago now. Which just went to show how far they had come.

CHAPTER FOUR

Freddie walked through the busy bookies to the back room, where he knew Sammy would be working in the office. He knocked briskly, then entered as he heard the deep voice granting him admission. Closing the door behind him, he kept his jacket on. As usual, Sammy had the temperature set to an arctic level. He seemed completely at ease in the cold, wearing nothing but a thin white shirt over his muscular torso.

Sammy's expression was animated, his big blue eyes glinting with excitement.

'I have some very interesting news.' Sammy dived straight in. 'Frank Gambino is making a trip to London. He arrives next week. He's staying here for a while on business.'

Freddie breathed out slowly, as he began to catch Sammy's contagious excitement. Frank Gambino, or Gambino the Gambler as he was commonly known, was the current head of one of the Five Families in New York. The Five Families were the Italian-American Mafia, and the firm who ran pretty much every major gambling enterprise in the western world, amongst other things.

Freddie picked up the stress ball which sat neatly in its own little holder on the desk and began playing with it absentmindedly, as a hundred thoughts whirled around in his head.

'You're right,' he said. 'That is very interesting news indeed. Where is he staying?'

'The Dorchester.'

'Who else will be with him?' Freddie asked.

'Just his own men – whatever he's here for isn't anything to do with the other families,' Sammy replied.

'Right. What are you thinking?' Freddie was pretty sure he already knew, but he wanted to see if they were on the same page.

'I think we need to get a meeting. We've been making money through the bookies and the back-room dens for a long time. We know the game inside out. Let's be honest, he's the only reason we haven't stepped up a level.'

Freddie nodded. Although the Gambinos resided in New York, they had also staked their claim years before on the high-level casino game in most major cities throughout the US and Europe. To open up a proper casino in London, the Tylers would need Frank Gambino's permission. They would also have to pay him a percentage of the profits. If they could get his approval to go ahead, it would mean moving up to a whole new level, professionally and financially. It wouldn't do them any harm to be seen to be making friends with their American superiors either. And superiors they were, for although Freddie was the biggest fish in London, the Five Families were one of the biggest fish in the world.

'Have you got an in?' Freddie asked.

'Sort of. I used to know a guy who does some work for one of the Gambino brothers. I can get him to ask for a meeting.'

'No.' Freddie shook his head. 'Ask him to extend an invite to dinner. A little welcome into the city, from us to them. He will have heard of us; he'll know this is our ground. He'll have to accept out of respect.'

Sammy nodded in agreement. 'I'll call him today.'

'Great.' Freddie sat down on one of the armchairs around Sammy's glass coffee table.

Sammy poured them each a neat whisky, passed one to Freddie and then eased his large frame into the chair opposite. He held his glass forward and chinked it against Freddie's.

'Here's to us and new ventures,' Sammy toasted.

'To us,' Freddie repeated. 'And hopefully a very lucrative friendship with the Mafia.' He knocked back the whisky, feeling the fiery burn slide down his throat. If they could get Gambino onside, the possibilities were endless. This could be the start of a much bigger future for them all.

*

Anna frowned in concentration as she walked through the hallway towards her front door, searching her handbag for keys. Pulling it up so that she could see inside, she pushed notepads and her purse out of the way. *They're in there somewhere,* she thought. She could hear them jangling. She tutted with impatience. *Why were they always the last thing you come across?*

Anna reached her door and stopped, still peering into the dark depths of the Louis Vuitton that Tanya had bought her for Christmas. She made a mental note to change to a smaller bag. As her fingers finally made contact with the bunch of keys, she exclaimed in triumph. She looked up to find the lock and stopped dead, her momentary elation fading away. The front door was ajar and the doorframe was damaged. Someone had broken in. She stepped backward. They might still be in there.

Silently she moved through the door that led to the stairwell and positioned herself so that she could see if anyone left. Whether this was a random break-in or an enemy of Freddie's trying to make a statement, she didn't yet know.

Anna pulled her phone from her back pocket and pressed Freddie's number. The line connected and began to ring. 'Come on, Freddie,' she muttered under her breath. It went through to voicemail and she groaned. Trying Paul's number next she swore as it went straight to voicemail too. Searching once more through her contacts she dialled another number and waited for it to be picked up.

'DI John Fraser.' The clipped voice sounded over a background of office chatter.

She breathed out in relief. Anna knew Freddie trusted this man explicitly and that she could count on him to deal with this. He had been on Freddie's payroll for years and Freddie had always told her to go to him should she ever need help.

'Fraser, it's Anna Davis. Can you talk?' Anna asked quietly.

'Sure, hang on.' There was a pause as he moved somewhere quieter. 'Everything OK? Is Freddie OK?' he asked.

'Freddie's fine. But someone has broken into the flat. I can't call the police officially – they'll crawl all over things. Can you come?'

'Christ. Yeah, I'm coming now. Where are you now?' Fraser asked. She could hear him moving as he talked.

'In the stairwell. I haven't been in. I just saw the door and called you.'

'Good. Stay there. I'm only five minutes away.'

As good as his word, DI John Fraser came through the door just over five minutes later. Anna breathed out in relief. Every second had felt like an hour as she waited tensely, keeping her eyes trained on the broken front door.

'Anyone come out?' Fraser asked, deep lines furrowing his forehead.

'No, not yet. I think they're probably gone.'

'Wait here.' Fraser pulled a small handgun out of his pocket and quietly made his way into the flat. *Well,* Anna thought, *they certainly didn't issue that at the police station.* She was glad he had answered. She couldn't have reported this properly and had a straight policeman going through their home. There was no telling what they might find.

Fraser came out and beckoned Anna over.

'They've gone. It looks like a random break-in; I don't think it's directed at Freddie. Come in and see if you can tell me what's missing.'

Anna walked into the hallway and looked around. There was broken glass on the floor where a vase had been knocked off the side table. Her heels crunched over it as she made her way through, trying to remember how everything was when she left earlier that day. Glancing into the lounge she could see the drawers on the dresser were open, but she ignored that. There was nothing in there. She walked into the kitchen first and opened the freezer. Pulling the top drawer out, she pursed her lips. The money they kept there had been taken.

'Five grand gone from here,' she said to DI Fraser. He raised his eyebrows but said nothing.

Anna made her way to Freddie's office. A quick check showed that their hidden safe was still intact but his drawers were all open and paperwork littered the floor.

'Freddie's iPad is gone,' she said, looking around to see if anything else was missing.

'Is there anything on it?'

'No, it's just for casual use, nothing incriminating.' Anna was glad that Freddie insisted on taking his laptop out with him every day. That had all his business dealings on it and would be very dangerous indeed in the wrong hands.

In the bedroom Anna gasped. Their belongings were everywhere. Her clothes were scattered all around, Freddie's too. The photo frames that used to sit on the bookcase had all been thrown off and most had smashed. Her dressing-table drawers were open and her make-up thrown out. She pushed her fingers to the back of the main drawer and felt around.

'Another five grand gone from here, too.' Her eyes rested on the mirrored jewellery box on top and she opened it. 'Oh no,' she groaned.

'What is it?' Fraser came over to look.

Anna pulled a sad face. 'I had some pearl earrings that Freddie bought me last year. They're gone. And a diamond necklace I bought from Hatton Gardens. And' – she rummaged through what was still there and then sighed – 'my grandmother's ring too. It wasn't worth much, but it meant a lot to me. It's all I had left of her.'

Anna stepped backward and sat down heavily on the bed. She suddenly began to cry. The break-in she could cope with. Money didn't matter; they could make more. Even the earrings from Freddie; sad though she was to lose them, she would get over their loss. But the ring that her beloved grandmother had left her was something she could never replace. It was the last thing she had given her before she died. Anna still felt close to her whenever she wore it, but now she would never feel close to her again.

Fraser sat down next to Anna, his expression sombre. He had been impressed by how calmly she had dealt with it all, as they had gone through the house. But clearly this ring meant a lot to her. Clearly family meant a lot to her, just like Freddie. Her devastated expression pulled at his heart and anger surged through him.

This was why Fraser had got into the force in the first place, to punish people who did things like this. Oh, he knew he was bent. He had been helping Freddie cover things up for years. But he had a moral code. Criminals like Freddie didn't bother him. He was just a businessman on the wrong side of politics, and when Freddie crossed the line it was justified. But Fraser waged war against the criminals who hurt people for no reason, with no care or concern for anyone other than themselves.

He looked around at the mess. This was someone's home. How could anyone come into someone's personal domain, their safe place, and treat it like this?

Anna sat upright and wiped her eyes. 'Sorry.' She was embarrassed. 'I'm fine. Just can't believe they would take that ring. They won't even get anything for it.' She shook her head sadly.

'Do you want me to call Freddie?' Fraser asked.

'No, it's OK. He's not answering at the moment. I'll track him down in a minute and tell him what happened. Thanks again for coming, John,' she said tiredly.

Fraser grinned.

'What are you smiling at?' she asked.

'That's the first time you've ever called me by my first name,' he replied.

'Yes, so it is.' Anna managed a small laugh. She stood up and brushed herself down, before walking back through to the other rooms to check she hadn't missed anything.

Fraser looked around. *What a mess.* He knelt down and started picking up the broken glass from the picture frames. *Might as well make myself useful,* he thought. If he knew Freddie, which he did, Freddie would want him to wait until he got here, to talk to him in person. They would decide how to proceed together, to find whoever was responsible for this.

Fraser pulled a face and his lips formed a hard line. He would not want to be in the thief's shoes when Freddie Tyler found him. Not for all the money in the world.

CHAPTER FIVE

A few days later, Freddie's tyres crunched to a stop on the stony ground of his new building site. He stepped out and waved to Tom, who was making his way over towards him.

'Freddie, good to see you!' Tom greeted him warmly. He had been on site in his new position for a week now and had settled in well. The men who now worked under him were happy with their new foreman and the owner of the building firm was pleased with how efficiently Tom was running things. The new arrangement was working out for everybody. Even Freddie was impressed.

Freddie had gone into this new development in partnership with Ralph, the owner of the building company. Ralph had the men and the building expertise; Freddie had the capital and the business contacts. The development was in an up-and-coming area of East London and was going to end up being sold as a mixture of offices and retail units. It had taken Freddie a lot of time and some hefty bribes to get the permissions pushed through. Certain legal technicalities had needed to be overlooked and buried, but he had managed to pull it off.

'How are you getting on? Enjoying it?' Freddie asked, as they made their way to the Portakabin that was Tom's site office.

'Yeah, I really am. This is a major project; it's nice to have something challenging to sink my teeth into.'

'Thought you already had that at home, mate,' Freddie joked. They both laughed.

'Oh, Tanya's challenging alright,' Tom replied fondly. 'Definitely keeps me on my toes.'

'It would be boring any other way, wouldn't it?' Freddie said with a wink.

'Indeed,' Tom replied, grinning. 'Anyway, how are things with you? Anna OK? Tanya told me about the break-in. That's rough, mate. You found out who done it yet?'

'No.' Freddie's reply was tinged with annoyance. 'I've got everyone out looking but not heard a dicky bird. It seems like a random break-in, from what Fraser found, but still, you never know.' He shook his head. 'I'm upping security on the place. Anna's really shaken up and I can't take any chances of a repeat performance. Hopefully we find the fucker soon.'

'Hopefully, mate.' Tom nodded supportively. 'So, you got the paperwork for me? My men are ready to break ground, soon as everything's in place.'

'I do. Some of it, anyway. But you don't need to worry about the rest, if you catch my drift.' Freddie stared at Tom levelly.

Tom took the paperwork from Freddie's outstretched hand. Freddie unbuttoned his jacket and made himself comfortable in the chair in front of the desk, as Tom sat on the other side to look through the documents.

Tom pulled the papers forward one by one and quickly identified those that were missing. There were a number of levels within the local council at which a development like this had to be signed off before work could begin. Two of the stages were not there – which he found pretty impressive seeing as the higher sign-offs shouldn't even have begun without the previous permissions being completed first. Freddie must have had to buy several people off to get this all pushed through as it was.

Tom knew that if it was ever uncovered that he had allowed the workforce to begin without the paperwork in order, he could be in big trouble. But, of course, Freddie Tyler hadn't got to where he was without being smart. If he was about to sink that sort of money into this development with such shaky paperwork, he must be pretty certain that it wasn't going to bite him in the arse. Tom figured this was his first test. Freddie needed him onside, to start the build.

Tom shuffled the papers back together and smiled at Freddie. 'All looks in order to me.'

Freddie grinned back. 'Good. So' – he clapped his hands onto his knees – 'get the men to break ground today and then tonight, we celebrate.'

Tom nodded and, still grinning, Freddie shook his hand. Tom smiled back and got ready to tell the men to begin. His test had been easy to pass. Hopefully it was only a matter of time before Freddie gave him the position he so badly wanted.

CHAPTER SIX

Tanya swept into Club Anya and threw herself into the bar seat next to Anna with a dramatic sigh. Anna couldn't help but laugh.

'OK, what's up?' she asked, amused.

'I'm so done with trying to appease comedians!' Tanya exclaimed, wringing her hands in the air in frustration. 'Flamboyant bastards. The showgirls here are so much easier. Can we swap shifts when I'm supposed to be there for, like, forever?'

Anna shook her head, laughing. 'No, we most certainly can't. We've barely been open a few weeks, and it will get easier. It's just new ground, that's all.'

'He wants a fruit sculpture, Anna,' Tanya stressed flatly. 'A fruit sculpture. Made to a specific design. In his dressing room.'

'His dressing room?' Anna raised an eyebrow and sipped at her drink.

'Yeah, exactly,' Tanya replied, rolling her eyes. 'Hey, Carl?' She waited until their bar manager and friend came over. 'Can you make me something really strong and super sweet?'

He grinned. 'Coming right up.'

'You're a babe. So anyway' – Tanya turned back to Anna – 'he's threatening not to perform if he don't get both a fruit sculpture and a dressing room.'

'Who is it?' Anna asked.

'Matt Harper.'

'OK. Well, tell him he can have a fruit *bowl,* and access to the same green room that the rest of the acts will be in that evening and that he can take it or leave it. He's probably just trying his luck,' Anna said.

'And if he isn't?' Tanya asked.

'Then we'll find someone else.'

Tanya nodded her agreement. 'How are you, anyway? You look tired.'

'Oh thanks!' Anna laughed. 'You're right though. I'm not sleeping well at all right now. Freddie isn't either to be honest.' She sighed.

'Why?' Tanya asked.

'Every time I fall asleep I end up having nightmares that there's someone in the flat. I end up jolting awake panicking that it's really happening. I still can't believe someone was in our home, Tan. You know?' She shook her head sadly. 'I used to feel so safe there. I didn't ever think it could feel like it does now. And Freddie, it's like he feels like he failed. I find him sitting up sometimes with his gun.'

'Shit, Anna, I didn't realise it had affected you so much.' Tanya felt awful – she should have checked up on her friend sooner.

'I can't stop thinking about it. Even with these new security cameras Freddie had put in and the new safety door. I mean, Christ, it has steel bolts now – a battering ram wouldn't move that thing! But I still can't shake the feeling. And Fraser hasn't found anything. Whoever it was, they wiped their prints. There's nothing to find. But anyway' – she smiled – 'there's no point dwelling on it in the daytime too. It already steals my sleep.'

'What are you going to do? Maybe you should talk to someone. Like, you know, professional,' Tanya suggested.

'And say what?' Anna laughed. 'My boyfriend is one of the biggest gangsters in London who would happily kill whoever broke into our home, except he can't find them and despite the fact I have this fierce warrior in the house and plenty of firepower, I just keep having bad dreams?'

'Fair point,' Tanya conceded.

'I don't know,' Anna said. 'I might broach the subject of moving and starting over somewhere fresh. Though I don't know how Freddie will feel about that.'

Carl came back with a tall pink sparkling drink and placed it in front of her.

'I call it the candy cane,' he said. Carl loved mixing up new cocktails, so their menu was forever changing.

Tanya took a sip and grinned, her eyes sparkling. 'Now that's what I call a drink,' she enthused. 'Can I chase it with a tequila? One for Anna too.'

'Hold your horses,' Anna protested, 'I have to go out later. I have dinner plans.'

'Oh, come on, one won't hurt. I need to take the edge off,' Tanya pleaded.

'Surely a bunch of comedians hasn't rattled you that much?' Anna replied. She nodded to Carl that she would accept the shot.

'No, not them. I'm a bit worried about Tom, to be honest,' Tanya said, her easy smile dropping. She ran her red manicured nails through her thick hair and pursed her lips. 'And I could bloody murder your Freddie an' all. No wonder the bugger's been keeping out of my way for the last few days.'

'Freddie? What's happened?' Anna frowned.

Tanya sighed. Initially, she had decided not to moan about it to Anna. It wouldn't help. But the feeling of worry hadn't passed and had only deepened when Tom had quietly told her about the contracts.

'We all know who Freddie is and we all love him for or despite it. But he offered Tom a job. And Tom took it.'

'Oh. I see.' Anna did see. They both drank from their glasses for a moment.

'Tom ain't from all this, ya' know?' Tanya looked at Anna. 'He might be rough around the edges, but he's a straight shooter. Or at least he has been, until now. It's worrying me whether he can survive in this world. Or, if he can, how it's going to change him and us,' Tanya admitted.

'Hmm. The way Freddie told it, it was Tom who asked him for a job,' Anna said.

'That's strange,' Tanya replied, frowning. 'Tom definitely said it was Freddie who brought it up. Said he was looking for this new build site.' Tanya bit her lip, looking confused.

Anna was quick to settle the conversation. 'Oh, I must have heard wrong then. Or got the wrong end of the stick – don't worry about it.' She hadn't heard wrong at all; Freddie had repeated the conversation back to her practically word for word, but the last thing she wanted to do was cause an argument between Tanya and Tom.

'Oh, OK, good.' Tanya laughed and leaned forward on the bar, signalling for Carl to top up her tequila.

Anna sat back and placed her arm across the back of Tanya's chair, in a subconsciously protective gesture. Her expression was sombre. She didn't know why Tom had needed to lie to Tanya about it.

'I just hope it is only the foreman job and not an in to the real business. I like Tom how he is. I don't want to lose him to all that,' Tanya said.

'I'm sure it is,' Anna replied. She knew Freddie wasn't keen on bringing Tom into the fold on that side, so hopefully nothing more should come of it and Tanya could keep her white knight.

'Well, it had better be,' Tanya sniffed, 'or I'll have his balls for earrings.'

Anna raised her eyebrows with an amused smile.

'Oh, don't worry,' Tanya said with a twinkle in her eye, 'I'll let you borrow them.'

The girls doubled over as their peals of laughter rang throughout the club.

CHAPTER SEVEN

Freddie paced slowly up and down the pavement outside the building, lost in thought. He didn't see Anna approach until she was almost right in front of him.

'Ah, there you are. You look amazing.' Holding her hand, he stepped away to appraise her fully. She really did look incredible. She always did, but tonight she looked particularly special in a black figure-hugging, knee-length dress that hung just off the shoulder. Perfectly flawless make-up and simple, well cut diamonds at her throat finished the look off perfectly. She was elegant and classy at the same time as being the sexiest women he had ever laid eyes on. She floored him, every time.

Anna smiled warmly and wrapped her arms around his neck, before kissing him softly on the lips.

'Sorry I'm late – Tanya needed a drink and a chat. She's very upset with you, by the way.' Anna's tone was matter-of-fact, rather than accusatory.

Freddie grimaced. 'I thought she might be. But it really is a good opportunity for him. And he's a big boy – he makes his own decisions. It's not like it's me chasing him into things.'

Anna kept her counsel and didn't mention Tom's version of it all to Freddie. She tucked her arm into his.

'You look good too, by the way.' She glanced sideways at him. Her compliment hit its mark and Freddie held his head a little higher.

As they walked up the steps to the elegantly carved double doors, Anna sensed another body fall into step next to her. She turned with a smile.

'It's been too long, Sammy.'

'Indeed it has. Good to see you, Anna,' Sammy replied.

In the end, Sammy had sent the dinner invitation to Frank Gambino at Freddie's request and it had been accepted. Frank had, however, insisted that he be the one to host them, in one of his elite casinos in Mayfair. In no position to refuse, they had agreed and had arrived at the specified time and place. The invite had been extended to partners, but as Sammy was still a terminal bachelor, this only included Anna.

They were greeted by a hostess who led them through to the main bar and left them waiting with a glass of champagne each. Freddie took note of his surroundings. The bar was tastefully decorated, with dim lighting and soft music. The colours were subtle and the walls were mirrored from waist height upward. He wondered if any of the mirrors were two-way, to allow for security to see into the room unobtrusively. There did not appear to be any CCTV cameras sticking out, as one would usually expect to see.

After a short wait, two men wearing black suits and wired earpieces entered the room and made a beeline over to them. The taller one smiled tightly in greeting.

'Mr Tyler, Mr Barker – Mr Gambino will greet you in one of our private rooms. Miss Davis.' He turned to Anna and handed her a silver-coloured satin bag that was pulled tight at the neck. 'Mr Gambino asks you to accept this gift from him to use at any of our tables here this evening, as an apology for stealing your companions away from you for a time before you all dine together later.'

Anna took the bag and opened it up. There was a small fortune in gambling chips inside. She raised her eyebrows and smiled, amused. Clearly she was expected to stay out of the way whilst the men talked business. She wondered why she had been invited at all. She mentally shrugged. It didn't matter. What mattered was that she was here to support Freddie. She smiled back at the man and answered pleasantly.

'Please tell Mr Gambino that I accept with gratitude and look forward to meeting him later.' Nodding at Freddie to indicate all was well, she took her leave and wandered into the connecting room. Out of the corner of her eye she watched Freddie hesitate, then follow the two men out of the room, along with Sammy.

For a few minutes, Anna strolled through the small maze of connecting rooms. It was a beautiful building, with high ceilings and ornate plasterwork. Dark red walls were filled with classic oil paintings and mirrors, whilst the chandeliers and finishing touches had been added with a modern twist, giving the whole place an air of sophistication. Anna admired the delicate balance of old and new that they had accomplished. So many places tried and missed the mark entirely.

Finding an almost empty blackjack table, she took a seat. Crossing her legs, she gave a passing waiter her drink order and began to place her bets. After the first round, Anna was the only player, the others having left to try their luck at another table. She was down so far, but it didn't bother her. Aside from the fact it wasn't her money she was gambling with, she knew the score. The house always wins. That was why opening a casino would be so lucrative for Freddie and Sammy.

Pushing forward another handful of chips, she laid her next bet and smiled politely as another man joined the table next to her. She waited patiently as the dealer dealt him in. The cards were played and she won, the payout replenishing her dwindling pile.

'Nice hand,' the player next to her said.

'Luck of the draw,' Anna replied.

'Ah, you're one of those,' he said knowingly.

'What do you mean?' Anna asked, with a polite laugh.

'One of those people who believe all gambling is down to luck.'

'Well, isn't it?' Anna asked, turning to face him. 'I mean, at the end of the day, it's a pack of cards that are shuffled into a random order. There are only so many chances you have of winning. Unless of course the casino is corrupt and the cards are placed in specific order in favour of the house.' She shrugged. 'Who knows?'

The man nodded slowly with an amused smile.

'So, you think we're being set up then? Do you think it's all just a big fix?' He grinned, showing even white teeth. His eyes twinkled as he leaned in conspiratorially. 'We could be being taken for all we're worth here.'

Anna laughed. 'No, I don't think that. But I do believe it's all down to luck. That's what gambling is all about, after all. The anticipation of whether or not your luck will come in.'

The man nodded slowly again and they played another hand in silence. Anna looked at the large clock in the corner. Freddie and Sammy had been gone for about fifteen minutes.

'I don't buy it.'

'Sorry?' Anna asked, with a frown.

'Your story. You say this is about luck, but of all the games in a casino blackjack is one of the most strategic. It takes a certain element of skill and thought, both of which you've displayed in your last three hands,' the man answered. They continued playing as he spoke. 'Considering you walked past all the actual tables of luck like roulette and headed straight here, that tells me that blackjack is your usual game. You gravitate towards it because you're a strategic thinker and like to believe you have some control. But you don't want to say that to me, a stranger, because that would draw me into a much deeper conversation, and considering you prefer to keep yourself to yourself, that wouldn't suit you very well, would it?' The man paused and Anna kept her eyes trained on the table, very alert to the subtle shift in the conversation. 'You're not the usual extrovert who favours blackjack, yet not exactly an introvert either. You are quite an interesting person, Miss Davis.'

'You seem awfully concerned with my personality type,' Anna replied coldly, 'and I don't recall giving you my name. Should I be concerned at your level of attention, Mr…?' She turned and raised an icy eyebrow at him.

He held his hands up and smiled in apology. 'I'm sorry; I haven't introduced myself. That was rude of me.' He held his hand out to shake hers. 'I'm Frank Gambino. And you're Anna Davis.'

Anna shook his hand and hid her surprise. He was supposed to be meeting with Freddie and Sammy. Frank turned back to the table to play the next hand. Anna followed suit, still unsure why he was here playing cards with her instead of being in the meeting.

'Well, it's nice to meet you, Mr Gambino, though if it's Freddie you're looking for—'

'Actually it's not,' he cut her off. 'I know what it is that Mr Tyler and Mr Barker want. If anything, I'm surprised they haven't come to me sooner.' The New York twang was clear in his tone and Anna kicked herself for not picking up on it sooner. 'I'm happy to come to some sort of arrangement with them, but there are certain things that I want in return and one of those things happens to be under your control, Miss Davis.'

The dealer dealt another hand and Anna tried to focus on the cards, her head whirling. What could he possibly want from her? She pushed her long hair back behind her ear and snuck a proper glance at him. He was looking at his cards. Tanned with deep-set dark eyes and perfectly slicked-back dark hair, he looked every inch the Italian-American she now knew him to be. He wore a blue suit and heavy aftershave and Anna gauged him to be nearing forty. His eyes flicked over and met hers and Anna quickly turned back to the table.

'I don't know what you could possibly want from me that Freddie can't give you,' she replied bluntly. She didn't like how this conversation was going.

'Then let me explain. A few years ago we helped out a man who ran a bar. In exchange for our help, he was supposed to do a job for us. We got some people off his back and settled some of his debts – and how did he repay us? Well, he didn't. And no one gets away with accepting help from my family and then not paying their dues. So, I made sure his business received no more custom. I liked the building and the location, and realised it would be perfect for a little venture I had in mind. Once he was bankrupt and no longer in a position to keep the bar open, I planned to swoop in and take the premises for a nice low price. It was to be a smaller, exclusive casino. High-rolling members only.' Frank picked up a chip and twisted it through his fingers, back and forth. 'The realtor he worked with was prepped and ready to bring it to me when he eventually came in. Only something went wrong. They had a new guy, some kid fresh out of college. It was his first week and he was eager to get a deal signed. He took the details when the call came in and without telling anyone he took two young ladies to see it later that day, even though it wasn't yet officially on the books.'

'Robert…' Anna breathed, realisation hitting her. She remembered how desperate the young agent had been for them to see the property, having rejected the first two he'd shown them.

'Those two ladies made arrangements there and then, and the contract was finalised before my guy even knew that the call had come in. Legally there was nothing I could do. It had been done.'

'And illegally?' Anna asked.

'Well, I could have forced my hand, but I respect the rules here the same way I expect them to be respected in New York. I knew it was Vince's ground and that you would be under their protection. I had no interest in starting a war over a stupid mistake. So, I decided to wait until a more delicate opportunity came along. And here we are.' He spread his arms out.

'You want my club,' Anna said flatly. Her heart turned to ice and hit the bottom of her stomach with a thud. Frank Gambino, one of the heads of the Mafia, wanted her club. She felt sick. This was why she had been invited. This was why she had been separated from Freddie. Frank would have known that Freddie wouldn't accept this.

'You're a clever girl, Anna,' Frank said. 'You've made a huge success of that club and I admire you for that. You've even moved on to a comedy club now too – that must be great fun.' Frank's tone was friendly, as if they were old pals catching up. Anna felt the bile rising in her throat, but she kept her expression neutral. 'I would be happy to pay you over the odds for Club Anya. I'm sure you can convince your business partner to sell her half of the club along with yours. After all, she wouldn't want to risk an unknown entity buying your half and becoming her new partner. I know that isn't what you had planned, but it would leave you very comfortable financially and free up your time to concentrate on your other venture. And if we can come to this agreement swiftly and quietly' – he lingered and stared at her – 'then I will grant your boyfriend the permission to open his casino and I will be generous in lowering the percentage I take. With what he's set to make from there, you wouldn't have to work anymore. That would be nice, wouldn't it? I'm sure after a long day in a man's world, every woman is secretly dreaming of the day she no longer has to fight her way through it.'

Anna stood up abruptly and straightened her dress. Picking up the satin bag full of chips, she placed it down in front of Frank and stared back at him coldly.

'Not this woman, Frank. You see, I don't believe that this is a man's world anymore. It's certainly not here in London, anyway. The only thing I dream of is making my empire bigger. Thank you for your offer, but the answer is no.'

Anna turned to leave.

Frank clicked his fingers and two men behind her blocked her way, giving her no choice but to stay and listen.

She turned back to face Frank in frustration. 'Ask your men to move themselves out of my way,' she demanded.

'I'm going to give you some time to think about it.' Frank's tone lost its charm. 'If you decline my offer, I will make sure Mr Tyler and Mr Barker have no place on the casino scene at all. I suggest that you keep our conversation to yourself, until such time as you have made a sensible decision.' Frank motioned for his men to move. 'It was lovely to meet you, Miss Davis. I hope you will still join us for dinner.'

Seething with rage at the corner Frank had her trapped in, Anna turned and walked through to the bar without another word. Taking a deep breath, she just about managed to stop herself from leaving. Freddie was expecting her to be here when he got out of the meeting and she didn't want to have to tell him about this yet. Not until she had worked out how to deal with it. She would put on her poker face and get through this evening. But after that, she had to figure out how she was going to take on the Mafia and still come out the other side breathing.

He might be one of the most dangerous men on the planet, but it would be a cold day in hell before she let a bully like Frank Gambino waltz in and take her club. He assumed she would just roll over and comply. Well, he was in for a sharp shock. Because Anna Davis didn't roll over for anyone.

CHAPTER EIGHT

Freddie's expression was thoughtful as he toyed absentmindedly with a pen at his desk in Club CoCo. It had been an interesting evening at the casino the night before. Frank was a good host and dinner had been spectacular. Anna had seemed a bit quiet, but then perhaps she was wary of this new alliance with the Mafia. She was sharply cautious when someone new came on the scene. It was a residual defence mechanism from her painful past. It took a lot for Anna to trust anyone new. But that wasn't necessarily a bad thing, in Freddie's eyes.

Freddie turned his thoughts back to Frank. He felt a little frustrated, because no matter how much he'd tried last night, he hadn't been able to manoeuvre the conversation towards the casino plans. Frank seemed strangely determined to keep away from the subject and when Freddie had tried to push, he had asked that they discuss it another time. The only business he'd been interested in discussing had been cocaine. Frank had just come from a stay in Mexico, where he'd been dealing with cartel business. The Mafia worked alongside the cartels importing drugs into America, but this wasn't something Freddie was interested in. He already had suppliers.

Freddie took a deep breath and sighed, reminding himself to be patient. Frank had just arrived; perhaps he was jet-lagged and needed to wind down before he jumped into another business venture. The man was only human after all. Or perhaps he needed more time to suss Freddie out before he gave his approval. This was hopefully the start of a long, fruitful relationship with the Mafia. If Freddie had to take things slow to gain their trust and respect, then that was what he would do.

The door to the office flew open with a bang and despite himself, Freddie jumped. DI Fraser bent over double to catch his ragged breath. He had clearly run from wherever he had come from. Freddie frowned and stood up.

'You alright, mate, running in here like your arse is on fire?' he joked, concerned.

'Not mine, Freddie,' Fraser panted, 'yours.'

'What? What's happened?' Freddie's half-smile disappeared and he quickly strode across the room to close the door behind John, who half fell into a seat.

'Viktor Morina. His body's been found.'

Freddie's blood turned cold and he sat back against the desk. Viktor Morina was an Albanian sex-slave trader in South London. Or at least he had been until just over a year ago, when Freddie had killed Viktor for trying to take out his younger brother Michael. His men had disposed of the body, as they had disposed of bodies many times before. This was the first time one had ever come back to haunt them.

'Where? How?' he asked.

'That's the weird thing, Fred. It was out in the open, dumped on the side of the nearest road from where they buried him. He'd been dug up. There's a big fuck-off hole left in the field.'

Freddie's eyes widened in shock. He couldn't believe what he was hearing. Who on earth would have dug up a decomposing corpse and left it on a public road for anyone to find? Who would have even known where the body was, other than himself and the men who had buried him? None of them would want this ever coming out, nor would any of them tell a soul, that much he was certain of.

Fraser waited and tried to calm his ragged breath as Freddie processed it all. The body had come in that morning. It hadn't been a red flag at the time – these things happened in London from time to time. But when they had identified the body, Fraser knew he had to tell Freddie and fast. Freddie had never outright told him that he had disposed of Morina, but Fraser knew the trouble that the slave trader had caused Freddie. When Viktor went on the missing list, he had quietly put two and two together.

Fraser knew the unspoken laws of the underground just as well as he knew the laws of the justice system. And though he didn't necessarily agree with murder, he wasn't going to mourn the death of a man who had ruined countless young lives. And he wasn't going to disagree with the fact that he deserved it either. If you play the game of the underworld, you accept the consequences when you make a wrong move.

Now, Fraser's priority was helping Freddie cover this all back up. And he had a plan – or half a plan anyway. It was risky, but there was no time to play it any other way.

'I think we can sort this out if we act quickly. The body's undergone a basic post mortem which has identified who he is and the basic cause of death, but they need a forensic examination to get anything further. The forensics team are tied up with a bunch of fire victims. They're busy trying to prove it was an insurance job. They won't get to this body until the morning. If we can get in tonight and take him, it can't go anywhere. Who have you got in your pocket at the mortuary?'

Freddie thought it over. It could work, if they executed the extraction properly. They didn't really have the time to plan it well, but this might be the only opportunity to get himself or one of his men out of a murder charge. If they found any trace of DNA at all, or anything that led them back to the house where they'd killed him, any one of them could go down for it.

'OK, I'll gather a crew,' he said eventually. 'Cheers for the intel – you might just have saved my arse.'

'Again,' Fraser added with a wry grin.

'Again,' Freddie agreed, nodding. 'Right…' He breathed out heavily. 'I've got Melrose on payroll. Can you find him and bring him back here at ten o'clock tonight? Ask him to swipe a visitor's security card from the front desk today, unregistered but with full access. I'll get Bill Hanlon in on this. He can clear their CCTV and help plan a route in and out. You're right that it's going to be risky, but it's all we've got.'

'On it. I'll go find him now. See you at ten.' Fraser stood up and left, already working out the quickest way to the mortuary.

Freddie picked up the phone to call Bill. He still couldn't believe this was happening; it was crazy. His mouth formed a hard line. For now he just had to focus on getting himself and his men out of immediate danger. But when this was dealt with, there were some big questions he wanted the answers to – like, who the hell was going around digging up dead bodies? Who could have known the remote, secret location where they had buried Viktor's body? And who wanted to see Freddie Tyler go away for murder so badly that they would risk a move like this?

*

Anna walked through the bar of Club Anya and froze as she caught sight of a group of men at one of the tables. Taking a deep breath, she casually sidled up to the hostess at the front.

'Louise, how long have those men been at table eight?' she asked.

'Oh, not long,' Louise replied, glancing over to them. 'Only about half an hour or so. Why, is everything OK?' She frowned slightly, aware of the tension in her boss's stance.

Anna quickly smiled. 'Yes, of course. Thank you.'

Louise smiled back and walked away to greet some new customers who had wandered in.

Taking a deep breath, Anna hid her irritation and approached the table. 'Frank, what a surprise to see you again so soon.'

'A pleasant one, I hope?' he joked, with a glint in his eye.

'Of course,' Anna lied. 'What brings you to my club?' She raised one eyebrow challengingly as she put emphasis on the word that signalled her ownership.

'Well, I heard that this was a great place to grab a jug of sangria.' He indicated towards the jugs on the table in front of them. 'And of course' – he dropped the pretence and his steely gaze grew hard – 'I like to get a feel for my new investments.'

Anna looked around the table at his men. Their expressions mirrored their boss's. She drew herself up to her full height and met his gaze coolly. They were here to intimidate her and although they were beginning to succeed, she wasn't about to let them know that.

'Enjoy the sangria,' she said with a tight smile that didn't reach her eyes. 'It's on the house.'

Walking away Anna held her head high and tried to hide her shaking hands. With a deep breath she fiercely reminded herself that she had overcome worse things than this. Frank could take his threats and tactics and shove them up his arse for all she cared.

CHAPTER NINE

Bill Hanlon was one of Freddie's oldest and most trusted friends. Due to his impressive technological skills, and more specifically his ability to hack into most surveillance systems, he was a freelancer throughout the underworld. He was sought after by all types of criminal firms pulling bank jobs, robberies and other tricky illegal ventures. He was a fairly neutral entity in the criminal world, though when push came to shove, as it sometimes had in the past, he placed his loyalty with Freddie above anyone else.

He took a last deep drag on his cigarette, then flicked it out of the van window. He was in the driver's seat, parked up just down the street from the mortuary. Freddie sat in brooding silence next to him, staring at the ugly grey building.

'Who was on the mop-up crew that night?' Bill asked, his deep, gravelly voice bringing Freddie's attention back inside the van.

'Dean, Simon, Reggie and Michael. None of them would have talked,' Freddie said.

'No, they wouldn't have,' Bill replied thoughtfully. He frowned and chewed his lip. It didn't make any sense. He was as flummoxed as Freddie was.

The light in the doorway flickered three times. That was the signal. Turning the key in the ignition, the old white van rumbled to life. Without turning the lights on, Bill crept forward down the road and through the gates. Someone ran out of the shadows and closed the gates again behind them, before jumping into the back of the vehicle.

'Alright, Seamus?' Freddie asked, without turning around.

'Grand, Mr Tyler, just grand,' Seamus replied, his voice charged with excitement. He had no idea why they were here, but he was thrilled that Freddie had called him in. He so desperately wanted to start showing his worth. Already he had run a few errands, but Freddie hadn't trusted him on anything big up until now. And Seamus could tell that whatever they were doing, it was definitely something big.

Bill pulled around the side of the building, just outside a fire escape. As they all got out of the van, the door swung open and a man in a long white coat ushered them inside. Freddie stopped and turned to Seamus.

'I want you to stand on the corner and keep an eye out. If you see anyone at all come through the gates, call me immediately. Have your phone out, ready.'

'Yes, boss.' Seamus pulled his phone out of his pocket and jogged over to the corner as he had been told.

Freddie and Bill followed Melrose in and through the labyrinth of corridors in silence. It was dark but the security lights from inside each of the rooms they passed lit the hallways enough to see where they were walking. Soon enough, they stopped at one of the doors and Melrose slipped the key card down though the scanner. The light turned green and the door clicked open, allowing them access. Melrose glanced worryingly at the CCTV camera facing them.

'Don't worry about that,' Bill said. 'I'll wipe them. They're closed circuit.'

'OK,' Melrose breathed. He held the door open for them to enter.

Freddie winced and wrinkled his nose. Despite the overpowering odour of chemicals that were clearly used to keep the place sterile, the unmistakable stench of death hung heavily in the air. It was a sickly, cloying smell that reminded Freddie of rotting meat. Which, he reasoned, was exactly what it was.

'Over here.' Melrose guided them to a wall full of body drawers. He pulled one of them open and the smell immediately intensified. Bill turned away, making a noise of complaint. Freddie pushed down the urge to vomit and looked at what was left of Viktor Morina.

The plastic sheeting they had buried Viktor in hadn't protected him much. His clothes had been removed, presumably by the coroner. Patches of mottled, waxy skin had sunk in and wrapped around his bones and a few strands of hair were still stuck to the top of his skull, but aside from that there was little left but greying bones. Freddie was surprised at how quickly his body had decomposed. He had never actually seen a body again after it had been buried.

Melrose handed Bill a large, full plastic bag.

'This contains everything else. The wrap he was in, his clothes, any loose parts, stuff like that,' he said. Bill grimaced and took the bag without a word.

Melrose opened a cupboard and pulled out a fresh body bag. He handed it to Freddie. 'We need to slide him into this, then we can carry him out. If you can get it over his head and shoulders, I should be able to tilt the tray and push him in.'

'Right, OK.' Freddie quickly pulled a pair of leather gloves out of his pocket and slipped them on. Aside from making sure there were no fingerprints left behind, he couldn't bring himself to touch Viktor's body with his bare hands.

Taking a deep breath, Freddie lifted the skull and slid the open neck of the bag underneath. Something cracked but he ignored it. Gently easing his fingers underneath the shoulders, he shifted the bag further, making sure that each side moved into it. He nodded at Melrose and Melrose lifted the metal base of the drawer. Freddie braced himself against the additional weight as the body slid into the bag. Melrose guided it down carefully until they finally pulled the bag over Viktor's decaying feet. Nothing remained on the slab of metal now except a trail of slime that would be removed later, when Melrose cleaned up.

Freddie let the bag slump to the floor and zipped up the open end. He breathed out in a sigh of relief. That hadn't been too bad.

Melrose closed the drawer and bent to pick up the end of the body bag. Freddie lifted the other end at the same time and they began their journey back out of the building.

Melrose's breathing became more and more laboured as they walked, not used to carrying such a heavy weight. He tried to quieten it, as he realised that Freddie wasn't struggling at all.

Bill opened the door ahead of them and dumped the bag by the van. Glancing sideways he checked Seamus was still in position. He was. Nodding at Freddie he disappeared back inside.

'Where is he going?' whispered Melrose.

'To wipe the cameras. Listen—' Freddie shifted the weight of the body bag onto one side so that he could open the back doors of the van. 'When I'm gone you need to clean down that room. It will be investigated.' Freddie dropped his end of the body into the van and helped Melrose push the rest of it in. 'You've got an hour from when Bill gets back here until the cameras start recording again. You need to be out of here before they start up. Got it?'

'Yeah, I got it,' Melrose replied shakily. He had been on Freddie's payroll for a while, slipping him information here and there. Tonight had been the first time he had needed to step up, and he was scared shitless.

'And get yourself an alibi. Familiarise yourself with the details,' Freddie said.

'I will do,' Melrose replied. He wanted nothing more now than to get back home, showered and in bed so that he could forget about all of this.

Bill came back out of the door and got straight into the van, starting up the engine.

'Right, go on,' Freddie instructed. He whistled to Seamus. 'Seamus, let's go.'

'Yes, Mr Tyler.' Seamus ran over and jumped up into the back of the van, next to the body. He paused as he registered what it was. Freddie waited, watching for his response. Seamus was still green, but Freddie had high hopes for the boy. Tonight was a test, to see how well he would cope with the less attractive side of 'the life'.

After a moment Seamus looked up at him with a carefully neutral expression. 'Ready when you are, boss,' he said.

Freddie nodded, impressed that he had taken it so well. Many great men in their world had baulked the first time they had been faced with something like this.

Melrose disappeared and Freddie jumped into the passenger seat.

'Where to now?' Bill asked quietly as they drove away. Freddie was silent for a minute as he considered his options.

'I have somewhere, but it will have to wait until tomorrow night. Can you keep him and the van hidden in the warehouse until then?' he asked. Bill nodded.

'OK. Drop Seamus and me off to my car then and I'll sort it out in the morning,' Freddie said. He took a deep breath. He wasn't sure Tom was going to be ready for this, but he had no choice. He couldn't afford Viktor making another appearance. This time, he had to stay buried for good.

CHAPTER TEN

He watched as the flames licked and curled around the pile of clothes they had dumped on the fire. The muddy material burned quickly, disposing of all the evidence that they had been the ones to dig up that body. Two pairs of clothes, two pairs of boots and the sheets that they'd laid down in the car to protect the seats. In just minutes there was nothing left, no sign that they had ever been there. The smoke rose up into the sky and drifted away over the rolling green fields surrounding them.

He turned as his accomplice came out of the house to stand with him. 'Is that everything?' he asked. 'Everything you were wearing, or touched.'

'Yes, of course,' the other man replied.

'And our new friend? He's definitely on board?' he asked, searching his companion's face.

'Oh yes, one hundred per cent. He almost bit my hand off for the opportunity.'

'Good.' He nodded, pleased with this result. It had been a gamble, but from his time studying the man in question, he'd been sure his offer would be met with excitement. And he'd been right.

'He'll meet with you tomorrow to discuss what's required of him,' the other man confirmed. He lifted his face to the sun, his olive skin soaking up its warmth.

'Perfect. Not long now,' the first man said, glancing at him sideways. 'Then you can go and enjoy some real sun.'

'The sooner the better,' came the reply.

'Patience, my friend. All in good time.' He smiled coldly at the dying fire. 'There's still much to be done. We must tread carefully, one thing at a time. Then, the world is ours.'

*

Tanya's heels cracked out a rhythm on the hard floor as she walked through to the bar of Club Anya with purpose. Head held high, she smiled broadly at Carl and Anna as she reached them.

Anna was sitting at the bar drinking coffee, and she and Carl had been in deep conversation but this ceased as they turned towards Tanya.

'Wow, you look amazing. What's the occasion?' Anna asked.

Tanya had gone all out today with a black bodycon dress that did every curve on her body justice. Finished with high leopard-print Louboutins and matching belt, she was dressed to kill. Not a single perfect curl was out of place and she sported what Anna knew to be her favourite fire-engine-red lipstick. Anna suddenly wondered if she had forgotten something important today.

'No occasion, I just needed to feel alive,' Tanya replied dramatically. She shot them a dazzling smile and Anna returned it warmly. 'I've had an idea. We need an adventure.'

She sat down next to Anna and pulled out an iPad from her handbag. 'I'm thinking we should go to Monaco for a week. Look at this,' she squeaked. Opening up a website she handed the device to Anna. 'Carl can watch over the clubs and we can go live it up in the land of crazy, rich people. What do you think?'

Anna laughed. 'Tan, we can't leave right now, we've only just opened at The Last Laugh – it needs us. And what about Tom anyway? Freddie might be able to move things around but Tom's just started on site – he can't leave the build right now.'

'I don't mean *them*,' Tanya tutted. 'I just mean us! A girls' trip, crazy adventuring, out in the wild.' Tanya swept her hand out, as though painting a picture for her friend.

'Crazy adventuring in the wild?' Anna asked with a laugh. 'Monaco isn't the wild, Tanya. If you want a crazy wild adventure we should go climb a mountain somewhere, or hike through a jungle.'

There was a pause as they exchanged expressions. 'No,' they laughed in unison, shaking their heads.

'Don't be ridiculous,' Tanya continued. 'I don't own the footwear for shit like that. I don't *want* to own the footwear for it either, actually.'

'Tanya, you don't own a passport,' Anna reminded her, amused. 'So jungle versus Monaco aside, you aren't going anywhere, babe.'

'Oh yeah,' Tanya screwed her lips to the side. 'Should probably get one of those. Oh, forget it,' she grumped. 'It was just an idea. I'm bored. I need some fun.'

Anna squeezed her arm. 'I know. Get a passport, then maybe we can look at booking something when everything's settled down with the new club.'

She knew Tanya had been itching for something different lately. She'd seen the signs. Tanya was a free spirit, who never liked to live the same day twice. It was one of the reasons she had been so excited to open up The Last Laugh. The comedy club hadn't been quite what Tanya was expecting so far though, and Anna could sense her disappointment and thirst for something else to light a fire in her soul.

'Coffee?' Carl offered, holding up the jug.

'Probably shouldn't, already had three,' Tanya replied.

'Clearly,' Anna said, hiding a grin.

'I just don't like sitting still, you know? I get this feeling sometimes like the world is moving so fast and I have to keep moving too or I'll get left behind and be that person who never changes and never evolves. Do you know what I mean?'

Anna laughed. 'Christ, Tanya, you've evolved faster than anyone else I've ever known! I mean, look around you.' Anna gestured around the club. 'Look at this place. Look at what we've achieved. Four years ago I was on the run with no job and you were a stripper. We lived in a tiny shithole and drank wine out of a box.'

'Hey, I liked that shithole,' Tanya said, pointing her finger at Anna in mock indignation. They both laughed and Carl shook his head with an amused grin.

'But seriously, Tanya, look at what we've built here.' Anna looked around at the club herself, fondly. She loved Club Anya. She knew Tanya did too. They had created it together from nothing. They had scrubbed and painted on their hands and knees, built a team of people around them, worked around the clock every hour God sent to make this the place they had both dreamed of. Every detail in the décor, every twist in their fresh new shows, every new face that joined the team of staff, all of it was down to them.

Tanya nodded. 'I know that, mate; this place is everything to me too. I just need a bit of fun. Maybe I need a hobby.'

'Maybe you do. I could just see you finishing a nice cross-stitch cushion cover,' Anna joked.

'Or painting perhaps. I'll model for ya, what do you reckon?' Carl pulled a pose, placing one hand behind his head and pouting for good measure.

'Well, how could I possibly refuse that?' Tanya winked at him from across the bar.

'Anyway, while you're here,' Anna said, changing the subject, 'I was looking at the line-up for next week. I was thinking about—'

'I'll buy a car,' Tanya cut Anna off as the idea hit her. 'Yeah, that's what I'll do. A Porsche or something really sexy. We can go on drives to the country and weekends away. I don't know why I didn't think of that before.'

Her energy renewed by this idea, Tanya stood up and grabbed her handbag.

'Tanya, you can't drive,' Anna said flatly, as Tanya made her way back out again.

'Yeah, I know that,' she replied, rolling her eyes. 'I'll book myself some lessons for it too, won't I? Catch ya later!' She flew out the door, leaving Anna and Carl staring after her.

'She defies all logic,' Anna said, turning back to Carl.

'Yep. Hurricane Tanya,' he replied.

'She does worry me sometimes,' Anna admitted.

'Ah, she'll be alright. She might be a bit crazy but that's not a bad thing. And she's got you. She might be a hurricane but you're the eye of the storm; the calm in the middle, keeping it all together. You make a good team, you two.'

'Thanks, Carl,' Anna said, warmth in her tone. Carl had been with them from the start and had been a good friend to them over the years. He was right – they were a good team. As long as they always stuck together, Anna knew they'd do well in this world.

Her smile faded as she thought back to the threat hanging over her head. There was no way she would ever hand this club over to Frank Gambino. A chill flashed through her body and she shivered. There were still battles ahead yet.

CHAPTER ELEVEN

Tom waved as he opened the door to his Portakabin. He had seen Freddie pull up out of the window as he was getting ready to finish up for the day. He was just waiting for the last few men to clock out before he headed home.

He had been counting down the minutes for the last hour or so. Tanya was off work tonight and had given him some very unsubtle clues as to what she had in mind for the evening. So far, he knew that it involved a lot of champagne and not a lot of clothes, both of which he was very much looking forward to. It seemed he would be delayed now, but that was OK. The anticipation would just make it all the more rewarding later.

Freddie's shoes crunched on the gravel as he approached and Tom stood back to let him in.

'Alright, mate, how ya been?' Freddie asked with a smile.

'I'm great, thanks. What about yourself?' Tom answered.

'Yeah, all fine…' Freddie walked past him and leaned back on one of the smaller filing cabinets to the side of Tom's desk. Tom frowned slightly. Freddie sounded tense and his movements appeared agitated.

'That's good.' Tom walked back to his desk and sat down in his chair. Whatever Freddie wanted to talk about, he would get to in his own time. He reached into the mini fridge underneath the desk and pulled out two cold bottles of beer. 'I keep these for finish time on Fridays usually, but you look like you could do with one.' There was a short fizzing sound as he popped each bottle cap off. He handed one to Freddie, who took it with a grateful look.

'I do, mate,' Freddie said heavily.

They sat in silence for a moment, each savouring the taste of the cold beer.

Freddie rubbed his eyes tiredly. 'You've been laying the foundation cement today, haven't you?' he asked.

'Yeah, got the north side down this afternoon. Nearly at the central stairwell, so stopped there until the morning. That area runs deeper, obviously, so best done in one shot,' Tom replied. He was happy with how things were going so far. Everything was running to schedule, no major screw-ups anywhere.

Freddie reached into his jacket pocket and pulled out a bulky brown envelope. He threw it onto the desk, in front of Tom. Tom gave him a quizzical look, then opened it and pulled out the contents. Two thick, bound wedges of twenty-pound notes fell out onto the table. He blinked and sized them up; there was a few thousand pounds in front of him. He looked up at Freddie and raised his eyebrows in question.

'I need you to be here with me tonight at midnight. You and I are going to fill the foundations for the stairwell.' Freddie looked him in the eye steadily. 'Some of my men will assist and anything you see tonight, you didn't actually see. It never happened.'

'Oh. Right.' Tom's head whirled and his heart began to beat faster with excitement. Finally Freddie was giving him an 'in' on something. He wondered what it was. What could they be burying under the foundations – money? No, not likely. It would be something he didn't need access to for a while at least. Incriminating files? That could be it. Tom's mind ran away with the possibilities. He knew he'd been right about the paperwork for the build. It *had* been a test and clearly he'd proven to Freddie that he was a cool customer to have on board.

He'd been worried that Freddie wasn't taking him seriously, that he would never be given the position of authority that he so craved. He couldn't bear to live in Tanya's shadow all his life.

He needed to be a man of his own standing. Now he could start showing Freddie what he was made of. He couldn't wait for the evening to start.

Freddie watched the emotions play out across Tom's face as he digested the request. Tom's poker face was atrocious, which was another reason he hadn't been eager to get him involved in the business. But that was before Viktor's body had turned up again out of the blue. The foundations were the only good place he could think of, where he could guarantee Viktor could not be accessed again. Once the concrete had set and the stairs had been bolted down, there was no going back.

Tom swallowed and put the money back into the envelope, trying to act casual, as if it was no big deal. He placed it in the top drawer of his desk.

'Midnight, did you say?' he asked, clearing his throat.

'Yes, midnight. Get the concrete churning, make sure there's enough of everything we need and I'll be here just after. OK?' Freddie said, his eyes searching Tom's for any sign of doubt.

'OK.' Tom nodded with a grin. 'I'll be here.'

Freddie stood up. He wondered how Tom would react when he saw the reason for this midnight meeting. He tried to remember what it had felt like to be a civilian faced with the demands of their world for the first time. He had never really been a civilian, at least not in his adult life. He tried to remember how the world had looked when he was a ten-year-old boy, right before this darker, harder life began to take over. It was so far in the past that he couldn't quite grasp the memory. Would he have felt fear? Would he have frozen?

'I'll see ya later then,' Freddie said.

'Yeah. See you then.' Tom grinned and Freddie walked out. He went back to the car, leaving the fuzzy memory of his ten-year-old self behind. That boy had no place in this world.

CHAPTER TWELVE

Freddie pulled up beside Bill's old van just after midnight and cut the engine. Seamus sat silently in the passenger seat. They stepped out of the car and waited for Paul and Bill to join them.

'Everything alright?' Freddie directed his question to Bill.

'Yeah, all's good,' he replied.

'Except for the fucking stink,' Paul added, looking far from amused.

'Yeah, well, he hasn't worn deodorant for a year, has he?' Freddie said. Seamus snorted. Freddie managed to share a grimace with his brother.

Freddie was pleased that Seamus was proving to be such a good gamble. One lesson that Freddie had learned from Vince, his mentor, was that if you take the right person under your wing whilst they're young, you can count on their loyalty for life. It was how Freddie himself had come into 'the life'. Vince had given him a chance when he was just a boy. Now he was underworld royalty and the time had come where he needed to bring others up the ranks. Others whose loyalty he could guarantee. Seamus was his first serious protégé.

Freddie patted Seamus on the back and the four of them began walking towards the light that was shining from somewhere in the middle of the site. As they passed the vehicle that was blocking their view, Freddie saw Tom already working away, churning the first big vat of cement.

'Oh, hey,' Tom called out in a cheery greeting. 'This first lot is ready to go when you are.'

'OK, great.' Freddie took off his sweatshirt and threw it to one side. He wore a simple tracksuit underneath. Joining Tom, he picked up the ballast and began measuring it out into the next empty vat. Tom glanced at him and blinked, surprise on his face.

'I worked on building sites when I was young,' Freddie explained. 'Helped out me mum, extra money and all that.' He shrugged and continued to mix up the cement.

Tom nodded and carried on mixing. He had only ever seen Freddie in nice suits and flashy cars. It was strange to see him working alongside him here. It was a side of Freddie that Tom found he liked. He could respect a man who didn't mind getting his hands dirty even when he was rich enough to not have to. It also bolstered his belief that if someone like Freddie had gone from labouring on a building site to where he was today, Tom could get there too. Whatever he had to do to get there.

Paul and Bill had disappeared to collect Viktor's body. Freddie had asked them earlier on in the day to make sure it was covered up, so that Tom didn't have to catch sight of the year-old corpse. Though maybe he should let Tom see Viktor, he mused. Perhaps it would show the other man how bad things could get in this life. Perhaps it would scare him back to settling for his comfortable day job and get him off Freddie's back.

'What do you want me to do, Mr Tyler?' Seamus asked.

'Pour that first lot in and make sure it's spread evenly on the bottom. Then wait,' Freddie replied, not looking up.

Seamus did as he was bid and then watched as Bill and Paul made their awkward way through the building site with Viktor. He was wrapped up in old sheets, but it didn't take a genius to work out that it was a body by the shape and size.

Tom paused and his eyes widened in shock as he clocked them coming through. He had assumed it was a gun, or a laptop or something. Some evidence they needed to get rid of. He hadn't for a second considered the possibility that it would be something as serious as this. His heart rate quickened and his palms began to sweat.

'Tom,' Freddie's stern voice cut through his racing thoughts. He turned. Freddie's gaze was steely. 'Focus. One part cement, five parts ballast. Come on.'

'Yes,' he heard himself say faintly.

Paul chuckled and exchanged amused looks with Bill as they saw Tom's face drain of colour. 'What's the matter, Tom? I thought you wanted to play with us big boys, no? This a bit much for your delicate disposition.'

'That's enough,' Freddie chided, though he grinned at his brother's words. He'd told Paul how desperate Tom was to get in with them and had found that Paul's opinions on the subject mirrored his own. Tom wasn't cut out for all of this. He wanted the pretty lifestyle that Joe Public saw them living every day, but he wasn't strong enough for the hard, dark work behind the scenes.

Not able to find an answer, Tom turned his back on Paul and Bill and tried to focus, like Freddie said. He lifted the cement bag. His hands were shaking but he ignored them. Taking a deep breath to try and calm himself down, he poured the dusty powder in.

What had he been thinking? He hadn't been prepared for this. Freddie knew that. Tom glanced over at his friend and saw the mocking smile that played on his lips. Anger coursed through his veins. Freddie was mocking him – they all were. He had come to them and offered to join them, to work for them and keep their secrets. That was what people like Freddie needed, men who weren't afraid to turn a blind eye or bend the rules to help him run things smoothly. He should have been glad of Tom's offer, grateful for it even. Tom would have happily helped out with the running of things, seen to it that money went where it should, or clients were looked after. That was what it was all about, right? Freddie had 'heavies' for the more gruesome stuff like this, surely?

Why on earth would he bring this to Tom's door? He could have at least pre-warned him.

As Paul and Bill walked towards them with Viktor, Paul suddenly tripped over a loose brick and stumbled forward. His grip loosened and he lost contact with his end of Viktor's body. Bill grasped the body bag tighter, trying to contain the situation and get a better hold, but he was caught off-guard. As he yanked the bag, the body slid out the other end, hitting the floor with a sickening crunch.

There was a shocked silence for a moment as everyone registered what had just happened and stared down at the mess of remains on the floor. Paul glanced over towards Freddie, his face frozen in surprise. Tom leaned over and violently threw up the contents of his stomach.

'What the fuck,' Tom wailed, in between final dry heaves. 'What the fuck is that, Freddie? Jesus Christ.' He put his head in his hands and crouched down. Strangled sounds came out through his hands. He couldn't breathe; true panic was beginning to set in.

Paul blinked and looked stunned. 'Is he fucking crying?' he asked Freddie in disbelief. 'Are you joking, mate? Seamus here is barely eighteen and he's not bawling like a baby!'

In truth Seamus was looking a tad green, but he was holding his own and styling it out as any hard man would be expected to. Freddie's respect for the boy rose up another notch.

'No, I'm not fucking crying!' Tom shouted, standing back up. 'I'm just trying to understand what the fuck is going on! What – I mean…' He looked at what remained of Viktor as he tried to find the words. 'What even *is* that? How long have you had… him? Her? Oh, Jesus…' He pulled his hair between his fingers and began to pace up and down.

'We shouldn't have brought him along, Fred,' Bill spoke up, his voice calm.

Freddie nodded. 'Tom, you wanted into this life. Well, this is it. This is the gritty, shitty work that goes on behind the scenes. Not every day, of course. This is rare, to be fair. But it does happen. And I need to know that the men on my payroll can just get on with whatever is thrown at them, no matter how bad. The cars and the money and the kudos on the street? That's just a small part of a very dark life. Now' – Freddie picked up Tom's shovel from the ground and handed it back to him – 'get moving. This cement ain't going to mix itself. What I said earlier still stands. Tonight never happened and you never saw a thing. You've been paid for a job, that's all. There won't be another one, so you don't need to worry about anything. Now let's get this done. Come on.'

Wiping the vomit from his chin with his sleeve, Tom tried to spit out the sour taste of bile that coated his mouth. He took the shovel from Freddie and carried on mixing. What else could he do? He turned away from Paul with his look of disdain and the teenage boy who was regarding him as though he was a complete weirdo.

They could have given him a proper chance, put him on anything other than burying rotten skeletons. But they hadn't. He'd been set up for a fall from the beginning. Well, that wouldn't be something he'd be forgetting in a hurry.

The small team worked together in silence. Tom turned away as Bill and Paul dropped Viktor's body into the thin layer of cement at the bottom of the pit. They carried on, him and Freddie, until all the cement needed to fill the section up had been mixed, poured and evenly spread. As Paul pulled the levelling stick away from the surface for the final time, Freddie turned to Tom and clapped him on the back.

'Thank you,' he said simply. 'You must be exhausted. Get off home; I'll see you in the week. If anyone asks about this tomorrow, tell them you had a night crew in, as we moved the schedule up.'

'Got it,' Tom said tightly. The atmosphere had calmed down and everyone nodded at him as he passed to leave. 'Catch you later,' he said, leaving the site hurriedly.

Freddie turned to Paul and Bill and blew out a long breath. 'Well. I'd like to see Viktor get out of this one,' he joked, trying to lighten the mood. Bill smirked tiredly, and Paul rolled his eyes. Seamus didn't respond this time, barely able to keep his eyes open.

'Come on, kid, let's get you home. Don't worry about training. You can have a morning off; I'll text Robbie,' Freddie said.

'Thanks, boss,' Seamus replied, too tired to argue.

They got in the car and Freddie drove out through the gates. Seamus was asleep before they even hit the road.

Freddie took a deep breath and exhaled wearily, worry lying heavily on his chest. Viktor's body was dealt with. But what about Tom? Was he going to take the casual dismissal OK? He had seemed to accept it, but Freddie had caught the resentment in his eyes.

And what were they going to do about finding the person who'd dug Viktor up? Whoever did it had known exactly where he was. What else did they know? And how long would it be before they found out he was gone again?

CHAPTER THIRTEEN

The key sounded in the door and Anna jumped. She closed her eyes and cursed at her overanxious response to the small noise. She felt as though she was on tenterhooks all the time now at home, since the break-in, and she hated it. She closed the door to the fridge and turned to greet Freddie as he came into view.

'You're home early,' she said, frowning at how stressed he looked.

'Yeah, I'm knackered. Need some downtime before tonight.' They wandered through to the lounge and Freddie flopped heavily onto the sofa. He held his arm out and Anna joined him.

'Everything OK?' she asked. She waited as he paused before answering.

'No, it's not really. Something came up that I wasn't expecting.' Freddie shifted slightly so that he could look at her.

They were much more open about Freddie's less legitimate work these days. They had nearly broken up a year before because of secrets he had been forced to keep from her, and when they made it through unscathed Freddie had been careful never to let himself get into a position like that again. These days he told Anna everything, even things she would be better off not knowing.

'Viktor Morina was the slave trader who tried to take Michael out last year, when we were all still looking for Katherine,' he said.

'Right,' Anna replied. She remembered him telling her about him after it had come out that Michael was the one who had kidnapped Katherine in the first place.

'He was dealt with and disposed of accordingly,' Freddie said.

Anna nodded but didn't say anything. She knew what Freddie meant by that and accepted it without question. She didn't exactly agree with murder, but she was well aware of the rules in Freddie's world. If you tried to kill one of the Tylers, they were within their rights to respond in turn.

'He was found a couple of days ago on the side of a road, near where he had been buried. He'd been dug up.'

'What?' Anna's face was aghast. 'Dug up? What the hell?'

'It's OK,' Freddie quickly reassured her. 'It's been dealt with. I've made sure he's now somewhere he can never be found and the police have nothing. It's done with. But what's worrying me is how he got there.' Freddie rubbed the bridge of his nose. 'Only a few people knew where he was, and none of them would have wanted that coming back to bite them. They hadn't told a soul – I checked. I can't work out who could have known Viktor was there and even then, why on earth they would want to dig him up and have him found. It doesn't make any sense.'

'Jesus.' Anna didn't know what else to say.

'On top of that, I don't know what else this person knows. If they were hoping to have me arrested it hasn't worked, so I'd guess they'll probably try again. Just wish I knew what to expect.'

'What are you doing about it?' Anna asked.

'I've got Bill and Sammy looking into it. There's not exactly a lot to go on though.' Freddie leaned his head back into the sofa and closed his eyes.

'You're tired. Get some rest now, worry about this later,' Anna said. She stroked his head, concern marring her face.

She bit her lip. Who would do something like this? It was extremely odd, even in their world. It was the last thing Freddie needed right now, especially as he was looking to expand the business. He would have to put that on the back burner until this had all been dealt with. Frank Gambino had been delaying their meeting anyway; Anna knew that. He was waiting for her to agree to his terms before he would help Freddie. Not that that would be happening any time soon.

Surely Gambino wouldn't go to such lengths to pressure her into agreeing to hand her club over, would he? Her heart skipped a beat. He wouldn't have got to his position by being nice, that was for sure.

Anna's lips formed a thin line as she reached for her phone. She needed to deal with this. She glanced at Freddie, who had already fallen asleep. She texted the number that Gambino had given her.

We need to talk. When can you meet? Anna

The reply came back almost instantly.

I can be at Club Anya in an hour

Anna bit her lip as she considered what she was doing.

See you there. Anna

She let out a long breath and slipped her arm away from Freddie's sleeping form. Tiptoeing through to the bedroom, she went to change and put some make-up on. For what she was about to do, she needed to be dressed to kill.

An hour later, Anna sat tensely behind the desk in her small office. Wearing a sleek pencil dress and with her war-face on, she felt ready to face Frank Gambino.

Carl knocked on the door and then opened it, announcing her visitor. Anna stood up to greet him. Frank walked in, his expression appreciative as he saw Anna. He smiled and his eye glinted as the door closed behind him.

'So nice to hear from you, Miss Davis. You have come to your decision?' Frank asked cordially.

Anna felt hot anger course through her veins at his smug expression. He thought she was here to bow down to him, give into his demands in return for an easy life. The good little woman, doing her bit for her man, scared by his tactics. Well, he was in for a surprise.

'I have indeed,' Anna replied curtly. She softened her tone with a tight smile. 'Won't you sit down?'

Frank took the offered seat and waited, still seemingly confident that he was about to get what he had come for.

'I might not be in your line of business, Frank,' Anna started, 'I may not have your sway or the fear and respect that you have gained over the years. But that doesn't mean that I'll cower when backed into a corner by a bully.'

'Excuse me?' Frank asked, frowning.

'Let's be open with each other, shall we? It saves dancing around the basic truth. You've surely figured out by now that I'm never going to hand the club over willingly. That's why you thought it necessary to threaten Freddie by having that body dug up and exposed. I imagine you knew he would have the network available to get out of it – just. But you thought it would scare me enough that I would agree to your terms.' Anna stared at Frank levelly from across the desk.

Frank's frown grew deeper. 'What are you talking about? What body?'

'Oh come on; please don't treat me like an idiot. We both know it was you. Freddie has no real enemies right now, no one threatening him, nothing. Life has been peaceful for us for over a year. You come along asking for my club and when I don't agree, this happens.' Anna raised her arms to the sides and shrugged. 'I know who you are, Frank. I know the Mafia don't mess around and I know that when it comes to the gambling scene, you are the royal family. But this isn't New York. This is London, and this is *our* world. And in our world people don't dig up other people's bodies to get other people arrested. You need to stop this now. There must be no more of this.' Anna held his gaze, hoping that her beating heart wasn't so loud that he could hear. As confident as she knew she sounded and looked, she was shaking like a leaf inside. In all her years, she had never thought she would have to confront someone in the Mafia. She wondered for a second if she was totally insane. He could kill her and get rid of her in an instant if he chose to.

Frank didn't respond straight away and the pair faced each other silently for a few moments.

'You think I'm trying to scare you into selling to me?' he said eventually with a slow smile. He sat back and shrugged nonchalantly. 'Sorry, I have no idea what you're talking about. After all, your personal life is none of my concern. What *is* my concern is this club. So I will ask you again, will you consider my offer? If you agree, I will make sure Freddie gets what he needs from me and you won't ever have to worry about money again.'

Anna seethed. She didn't believe him for a second. It had definitely been him – there was no other person who would need to do this sort of thing. They had achieved peace with the other firms and had formed valuable alliances. And if it was a young try-hard attempting to jump the ranks, Freddie would have been able to find that out already through the grapevine. Taking a deep breath, she broke eye contact and sat back in her chair. She folded her hands in front of her.

'Even if I did want to agree to your terms, I can't. The club isn't mine anymore. It hasn't been for a while.'

'What do you mean?' Frank asked, his tone taking a hard edge.

'I mean that I'm not the owner of Club Anya. I'm not even part owner. The club belongs solely to Tanya. I just work here.' Anna pushed a file across the desk to Frank, who opened it and pulled out the contents. 'This is a photocopy of the legal document drawn up a year ago, transferring my half of the business into Tanya's name. It's all legal and binding. So, as you can see, even if I did want to sell this business, it's not mine to sell.'

Frank's jaw dropped as he scanned the pages. It was as Anna had said – she no longer had any legal right to the club.

It was genuine, the information she had given Frank about the club. Just over a year ago they had been in a situation where she and Freddie might have had to flee the country and start again under new identities. If that had happened, she would never have been able to come back and her assets would have been seized. To ensure Tanya and the club were both protected, Anna had hastily had the papers drawn up and transferred ownership to Tanya. No one had known about it, not even Tanya. She had forged Tanya's signature on the documents knowing that this would be fine with her friend, should it ever come up.

When they were in the clear and no longer needed to consider running, Anna had shelved the document away in her personal files. She wasn't sure what had made her keep it. It was the only copy; if she had destroyed it the club would still be hers. But something in the back of her mind had told her to keep hold of it, in case she ever needed it again. And now she was glad she had.

'But… why?' he asked, confused.

'That is none of your concern. I do have a counter-offer though.' Anna tried to sound friendly, despite the hatred she felt burning inside. She needed to keep relations civil between them. Frank could still destroy all of them in an instant if the mood took him. 'I still get half of the profits from the club each month. I'm willing to give you ten per cent of that for the next five years, as a gesture of goodwill and friendship between us, in exchange for your support towards Freddie's casino.'

Frank barked an incredulous laugh.

'Please,' Anna continued. 'I know you're disappointed and that you haven't got what you came for. But that is all I'm able to offer you. You can see that. I don't wish for bad blood; I'm hoping that we can all move forward benefitting from this.'

Frank stood up, a look of amused shock on his face. He stared at her and nodded slowly. 'Well, you certainly are full of surprises, aren't you, Miss Davis?' He leaned forward over her and Anna had to force herself not to shrink back under his intimidating stance. His words were cold. 'I don't care what legal games you and your business partner are playing, nor the reasons why. I want this club. Now, let's negotiate, shall we?' His hand shot forward and he seized Anna's face in a vice-like grip. She gasped in shock. 'It appears my offer wasn't quite juicy enough for you. But everyone has a price. So, what's yours, Anna?'

Anna swallowed hard and tilted her chin up at him in defiance, her eyes burning. 'There is no price on this club,' she said through gritted teeth. 'No amount of money in the world would force us to give it up. Especially to someone who thinks they can walk in here and force our hand like this. I've known bullies before, Mr Gambino.' Anna leaned forward despite his grasp, forcing him backward. 'I lived with a bully like you for years, making the same mistake over and over – and that mistake was letting him push me around. I won't make that same mistake again, not with anyone.' She tried to shove his hand away but he held fast, with venom in his eyes. 'You made me an offer and I have refused. I've made you a counter-offer, one that benefits everyone. If you choose not to accept, that's your choice.' Anna's hard gaze didn't break as Frank squeezed her face in anger.

'Do you know what they do with women who act out of turn in Mexico?' he hissed. 'They cut out their tongues.'

'Well, you're a long way from Mexico and I don't think anyone would take kindly to any harm you inflict on me, Mr Gambino.'

Frank pulled his hand from her face and pushed her away from him. He stood back and straightened his suit. 'I don't accept your offer. I don't take kindly to being told what I can and cannot have by some little woman,' he spat. 'You play at hostess in this club, running around like you own the place, but at the end of the day it's your man whose life you're messing with. It's your man who will pay the price for your stupidity.'

'Firstly' – Anna's eyes flashed – 'the only reason Freddie could suffer from one of my business decisions is if you put him in that situation. That's on you, not me. Our businesses are and always have been completely separate. And secondly, your sexist bullshit is not welcome here. If you ever touch me again I will ensure you regret it. The door is that way, Mr Gambino.' Anna pointed. 'This meeting is finished.'

Frank nodded with a cold smile. 'I'll let you tell Freddie why he won't be opening his casino and why his ambitions of forming an alliance with the Mafia are now hopeless. You can watch his face crumple as you tell him what you've done to him here today. And I'll be sure to leave him a little message of my own before I go. I'll see you again soon, Miss Davis.'

Frank walked out and as the door shut Anna sank back into her chair. She reached up and rubbed her sore chin and cheeks. Her heart was pounding and her hands were shaking. What had she done?

She reached into the bottom desk drawer and pulled out Tanya's stash of cherry vodka. Taking the top off she poured some into an empty glass on the desk and downed it in one. She grimaced as the sharp bite hit the back of her throat.

She needed to tell Freddie. Anna grabbed her phone and began scrolling through her call list before she paused. Her thumb hovered over his name. What was she going to say to him? Frank's words crept into her head, creating a sliver of self-doubt. She had done the right thing, hadn't she? She couldn't cower to Frank;

she couldn't be bullied into handing over all her and Tanya's hard work. It was her livelihood, their work baby. They had built this place up with their bare hands, from nothing. Why should they allow it to be stolen from them? But refusing to sell to Frank meant that Freddie's business suffered.

What if Freddie was angry? What if he felt that she had let him down? The Mafia weren't normal people; there weren't normal rules at play. What if she *was* expected to make the sacrifice, so that Freddie could move forward? What if now there were other consequences? Frank had said something ominous about leaving Freddie a message of his own.

Anna jumped as her phone began to ring in her hand. It was Freddie. A stone forming in her stomach made Anna realise she couldn't bring herself to tell him. At least not yet. Not until she had got her head around it herself. She let the call ring out.

CHAPTER FOURTEEN

Shelley Mitchell glanced sideways at the man who'd picked her up off her usual corner as they mounted the stairs in the house he had taken her back to. He was a bit of alright, she thought. She'd lucked out tonight. She wouldn't mind shagging this one at all. She had been surprised that he hadn't gone with one of the younger, prettier girls on the main strip. Shelley wasn't deluded – she knew she was past it these days. After four kids and too many years on the game to remember, she was puffy around the middle with stretch marks and saggy tits. Her face was weathered and deep lines made her look older than she was. Still, in the dark with some decent make-up on she was still alright, even if she did look a bit rough around the edges.

Shelley figured it was probably his first time, or that he was nervous about being seen. That would explain why he hadn't gone to the main strip. It was too busy. Her little corner around the back of The Swan pub was quiet and secluded. It offered that extra bit of privacy, something she always made sure she mentioned to her clients.

He wasn't much of a talker, but that was OK. They weren't here to hold hands and exchange life goals – they were here to empty his balls and line her pockets.

Entering the bedroom, Shelley sat back on the bed and pulled her legs apart, showing him the goods. She wore a lacy red thong underneath the denim miniskirt, but it didn't hide much.

'Fancy what you see, darlin'?' she asked with a saucy smile.

'Looks good to me,' he responded.

'Got somewhere I can quickly clean up before we start?' Shelley asked. He was her third full-package customer of the night and she was feeling a little stale. Best to have a little wash down there before he got started. It didn't matter so much when she'd had a string of blowies. There was usually more of them than anything else, a quick, cheap release on their way home from a night out. But tonight had been quite busy, which she was pleased about. Her youngest son Kyle had been pestering her for a new PlayStation game. She could get it for him now.

'Through there.' He pointed to the en suite and waited tensely whilst she cleaned herself up.

He hadn't been with a woman in ages and although he had been suppressing his natural urges for a while, he couldn't ignore them forever. She wasn't exactly up to his usual standard, but she had been the easiest one to pick up in an area with no cameras. And that was important.

Shelley came back out of the bathroom in just her underwear and laid herself on the bed. He looked down at her. Rough as she was, it had been a while and she still had all the right parts, so it wasn't difficult for him to get a hard-on.

Pulling down his trousers, he didn't bother to get undressed, just knelt down on the end of the bed and drew her thighs up. He plunged into her, closing his eyes and ignoring her fake noises of pleasure as he focused on getting to where he wanted to be. The warm wetness of her body around him spurred him on and his thrusts became faster.

Barely a couple of minutes passed and he felt himself reaching a crescendo. With a deep groan of relief, he released all of his pent-up frustration and was done. He let go of her legs and pulled himself away.

'Wow, that was amazing,' Shelley lied. She was half glad and half disappointed that he was done so quickly. It gave her more time to earn, but on the other hand she wouldn't have minded a bit of extra bump and grind with him. 'Best I've ever had, that was.'

'Yeah?' he barked a laugh at the blatant lie. 'Well, that's good,' he continued quietly, leaning forward over her again. She grinned excitedly, assuming he was gearing up for round two. 'Because it's the last one you'll ever have.'

'What?' she asked. Her eyes bulged as he wrapped his large hands around her neck and began to squeeze, hard. She grappled with his hands, trying to prise them off her throat but it was to no avail. He was too strong.

'Thing is, you've seen my face and where I live,' he explained conversationally, as she struggled beneath him. 'And that's a problem. Because when the police come round and start asking you girls questions there's a good chance you'll mention this and then they'll find me and all my careful planning would have been for nothing. And I just can't risk that. So we're just going to have to put you down to collateral damage.'

Shelley tried desperately to shake her head, to tell him she wouldn't say a word, but she couldn't even do that. He was holding her too tightly. Her windpipe was fully closed; she couldn't pull in any breath at all. Her lungs were burning and she could feel her face turning red. His body and legs were pinning her down and she couldn't get a hold on anything.

Shelley stared into her killer's vacant eyes and wished to God she had never got into the car. He was going to murder her and there was nothing she could do about it. Tears escaped the corners of her eyes as she thought about her kids waiting up for her at home. They would never know what happened to her. They'd think she had abandoned them.

She wished she had just taken that cleaning gig the Job Centre had offered her. She might not have been able to afford new PlayStation games, but at least her kids would still have a mum.

Shelley's vision turned dark as her body finally gave in to the lack of oxygen. *Who the hell was this evil bastard?* It was the last question that ran through her mind before he squeezed the last few fighting beats of life from her body.

CHAPTER FIFTEEN

It had been a few days since Tom had come home as white as a sheet. He hadn't talked to Tanya about why, and she hadn't asked questions. But something had shaken him up, she could tell. She was preoccupied, still thinking about it all as she walked through Club Anya. She barely heard Carl's warm greeting, not turning until he repeated himself and asked if she was OK.

'What? Oh, sorry… Yeah, I'm good as gold, mate,' she said, forcing a tight smile.

'Yeah alright, pull the other one. What's up?' Carl was concerned. As good a businesswoman as Tanya was, she rarely seemed serious. Even when she was juggling both clubs on the busiest night of the week, she always had a joke on the tip of her tongue and a cheeky wink at the ready. Something about her wasn't right today.

Tanya paused for a moment and seemed to regard him thoughtfully. After a second she looked away and pulled the same tight smile again. Whatever she had been going to say, she had clearly decided to keep to herself.

'Nah, honestly, I'm good. Far too sober though. Think I'll stick about for a cocktail or two once I'm done with Anna,' she said brightly.

'You realise it's eleven in the morning?' Carl asked with an amused expression.

'It's twelve o'clock somewhere, Carl,' Tanya replied over her shoulder as she walked through to meet Anna in the office.

She pushed the door open and found her best friend bent over the desk, frowning at an invoice. Anna looked up at the noise and immediately her face cleared into a warm smile.

'How are you?' she asked as Tanya sat down in the chair opposite her.

'I'm OK, mate. But Tom isn't. That's what I wanted to talk about.' As blunt as ever, Tanya cut straight to the point. She rubbed her forehead, worry lines appearing. 'Do you know anything about what's going on at the moment, with the stuff Freddie has got Tom involved in?'

'Yes,' Anna answered carefully.

'OK. *I* don't know anything, for the record, and I'm not asking either. But whatever it is, it's riled Tom right up. He hasn't slept or eaten properly since he came home the other day. He just keeps staring at his phone all tense and chain-smoking like a fucking chimney.' Tanya sighed heavily. 'Is he alright? That's all I want to know.'

Anna took a deep breath and sat back in her chair. She bit her lip as she thought about how to frame it.

'Listen, you know Freddie. Yes, there are risks to getting involved with him like Tom has, but he's not top of his game for nothing. He hasn't been taken down yet and I doubt that today is his day of reckoning. He faces new problems and threats all the time and he always finds a way to overcome them. That's "the life". You know that. Tom's just new to it all. And from what I understand, Freddie isn't keen to bring him into much more on that side of things anyway. So just let it settle. It'll be fine,' Anna said, her gaze unwavering.

'OK.' Tanya nodded. 'Fair enough. But with all that goes on, how do you always keep such faith that things will be OK for Freddie?' she asked.

'Because I know Freddie, and I trust that he knows what he's doing. And,' she added, 'because I have to. Otherwise I would just go crazy.'

'Christ, Tom's only been working for him for five minutes and I'm halfway to crazy town,' Tanya joked, breaking the sombre atmosphere. Anna grinned.

'Babe, you arrived there years ago,' she joked back. 'They've built you a castle and crowned you mayor.' She laughed and pulled back to escape Tanya's friendly swipe.

'Oh, get out of it. I'm the sanest person I know. It's everyone else who's nuts,' Tanya replied indignantly. 'Anyway. OK. If you say things are fine, then things are fine.'

'Yes... Tanya, there's something else I think you should know.' Anna's face clouded over into an expression of worry. 'I think I know who's responsible for the issues that Freddie's had to deal with lately.'

'What do you mean?' Tanya asked.

'Have you heard of Frank Gambino?'

'Gambino the Gambler, yeah of course. He's the Billy Big Balls of the casino scene,' Tanya answered.

'Right. Well, I met him recently.'

'Ooh, what's he like?' Tanya's eyes widened in excitement.

'Tan, please! That's so not the point right now,' Anna said, rolling her eyes.

'Oh right, yeah. Go on,' Tanya said, curbing her curiosity.

'Freddie wanted to meet him, talk about the possibility of working together on something. We were invited over to one of his casinos in Mayfair for dinner, so we went and Freddie was taken off to a meeting room. I was keeping busy with a bit of blackjack and he joined the table. He wanted to get me alone, away from Freddie, to ask me to sell him the club.'

'This club?' Tanya asked, surprised.

'Yes. Apparently, we jumped the queue when we signed the lease. He had set his sights on it. He said he would give Freddie what he wants, in exchange for me selling him the club,' Anna confirmed.

'Wow.' Tanya wasn't sure how to respond to this revelation. 'What did you say?'

'I told him no, obviously. This is our club. We've worked hard for it, why would we sell it?' Anna said vehemently.

'Well… yeah, but he's the Mafia, Anna,' Tanya replied gently. 'He's technically offered you a fair trade. In their world I'm not sure where we stand on not accepting that. I take it you were to get me to fall in line too?'

'Well, I don't live in their world, Tanya. I live in the normal world where if I don't want to sell my business, I don't have to. But anyway, I told him no and then he got angry and informed me that I would regret the decision and that he wouldn't work with Freddie unless we sell out.'

'Shit,' Tanya breathed. She looked very worried.

'When I first suspected, I met with him and told him that even if I wanted to sell to him, I couldn't. Because the business isn't mine. I just work here,' Anna continued. 'I made him a counter-offer to try to appease him, but he declined.' She chose not to share how nasty things had got in their last meeting. There was no way she was going to be seen as some sort of helpless victim, just because Frank had tried to intimidate her.

'But hang on, that's not true, about the club not being yours. Surely he saw through the lie immediately,' Tanya replied.

'Actually…' Anna pulled the file out from underneath the invoices. She had prepared for this moment. 'It is true. Take a look at this. You remember a year ago, all that stuff with Katherine Hargreaves?'

'Yeah…' Tanya opened the file and looked at the photocopy of the document inside with a confused expression.

'Well, there was a point at which we were ready to run, if the worst happened. Ben Hargreaves was going to fit us both up, everything left here would have been seized, including the club. I couldn't leave things like that; it would have been a nightmare for you. So I had papers drawn up transferring my half of the business into your name.' Anna pointed at the details on the document. 'I, er, forged your signature. Figured you wouldn't mind if it was between that and losing my half of the club to the government.'

'Oh my God.' Tanya was shocked. 'Why didn't you destroy this when everything was OK again? Why didn't you tell me?'

'Well, I knew as long as it was only me who knew about it, that the choice was in my hands. I could destroy it or keep it that way if the need arose. And I had a feeling it might. Turns out I was right. The offer Gambino made to me may have been "fair" as you say, but it has no bearing on you, does it? It's not a fair deal to you; he has nothing to offer you in exchange for the club. So I told him and showed him that it's out of my hands. I had hoped that it would put an end to the problems Freddie's been facing. But I think if anything, I made it worse.'

'Christ, Anna.' For once Tanya was at a loss for words. She closed her mouth, aware that it had dropped open. This was not good. 'What did Freddie say?'

'I haven't told him,' Anna admitted.

'What?' Tanya said, aghast. 'Anna, you need to tell him.'

'What can he do, Tanya? Gambino was pretty clear – either we sell him the club, or he won't do business with Freddie.' She took a deep breath. 'There isn't anything Freddie can do to change that. If anything he'll just get angry and it will start an all-out war. I think we need to sit on it and just wait for it to go away. He said he would let me tell Freddie myself, so I don't think he'll talk to him about it.'

'Anna, people like Frank Gambino don't just go away. There will be consequences.' Tanya's tone was deadly serious.

Anna remembered Gambino's parting words. *And I'll make sure to leave Freddie a message myself.* She shook it off. It wasn't going to make a difference if Freddie knew that he'd said that or not. In his line of work he habitually watched his back.

'Look, he's not here for long. Soon he'll be gone back to New York, back to his real business and this crap will all be forgotten about. And I will tell Freddie why Gambino won't work with him. I just...' She sighed heavily. 'I need to find the right time.'

Tanya nodded and bit her lip in worry. 'I hope you're right,' she said eventually.

'So do I, Tan,' Anna replied. 'So do I.'

CHAPTER SIXTEEN

Freddie knocked on the door of the Portakabin as he entered. 'Alright, mate?' he asked Tom cheerily. He held out a takeaway cup. 'Bought you a coffee. Thought you could use one.'

'Thanks.' Tom took the cup gratefully.

'Hope you don't mind me saying, but you don't look like you're getting much sleep,' Freddie remarked. He looked Tom over with a critical eye. 'Everything OK?' The question was loaded.

Tom nodded. He knew what Freddie was doing – he was sussing out how well he was coping with the knowledge of what was now underneath several tons of concrete stairs. He hadn't been sleeping well, but not for the reasons Freddie thought. Freddie believed he was weak, that the guilt was keeping him up at night, perhaps the fear of hell and damnation for his soul. But it wasn't that. Tom had never been the religious type and viewed life and death in a pretty factual manner. You came, you went, your body was recycled through the earth and the world kept moving on.

Sure, the realisation of what Freddie was capable of and had done had been a shock. The sight of that rotting body had made him sick to his stomach. It had been gross and something he had never seen before. Who wouldn't be sick and shocked? But that wasn't what was keeping him up. He'd talked himself through what he'd seen and had placed it neatly in a box at the back of his mind.

What *was* keeping him up was the memory of how they'd all laughed at him. The look in Paul's eyes when he'd regarded

Tom. It filled him with embarrassment and anger, every time he thought back to that night. Perhaps if Freddie had told him what was going to happen, he could have prepared himself. The others had known, but he had been thrown in at the deep end. He'd been made to look like an idiot, when all he was trying to do was be taken seriously. That was something he wouldn't forget.

'I'm fine, Freddie. You don't have to worry about anything. My lack of sleep has nothing to do with what you're thinking,' he said, looking Freddie in the eye. 'It's all good.' Tom gave him a friendly grin to prove his words.

'OK, if you're sure,' Freddie replied.

'I am. It's just work driving my mind a bit mad. I need to chill out a bit. Maybe catch you for a drink later?' Tom asked.

'Can't, mate, sorry. Got a lot on today. But we'll do it soon, yeah?' Freddie looked at his watch and missed the look of disappointment that flitted across Tom's face.

'Sure, just text me when you're free,' Tom replied.

'Yeah, will do. Alright, I'll see ya later; I've got to go.' With that, Freddie walked out into the sunshine.

Pulling away in his car with the tyres crunching on the gravel, his phone began to ring. He glanced at the screen and answered the car phone.

'Marco, how's things?' he said.

Marco was his main cocaine supplier, an eccentric Spanish importer who had a business model Freddie had come to admire. If he had any interest in importing drugs from South America himself, he would have tried to partner up with this man. But he had enough on his plate at the moment, without getting involved in cartel business.

'Things are good, Freddie, very good. The sun is shining, the coffee is fresh and business is booming. I cannot complain.' His thick accent curled down the line. 'I thought I should let you know though, your guy did not turn up last night. I left it until now, in case he was merely late, but there is still no sign. He is usually very punctual. I hope there is no cause for concern.'

Freddie frowned. Dale Matthews was one of his top-end dealers. He would pick up the order for his area, repackage it and send it down the chain to the next level. There they would cut it and send it trickling down the drugs tree again and again, until it hit the street and was sold to Joe Public. He had never missed a pick-up, in all the years he had worked for Freddie.

'That is strange,' Freddie mused. 'Thanks for the heads-up – I'll look into it. Can you hold the order until I can get it collected?'

'Of course, there is no question. No rush, it will be here waiting for you,' Marco replied.

'Thanks. I'll be in touch.' Freddie ended the call and stopped the car at the traffic lights. Scrolling through his phone, he found Dale's number. It rang out without being answered. Freddie thought about calling Paul to investigate it but then decided against it. He wasn't far away; he would drive over and look into things himself.

Driving into a large, rundown estate full of high-rise flats, Freddie slowed to a crawl. He nodded to a couple of groups of young lads hanging around on the corners. They looked to be minding their own business, but Freddie knew they were lookouts for various gang heads on the estate. He passed with no issue. They all knew who he was, despite the fact he rarely came down here in person.

Somers Town, a sink estate oddly butted up against some of the wealthier homes of Regents Park, was a notorious estate, rife with crime. The police rarely entered, and when they had to it was with caution. Freddie knew the ins and outs of the rabbit warren of buildings like the back of his hand. Although he hadn't lived there as a child, Sammy had, and they often used to knock about there after school and in the holidays. When he had first begun working for Vince as a teenager, a lot of his tasks had involved delivering goods and information to people within the estate. These days, it was some of the men who worked for him who resided here.

Pulling around the side of a building, Freddie parked up and got out of the car.

'Watch that for me,' he said to one of the kids nearby. He only looked to be about ten or so, but Freddie knew that didn't mean much around here. He would already be streetwise and more than capable of telling any interested parties that this was Freddie Tyler's car, should they get any ideas. The boy nodded and laid his bike down on the ground, before sitting beside it. He pulled a packet of cigarettes out of his pocket and lit one.

Freddie skirted around the building, then crossed the road to the next block. He wasn't sure what was going on with Dale, so parking his car away from the front was a bit of extra caution. Keeping his head down, he swiftly entered the building and started to mount the stairs. There were no lifts in this building, nor in many of the others.

Freddie grimaced. Nothing had changed over the years. The cheap plastic covering on the stairs was half ripped up, marked and even burnt in some places. Debris littered every corner – empty cigarette packets, cans and the odd needle. The smell of piss in the stairwell was overpowering and Freddie tried to breathe through his mouth to avoid the worst of it. He jogged up the steps as quickly as he could.

Slowing down as he reached the seventh floor, Freddie was struck by how quiet it was. Dale was a prominent drug dealer on the estate, and by this time of day he usually had at least a couple of his gang on the stairs, keeping an eye on the comings and goings. Stopping outside Dale's front door, Freddie tilted his head to listen. There was nothing, not even the buzz of a TV from next door. Freddie reached into his pocket and pulled on his leather gloves.

He tried the door handle and found it to be unlocked. This much he had expected. No one would try to rob Dale Matthews. His reputation was enough to deter anyone with bad intentions. Walking in with caution, Freddie looked around.

The front room was dark, the curtains still drawn and the light off. Freddie flicked it on, revealing nothing of much interest. A couple of La-Z-Boys sat on one side of the room, facing the large flat-screen TV. A few controllers and a PlayStation sat on the floor in front of a big leather beanbag. Next to this was an overflowing ashtray, no doubt the source of the heavy stench of weed, and a couple of empty cans of beer. There were no frills in the room, and no other signs of life. It was a simple bachelor pad.

A quick glance into the kitchen and bathroom showed them to be unoccupied, so Freddie turned his attention towards the bedroom door. He pushed it open and let the light flood in from the lounge.

'Ah shit…' Freddie groaned and looked up to the heavens as he finally located Dale.

He was sprawled out on the bed, face down, still fully clothed. He would have looked like he was sleeping, were it not for the pool of blood that now soaked the beige duvet cover underneath him. Freddie didn't need to double check; Dale was definitely dead. There was too much blood for him to still be clinging on to life.

Stepping forward, careful not to touch anything, Freddie knelt down for a closer look. Dale's throat had been cut, a deep gash almost from ear to ear. Dale's eyes were still open, a look of shock etched onto his face. He had not been expecting it.

Freddie sighed heavily, the lines on his forehead deepening. He had liked Dale. He had always been efficient and reliable and, as far as he knew, his gang had always been happy with their leader. Now, there would be a mass of young boys and men with no one to look to, and on the Somers Town estate that wasn't necessarily a good thing.

Turning his thoughts back to his own business, Freddie moved back through to the bathroom. Crouching down, he lifted the top off the toilet cistern, reached in and pulled out a plastic sandwich bag that was sitting half submerged in the water. Inside there were a few rolled-up fifties, a passport and a small notebook. Freddie took only the notebook and slipped it into his pocket. He replaced everything to its former position and walked back out into the flat.

Freddie walked out the back door onto the small balcony that was typical of all these flats. Like most of the other residents, Dale had his washing strung up to dry in whatever sun could make its way down through the buildings. Leaning over, Freddie looked around for someone he could talk to. He needed to find Dale's men, see if anyone knew what had gone down. In the building directly opposite, curtains twitched. Down below, a few groups of men stood around in the shadows and at the mouth of the alleyways. One in particular was looking up towards him, not attempting to hide his interest.

Just as Freddie was about to descend and find out who it was, the wail of sirens sounded through the air. The atmosphere changed instantly and all the people who had been milling around scarpered. Three police cars screeched to a halt, directly by the main entrance to the building.

'Shit!' Freddie cursed. He needed to get out. There would have to be a good reason indeed for the pigs to show up like that here and he figured right now it was most likely due to a murder tip-off. He might have some sway with the police, but nothing was going to help him if he was caught alone with a dead man and no solid reason for being there. As he watched, six armed men ran into the building, shouting to one another. They would be running up the stairwell and onto this floor at any moment.

'Oh f—' Freddie mashed his lips together in a hard line and took off running, back though the flat into the main hallway. He started towards the stairs but could hear they were close. It was too risky to get onto the stairs now. His heart hammered against his chest as he weighed up his options. If Dale was wise, he would have had a backup escape route in place with one of the end flats, but which he couldn't tell. Glancing to each side, he made a decision. He knew these buildings and the people in them knew him. He just hoped that was enough right now. He pushed off and ran as fast as he could down the long hallway, not pausing for breath. He urged his body on, ignoring the complaints from his muscles.

Going faster and faster, the sound of the police getting louder behind him, Freddie was nearly at the end of the corridor. Grimacing, as all he could see were grubby walls and closed doors, Freddie prayed to God he had made the right decision.

As he reached the full length of the hallway and a dead end, Freddie slowed and was about to panic when the very end door opened and a weathered arm shot out. It beckoned him in and he ran straight past the occupant without stopping. The old woman shut the door again quickly and pulled the bolt across.

Freddie bent over double to catch his breath and they both listened as the police reached Dale's flat. He closed his eyes momentarily in relief. He hadn't been seen. But he wasn't out of the woods yet. He needed to get out of here. He didn't want to be framed for Dale's murder. The question was, though, who had done it, and why? And who had tipped off the police?

'Thanks,' he whispered to the old woman whose house he was in.

'That's OK, them bastards'll screw anyone over they find. Don't matter that it weren't you.' She threw a dirty look at the closed door and pulled her crocheted shawl tighter around her shoulders.

'Do you know what happened?' Freddie asked.

She shook her head. 'All I know is a couple of the other lads found him about an hour ago. Don't think they knew what to do; they were only young 'uns. They went to find Jay.'

Freddie nodded. Jay was another of his men who lived in this estate; he and Dale were both high-ranking members of the same gang and worked together on a lot of things.

The old woman beckoned him to follow her. They walked out onto the balcony and she pointed towards a thick wooden plank. Freddie immediately knew what it was for. This balcony was on the corner of the building and was only a few feet away from the corner balcony on the next. The wood was to form a bridge to get across. He hoisted it up and laid it flat, connecting the two. He judged the distance to be only about three feet. It was a short distance but even so, his stomach flipped at the thought of the drop. Swallowing his fear, Freddie jumped up onto the concrete ledge and tried to focus on the plank. It would be two steps, three at most. The door on the other balcony was opening and a middle-aged woman peered out, her eyes wide and tense.

'That's Bridie. She'll let you out the other side. Go on, quickly now, or they'll be here.'

Freddie swallowed and carefully stepped forward, not taking his eyes off the other ledge. One step, two. He was more than halfway now. The wind stepped up a notch and Freddie almost lost his balance, but he surged forward and his foot finally connected with the next ledge.

'Take the plank,' the woman called after him. He pulled it over and placed it down out of sight on Bridie's balcony. He turned to say thanks, but the door was already closing, the old woman gone.

Freddie walked in and followed Bridie through to her front door. She opened it without comment and nodded at him as he went through.

'Thanks,' he said.

'No one saw ya,' she replied with a quick smile, before closing the door behind her. Freddie took off and contemplated how he was going to get back to his car without being seen. It was out of sight, which was a good thing, but the police were still swarming around. He felt for the notebook in his pocket and found it was still there, to his relief. All his dealers had a contact tree. They had all the numbers, names and drop points for the next level of the tree recorded in a notebook. Freddie advised them to hide these in the cistern so that they could be easily located by one of their own, in situations such as this.

As he wound his way down the stairwell, Freddie was stopped by a small kid who looked about seven or eight, if he were to hazard a guess. He was chewing gum and dressed in scruffy clothes, his Afro hair framing his face almost like a halo.

'You Mr Tyler?' the boy asked.

'Yeah, that's me,' Freddie answered.

'Jay said you might be down here and to come through here if you were.'

'OK, lead the way.' Freddie was relieved. He had been wondering how he was going to find Jay if he had been intent on laying low. But he must have seen him enter and figured out the rest. The boy walked down another set of stairs and then into one of the flats on a lower floor. Freddie knew this wasn't where Jay lived, but it was obviously where he planned to hide out whilst there was so much going on.

He walked into chaos, all the room in the small hallway taken up by a large pram, toys littering the floors and the sound of a baby wailing. Two toddlers squabbled over a teddy in front of the blaring TV and their mother, a slight, mixed-race girl who looked exhausted, was screaming at them, trying and failing to gain some control. The boy didn't seem fazed by any of it. He walked over to the toddlers and passed one of them the teddy, then picked the other up in his thin little arms and pulled him onto his lap on the faded old sofa, distracting him with a new game. Freddie watched the encounter with a half-smile. He had grown up quickly, helping his mother Mollie with his younger siblings from an early age. It had been the making of him, taking responsibility for his family. Hopefully it would be the same for this boy too.

'Freddie.' The relief in Jay's voice was tangible. 'Glad you're here.'

'Yeah, not so sure *I'm* glad I'm here though,' Freddie replied with a humourless laugh. 'What the hell happened? Who did that to Dale?'

'No idea. No one's seen nothing,' he spat. He threw the TV remote into one of the armchairs across the room and ran his hands over his head.

His anger was understandable, Freddie thought. He had just found out one of his best mates had been murdered.

'What do you know so far? Walk me through.'

'I left his flat about midnight – we'd been chilling out with some weed, played some *GTA*, nothing major. He was fine. He was supposed to go for a pick-up this morning.' Freddie acknowledged this with a nod and Jay continued. 'Then we was supposed to meet at mine to start splitting the bags.' Jay threw a look at the girl still rocking the screaming baby. 'Cassie, get us a coffee.' He turned straight back to Freddie, missing the resentful look she returned him.

Freddie figured the baby was probably Jay's, which was why he was down here. From what he had heard, Jay had a few children littered around the estate.

'He didn't turn up, so I sent a couple of the boys to find him. Figured maybe he forgot the time. They found him. They told me the news and I was about to come see you. I'd just got out the building when I was told you were already here, so I waited down below. Then the pigs turned up and here we are. Don't know who tipped them off. None of mine, that's for sure. They know better. That's all I got so far, it's all happened so fast.' He held his hands up helplessly. He still hadn't got his head around it. 'Whoever did it is gonna fucking pay. I'm gonna make damn sure of it.' He cracked his knuckles and breathed heavily.

Freddie sighed. This was the last thing he needed on his back. Dale had been one of his men, so it was his responsibility to find out what had happened and make the culprit pay. If you worked for the Tylers you were protected. He couldn't let this go unchecked, or people would start questioning his authority.

'Just find out as much as you can and get the information over to me. Don't do anything else. We'll sort it out. OK?'

'Yeah, yeah...' Jay nodded distractedly.

Freddie stood up. 'I've got to go. Good luck when they pull you in for questioning. Contact me once the heat's off. You remember where to call if you need a brief, yeah?' They both knew Jay would be one of the first pulled in by the police.

'Yeah, course. Thanks, Freddie.'

'No problem. And I'm sorry about Dale.'

'Yeah, me too.' The deep sadness on Jay's face stayed with Freddie as he left the building. His lips formed a hard line. He would find whoever had murdered his dealer and make sure he could never do that to anyone else again.

CHAPTER SEVENTEEN

Anna's soft voice wafted down the hallway as Freddie entered their home. The sound was like a balm to his soul. So many things kept going wrong, but Anna was the one thing he could count on to be right and good in his life. He felt tired. All he wanted to do was curl up with her in his arms and forget about everything else. But he couldn't.

He walked through to the big open lounge and threw his jacket onto one of the empty armchairs. Anna looked up at him from where she was curled up in the corner of the sofa. She was on the phone, so he kept quiet.

'OK, yeah. I'll think about it. I've got to go, Freddie's just got in. OK, sure. Bye.' Anna ended the call with a sigh and Freddie sat down next to her. 'What's up?' she asked. 'You looked like a cat with two tails this morning, now you look more like a dog with no bone.'

Freddie laughed, despite his worries. 'Ahh, just more shit landing on my plate.'

'What happened?' Anna asked.

'You really want to know?' Freddie gave her a questioning look. Anna paused before answering.

'Yes, go on.'

'One of my men was murdered today. Or last night, I think. I'm not sure.'

Anna gasped. 'Christ. Why? Who?'

'Dale Matthews. I don't know why yet. I've got Bill looking into it.'

'Will you be pulled in?' Anna asked.

'Nah, there's no connection. Not one they'll find anyway.'

'OK.' Anna nodded, her face serious.

'Come on, have a drink with me. I need one.'

'I'm OK actually, still a bit delicate from last night.'

'Ah, come on,' Freddie tried to sway her. 'You can't make a man drink alone with his problems, now that's just cruel,' he joked.

'I said no, Freddie. I don't want a drink,' she snapped. There was an awkward silence and Anna instantly regretted her shortness. It wasn't Freddie's fault she was so stressed out. She forced a tight smile. 'Sorry. I've just got a lot on right now and I want to keep a clear head.'

Freddie nodded and shrugged. 'Well, why don't you tell me what's going on with you then? It'll take my mind off my own issues,' he offered.

'It's nothing, just normal stuff,' she replied quickly.

'You just said you had a lot on.' Freddie frowned and looked at her. 'So, which is it?'

Anna sighed in frustration. 'It's nothing, Freddie. I don't want to talk about it right now.' She looked away and clamped her jaw shut.

Anna knew she should tell him, but she couldn't. Not yet, anyway. He had enough on his plate: if he knew everything that was going on with Gambino, he would hit the roof. It was the last thing he needed. She was protecting him from information that he couldn't do anything about even if he did know.

Plus, there was the small knot of worry in her stomach still that he might blame her. Even though he would agree with her decision, and she was pretty certain he would, the fact that she had been the one to close the door on his next big goal would be hard to swallow. She couldn't bear to see the disappointment in his eyes just yet.

Freddie watched her expression close up and suddenly felt cold. *What is she hiding?* Anna wasn't good at hiding things, not from him anyway. There was something bothering her greatly. *Why won't she just tell me?* he wondered. Anna never usually kept anything from him. Because of how complex their lives were, they made sure to be completely open with one another. The one time he had kept something big from her, it had nearly broken them. Now, more than ever, they told each other everything. And when there was nothing they couldn't share – not even dead bodies and drug runs – what could be so bad that Anna felt the need to hide it from him?

Anna turned back to him, a look of pure guilt marring her beautiful face. This alone sent Freddie's heart crashing into his stomach. *Why the guilt?* He stopped his brain from making any connections, too afraid of where they might lead.

'Listen.' Anna's voice was softer now as she regained control of her emotions. 'I think we both need a little fun, to let our hair down a bit. Why don't we have a day off tomorrow, get everyone together and just go have a load of drinks, get blind drunk and forget all our troubles? What do you say?' She was grinning now.

Freddie bit his lip and studied her. He couldn't make sense of her yo-yoing emotions. 'OK,' he replied finally. 'I can do that. I'll see who's around.'

Anna squeezed his arm and put her forehead to his. 'Great. I'll see if the girls are free.'

'I'll still have things to do in the evening, so let's call it an afternoon thing, yeah?' Freddie said. 'Tell them to come to Ruby Ten, that's open from lunchtime. We can take over the VIP area.' He stood up. 'I'm going for a shower.'

'OK.' Anna nodded.

'Anna.' Freddie paused by the door and looked back at her. 'You'd talk to me, if there was anything serious going on, yeah?'

Anna swallowed and forced a smile. 'Of course,' she said. 'I'm just really tired at the moment and there's *both* clubs to run. Really, it's fine,' she lied.

'OK.' Freddie walked through the hallway towards the bedroom, his mouth forming a frown. Anna had just lied to him. The question now though was why?

CHAPTER EIGHTEEN

The rhythmic bassline of the chilled house music underlined the relaxed, fun atmosphere around the full VIP table the following afternoon. Tanya sat chatting animatedly with James and Amy, Bill's wife, keeping their champagne glasses topped up. Carl was taking full advantage of his day off and inclusion in the afternoon fun, and was plying Sophie with shots of something neon blue. Bill and Paul were swapping inappropriate jokes over glasses of whisky and Thea swayed along to the music, talking to Seamus about his love for boxing. Sammy hadn't been able to come to the club. Work never ceased and there were certain things he couldn't push to the evening.

Anna sat to the side of Tanya with Tom, listening quietly but not quite joining in. This wasn't exactly out of the ordinary; she was known to be the quieter of the two friends and business partners. But Freddie knew that this wasn't all it was today. Her expression was tight and wary underneath the fake smile. Occasionally she and Tanya exchanged glances and Freddie realised from their unspoken communication that Tanya knew exactly what she was hiding from him. He filed this realisation away for a later date. He wasn't sure how he would use it yet. Tanya's loyalty would always be to Anna, but he would figure it out somehow.

Taking a deep breath, he caught the waitress's eye and signalled for her to come over. 'Rachel, I'll have two rounds of Patrón for everyone.'

There was a cheer from James and Tanya, and Freddie grinned. The grin didn't quite meet his eyes though. He hadn't planned on getting drunk today, not really. He still had work to do tonight. But for once he decided to cut himself some slack. There was a lot on his shoulders and none of it was going anywhere tonight. Whatever Anna was hiding was eating away at him and he just needed to let it all go and relax for a bit.

An hour later Anna saw Bill go to the bar and she glanced over towards Freddie. He was busy laughing with Thea. She took the opportunity to quietly join Bill at the bar.

'Hey, how's it going?' she asked, checking that no one was heading over to join them. They weren't.

'Good, thanks. What about yourself?' he replied with an easy smile.

'Things are OK, I guess.' She bit her lip, still not sure if she was making the right gamble. She went for it anyway. 'Bill, I need to talk to you about something, but it needs to stay between us,' Anna said.

Bill frowned and shifted his weight, waiting for her to continue.

'I know your loyalty is to Freddie. I'm not asking you to go against that, but this isn't something he needs on his plate right now.'

'OK. What's up?' Bill asked carefully.

Anna took a deep breath and began telling him all about her dealings with Frank Gambino.

'… so I thought that it was dealt with. Mostly at least. But then the dealer was killed. And I know that neither you nor the police have found anything so far, which means it was definitely someone who knew what they were doing. It wasn't just an accident or an argument gone wrong. It was calculated and deliberate.'

Bill shook his head. 'I don't think it's Gambino. I think you're barking up the wrong tree. It don't make any sense for him to cause such extra trouble for Freddie.'

'But it has to be him, Bill. He's doing it to pressure me into the sale. Who else could it possibly be? He's the only wild card in play right now. No one here would do all this, would try to get Freddie caught and locked up. It just isn't done.'

'I hear what you're saying, but I still don't think it's him. He's a clever bloke, Anna. And one who has a strong sense of rules – rules that are very similar to ours. If he was out to ruin Freddie for *any* reason, this wouldn't be how he'd play. He's already told you what he's going to do – Freddie won't be able to open his casino. Frank has no need to do anything else.'

'Well, *someone* is out to ruin him, Bill. Don't you think? There are an awful lot of strange coincidences happening at the moment.'

They stood in silence as each mulled over the other's opinions. Anna forced a smile and waved as Freddie began to make his way over to them.

'Listen, I'll look into it, OK?' Bill said. 'I'll see what I can find out, see if there are any connections between anything. Try not to worry about it. If it is someone trying to fuck with him, it won't be because of you. I'll let you know if I get anything.'

'OK. Thanks.'

'No worries.'

Freddie walked over and immediately stumbled into a bar stool. He laughed at himself and Anna smiled in amusement as she realised how drunk he was.

'Having a good time?' she asked.

'Yeah, more than you seem to be. You don't seem anywhere near as under the influence as I am,' Freddie said.

'I've had a couple. I'm just not feeling well, to be honest. I don't think the bubbles are agreeing with me again,' Anna replied.

Freddie bit back the drunken accusation on his lips. He was tempted to demand she tell him what she was hiding right there and then. It was bothering him even more than he'd realised. But this wasn't the time or the place. Charging in and demanding something from Anna wasn't going to do him any favours. She didn't respond well to tactics like that. Instead he reached into his pocket and pulled out his cigarettes. Lighting one up, he turned and leaned back against the bar.

Bill frowned. Freddie didn't usually smoke in his clubs. He smoked in the back office and was known to smoke in one or two of the pubs frequented by people in their line of work, but never in the bar of his clubs. He didn't want to set a bad example or put people off. It just wasn't that sort of place.

Sure enough, a man on a nearby table stood up and walked over.

'Er, mate, you're supposed to go outside. You can't smoke in here,' he said, his tone irate. He turned up his nose and tried to wave the smoke away.

'I can do what I fucking like,' Freddie spat, standing upright. 'This is my fucking club, mate. I own the place.' He began approaching the man but Bill strategically stepped in his way without looking like he was trying to stop him.

'Come on, Fred, leave this no-mark to it,' he said, gently turning his boss back towards the VIP area.

'No-mark? Who do you think—' the man began to speak but Bill shot him a dangerous look. The man retreated, suddenly aware that he wasn't sure what he'd stumbled into.

'Fuck off,' Bill ordered. The man did as he was told, walking back to his table, muttering under his breath about psychos and law-breakers.

'Whatever, get off me, Bill, I'm fine.' Freddie shook Bill off him and tersely straightened his jacket, aware he wasn't acting like himself. He dropped the cigarette into an abandoned half-empty pint glass at the end of the bar and turned back to the barmaid. 'Another round of shots. Make it something decent.' He returned to the VIP area with Bill close behind him.

Anna watched him go and shook her head. Freddie was always so cool and collected, even when he was pissed off. He must be really feeling the pressure with this latest murder to act out in his own club. He wasn't sleeping well either; they were both still stressed about the break-in. Fraser hadn't got anywhere and they still didn't have a solid list of possible suspects. This thought just cemented Anna's conviction. There was no way she could tell him about Frank right now. It was the last thing he needed.

The worry bubbled up in her stomach and she took another sip of her drink to try to quell it. This didn't work and only served to make the bubbling worse. The sudden realisation that she was going to actually throw up spurred Anna into action and she launched herself towards the toilets.

As she reached the nearest cubicle she didn't have time to lock it behind her before the first wave of vomit spewed from her mouth. She steadied herself against the back wall with one hand and grabbed at her hair with the other, trying to keep it out of the way as she heaved again and again.

The door banged open behind her and suddenly there was a pair of cool hands on her neck, scooping up the hair that was slipping from her grasp.

'Jesus, I didn't realise you'd had that much,' Tanya said with concern as she stood with her friend. She'd watched Anna's mad dash into the ladies' and had followed to find out what was wrong.

'I haven't,' Anna managed between heaves. 'Just… two.'

Tanya didn't say any more until the heaving stopped and Anna stood up straight again. She wobbled and Tanya righted her. Ripping off some tissue, she handed it to Anna, who wiped her mouth.

'Thanks,' she said heavily. 'I was ill yesterday too. I put it down to the takeaway the night before, but actually I think the stress of everything's just getting to me now.'

'Really?' Tanya frowned. 'That's not like you. I mean, it's not like you haven't faced screwed-up shit like this before. I don't remember any of that making you sick.'

'Well…' Anna trailed off. Tanya had a point. 'Things change, I guess.'

'Are you sure it's not something else?' Tanya stared at her and Anna's brain began to tick. She looked down at the mess and shook her head slowly. No, she wasn't sure. She wasn't sure of anything anymore.

CHAPTER NINETEEN

Anna stepped behind the bar in Club Anya and stared at the spirit bottles wistfully. Twisting her mouth to one side as she considered her options, she eventually yanked a carton of orange juice from the mixers fridge and poured herself a glass. It was early evening and the place was too quiet for her liking. Not that they didn't have customers in, there was a good general buzz, but usually Carl or Tanya would be around doing something, or Sophie would be getting ready for her acts on the rings. But none of her friends were here tonight. Of course they were all likely to still be in bed – or perhaps had made it no further than their sofas, still suffering the wrath of stinking hangovers from all the fun the day before.

The door opened and Anna glanced over expectantly.

'Oh, what are you doing here? I thought tonight was going to be a complete write-off when I saw the state of you this morning,' she said in surprise. Freddie looked awful. In fact she didn't think she had ever seen him look so ill and dishevelled. His skin was almost green and she couldn't help but feel sorry for him. She laughed as he gave her a pained look, before collapsing on a bar stool in front of her.

'I'm dying. I don't think I've ever had so much to drink.' He pulled a face at the Martini one of her barmen was pouring a customer next to them.

'Yes, well. That was kind of your own fault. You geared everyone up into a crazy party frenzy,' Anna replied.

'Yeah, I got a bit carried away. But you know what, it's not like we do that very often. Doesn't hurt to let loose once in a while.'

Anna smiled and reached across the bar, touching his face affectionately.

'Want some orange juice?' she asked, sliding her full glass over to him. He took it and gulped it down gratefully. Anna poured herself a fresh one.

'Thanks.'

'Listen, I wanted to talk to you about something. It's about the flat,' Anna said. She worded what she wanted to say carefully, trying not to offend Freddie. 'I know you keep us safe and that you've done everything you can with regards to security after what happened. I have every faith in that. But ever since the break-in, home just hasn't felt the same. I feel like I can't relax and I just can't shake that horrible feeling that came from someone coming into our private space and going through our things…' She trailed off and shuddered. 'I don't know about you, but I don't feel happy and secure there anymore. It feels tainted somehow.' She sighed. 'I know this was our first place together and we've put a lot into it. And it will always be special because of that. But how would you feel about maybe selling up and buying somewhere else?'

Freddie nodded, his expression serious. He had been expecting this conversation to come up. Anna's nightmares weren't diminishing and she had lost her ability to relax in their home. He'd had a CCTV system put in and a thick safety door installed. At nights when he knew she was home and he was working, he had one of his men posted outside and made sure she knew who was there. But it was no use. Someone invading her privacy like that had crossed a sacred line.

Freddie felt useless. There was nothing else he could do and Fraser still hadn't come up with anything either. He'd had forensics in to sweep the place but whoever it was had been a professional. There was not one cell of DNA left behind and there were no cameras anywhere near the front of their building. It was something Freddie had always valued up until now. If the police ever needed to prove he wasn't at home they wouldn't be able to. But his measures had worked against him in this instance.

Freddie didn't want to leave the flat. He liked it there and was proud of it. They had spent a lot of time and money getting it just right. But Anna's happiness and security was more important. He'd do anything she needed to get back to how she should feel in her home.

'If that's what you want to do, that's OK with me,' he said.

Anna visibly relaxed. She had been holding her breath, waiting to see what he would say. She had been dreading his answer, expecting him to ask her to give it more time. She was so glad he hadn't.

'Are you sure?' she checked.

'Yeah. Why don't you start having a look around at what's on the market tonight, see if there are any you like the look of and we can go over them tomorrow,' Freddie suggested.

'OK, I'll have a look. Are you out this evening then?'

'Yeah, I've got to go sort out a problem with a shipment. No rest for the wicked. Feel like death warmed up, but…' He laid his head in his hands for a moment and sighed.

'I won't lie, you look like it too,' Anna said.

'Great, thanks for the vote of confidence,' he said with a laugh. 'Right, I'm off. Catch you later.'

Anna waved him off and bent down to put away the orange juice. As she stood up a wave of nausea swept over her and she groaned. Darting around the bar, she made her way to the bathroom and got there just in time. The contents of her stomach splattered all over the basin of the toilet as she heaved violently. She closed her eyes. *Not again,* she thought. She felt awful.

After a minute or two she wiped her mouth and the beads of sweat that had formed on her forehead and stepped back out of the cubicle.

'Hey, um…' A concerned, young Latino-looking woman stood just outside. 'Are you OK?'

'Yes, I'm fine. I'm so sorry you had to hear that.' Anna laughed, embarrassed. 'I ate something that disagreed with me a couple of days ago. It doesn't want to give up the fight.' She pulled a face.

The other woman laughed lightly, but the concern was still on her pretty face. 'Well, hopefully you're winning,' she said. 'You are really pale though. Why don't we go and get you a glass of water?'

'Oh, no, I'm fine,' Anna protested, 'really.'

'No, I insist,' the woman said strongly in what sounded to Anna like a Spanish accent. She guided Anna forward gently by the arm. 'I used to be a nurse – it's pretty much my duty to make sure you're OK. Come.' She led Anna back out to the bar and found two empty stools for them to sit on.

Anna signalled the barman over and ordered herself a water. 'And what can I get you, err…?'

'Izobel.' The woman smiled, showing little, even white teeth. 'I'll have a small white wine, whatever the house wine is. How much will that be?' She directed the question to the barman but Anna waved him away.

'No, no. The wine is on me. For your kindness,' she said with a smile.

'Oh no, I couldn't accept that; it's nothing to show concern.' Izobel shook her head, but Anna held up her hand.

'I insist. This is my club, it's nothing.'

'Oh, wow.' Izobel's eyebrows shot up. 'Well, I like your club. It's the first time I've been here actually.' She looked around.

'Are you from London?' Anna asked.

'No, I moved here about six months ago with my boyfriend. Well… my ex now.' She pulled a face.

'Oh, I'm sorry,' Anna said.

The barman brought their drinks over and Anna sipped at the cool water gratefully.

'No, it's fine, really,' Izobel rushed to reassure her. 'He was an asshole, to be honest. I'm better off without him. He's making someone else's life miserable now. But I decided to stay and see how things went. I have another six months left on the rental contract anyway.' She shrugged.

'Well, how do you like it around here so far?' Anna studied the girl beside her. She was blessed with deep olive skin, dark almond-shaped eyes and a mass of thick wild curls. She was a natural beauty and Anna guessed probably a handful of years younger than herself.

She knew how Izobel must feel. She had been that girl once. It was only four years ago that she had rocked up in East London one night, having run away from her psychotic ex with all her worldly belongings in the back of her car. She'd known nobody in the city and had no plan as to what she was going to do. It had been by pure chance that she had met Tanya, who had befriended her and helped her find her way again. Tanya's offer of friendship had meant so much to her, at a time where she had nothing and nobody else.

'It's OK. It's going to take some adjustment, I think. But I'm hoping I'll like it.' She looked at her watch. 'I think I've been stood up.' She gave Anna a sad smile. 'Just my luck.'

'Who were you meeting?' Anna asked.

'Oh, just this girl who lives down the road from me. We got chatting and she said she would be in here tonight with some friends if I wanted to join them. But they were supposed to be here an hour ago now, so I guess they changed their minds. Maybe they went somewhere else.'

Izobel tried to hide her disappointment and Anna's heart reached out to her. 'Hey, well, I'm actually not doing anything tonight if you fancy hanging out?'

'Oh, no it's OK; you don't have to do that, honestly. I don't want to bother you. I shouldn't have said anything.' Izobel flushed crimson with embarrassment.

'It's not bothering me at all, I really don't have plans and' – she smiled warmly – 'you know, I was in your position once. Sometimes all you need is someone to just be a friend when you're alone in a cold, alien city.'

'Yes.' Izobel nodded vehemently. 'That is exactly how I feel. You get it.'

'I do.' Anna laughed. 'Trust me, I really do. Listen, have you eaten? Because I know a great Italian round the corner. We could grab some dinner, if you fancy it.'

'That sounds perfect,' Izobel said, her tone brightening. 'I'm starving.'

'OK then, let's go.' Anna grabbed her purse from behind the bar and led the way out of the club. She felt good befriending Izobel, like it was karma somehow after Tanya had befriended her all that time ago. She stepped outside into the cool evening air and waited for Izobel to fall into step beside her. It was also refreshing to be around someone who wasn't linked to any of her worries. She pushed everything else to the back of her mind and walked forward, determined to escape her own head for the evening.

CHAPTER TWENTY

The next morning, Freddie, Bill and Sammy walked out of Sammy's office together.

'So, there's still nothing? That's odd, Bill. Surely there has to be someone on that estate that saw something?' Freddie said.

'No, no one saw a thing. Or if they did, they ain't talking to us. Which is strange in itself. Jay's in custody at the moment – they're trying to pin it on him. He was the last one who saw him alive, last to leave his flat. His prints are everywhere. Only reason they haven't charged him is because they can't find the weapon, or traces of Dale's blood actually on him.'

'Fuck sake.' Freddie shook his head. 'He got the brief?'

'Yeah, Toby. I've asked him to keep me up to date.'

'Tell him I'll pay the bill at the end, cash. And to keep that quiet.'

'Will do. He figured that was the case anyway, when I went looking for information,' Bill said.

'I still can't work out who would have called Old Bill,' Sammy said. 'At exactly the moment you were standing in his flat. Bit coincidental, isn't it?'

Freddie bit his lip. He had been asking himself the same question for days. But he had no answer. Everything that was happening was suspicious, but he couldn't think of anyone who would want to cause him such trouble. Even his enemies lived by a code. No one would go around trying to get a rival caught by the pigs. You went for the throat or not at all in their line of work.

He changed the subject. 'Sammy, have you heard back from Gambino?'

'No, nothing. He's gone cold. It's really strange. I got a tip-off that he's planning on heading back across the pond soon though,' Sammy said with a grimace.

Freddie groaned. Gambino had been eager enough to meet and he had been the perfect host at dinner, but after skirting around the conversation of business that night, he'd gone cold for some reason. It was like he wasn't interested in working with them, but if that were the case, why would he have gone to all the trouble of entertaining them? Perhaps this was all some sort of test. Freddie let out a long, frustrated breath. There was nothing he could do but be patient and wait to hear more.

'OK, well let's hope he returns soon. He was supposed to be staying over here for a while, maybe he'll come back.'

The three men walked down the high street on their way to a restaurant for lunch. It had been a long morning and they were hungry. As they passed a newsagent's, Freddie paused.

'You go on, I'll catch up,' he said, entering the small shop. The door closed behind him, the little bell that tinkled above it alerting the shop owner to his presence.

Going to the till he pointed to the cigarettes he favoured. 'Twenty, please, mate.' He handed over his card and waited. A noise sounded and the man who had pressed it to the reader handed it back and pulled a face.

'It has declined, sir,' he said.

'What? Nah, it must be your machine.' Freddie frowned. He had around fifty grand in that account. It was his legal float, the only money he could have access to through an account that would pass any investigation. 'Here, I'll try the PIN.' He slotted the card into the machine and entered his PIN. Another message came through the reader, stating that it was declined. 'What the hell?' Freddie exclaimed.

Tutting, he reached into his pocket and pulled out a twenty-pound note. He handed it over. 'Keep the change.' He picked up the cigarettes and left the shop, heading straight for the cash point next door. He quickly tapped in his pin once more and waited to see his balance on screen.

Freddie gasped as the account came up as empty. The balance was at zero. It had been cleaned out. 'What the hell is going on?' he exclaimed in disbelief.

He strode back down the road towards his parked car and called through to Sammy's phone. 'Go ahead without me. Something's come up that can't wait.'

Forty minutes later, Freddie sat in the back office of his local bank branch. The manager knew him there, so all it took was an exchange of a few notes and he was settled in front of the controls to the CCTV.

'So you say it was the day before yesterday, at 4.45 p.m.?' he clarified.

'Yes, that's when the money was withdrawn, in full, over the counter,' the bank manager confirmed. He cleared his throat and swallowed nervously.

'And you say that it was me who took it out?' Freddie asked, completely confused. The manager nodded. 'But it couldn't have been. I was at a party—' Freddie trailed off.

He had been absolutely wasted that day. Had he left at some point and drawn all the money from his account? *But why would I do that?* he wondered. *And even if I had done that, where is it now? And surely I would remember?* He shook his head. There was no way in hell that he wouldn't remember clearing fifty grand out of his bank account.

'Play the footage,' he demanded.

'Of course.' The manager had already found the time on the video and had it paused, ready to go. He pressed play and they sat back to watch in silence.

The camera was above the door, trained on the cashiers' desk. It wasn't great quality, quite grainy, but clear enough that he should be able to make out who it was that had emptied his account. The seconds passed and he shifted in his seat, impatient. Eventually the light in the picture changed, signalling that the door had been opened and a man came into view.

Freddie leaned forward, a deep frown of concentration forming on his face as he watched. The man walked forward confidently towards the desk.

Freddie shook his head in disbelief. It looked exactly like him. The camera had only picked up the back of him so far, but it was uncanny. Whoever it was had the same muscular trim frame, the same styled dark hair and even the same dark grey jacket. Freddie's gaze fell to the bag the man was carrying and his jaw dropped open. It was his spare gym bag, the one he kept at the bottom of the wardrobe at home.

Rage began to build up inside him as the realisation hit him. This bastard was the one who had broken into his home. He had to be. There was no other way he could have had that bag. Freddie hadn't even noticed that it was missing. He wouldn't – it wasn't something he had thought to check.

Freddie ran his hand through his hair, his mind whirling. The man on the screen turned with the bag full of money and walked out, his face down, his attention focused on the awkward zip of the bag as he went.

'Well, we don't exactly get a clear view of the face here,' the bank manager said, 'but from what I can see—'

'From what I can see, you've let some fucking stranger walk out of your bank with fifty grand of my hard-earned cash,' Freddie exploded.

'Wh-what?' The bank manager swallowed hard, his Adam's apple bobbing up and down. 'It can't have been. That's you.'

'No, it fucking isn't,' Freddie yelled, standing up and knocking over the chair he had just vacated. He grabbed the man by the scruff of his collar and pulled him forward so that his face was only inches away from his own. Freddie's voice turned dangerously low. 'How on earth did you let something like this happen? Eh? Are you in on it? Is that it? Someone lined your pockets, to let them have a rummage in my account?'

'N-no, I would never—' he stuttered, his voice wobbling.

'Do you know who I am?' Freddie cut in. 'Do you know what I do to people who steal from me?'

'Yes, I-I, please—'

'Then you'll know how quickly I can find out everything about you, including where you live. You'll know how easy it would be for me to have your throat slit in the middle of the night, so quietly that your missus wouldn't find out until she woke up next to you in the morning, in a pool of your blood.'

The manager started to shake and an acrid smell wafted up to them. Freddie looked down and curled his lip in disgust. The man had wet himself.

'For Christ's sake.' He shook his head and sighed. This man didn't have the balls to try to steal from him, he was sure of it. He let go of his shirt but his face was still hard and cold. 'What's the procedure for taking out that amount of money over a counter?'

'We check ID,' he replied hurriedly. 'We take a copy and sign to say we've seen it and it matches the records. It all gets scanned into the system and attached under your file.'

'Check it.' Freddie pointed to the computer.

The manager hurriedly sat down and signed into the system. He clicked into their internal software and after a couple of minutes got through to Freddie's file.

'Here,' he said, pointing to one of the files. 'This matches the date.' He clicked on it and a PDF flashed up on the screen. It was Freddie's passport and was signed at the bottom to say it had been checked.

'Who checked this?' Freddie asked.

'Susan.' He swallowed and looked up at Freddie fearfully. 'My wife. She works on the cashier desks.'

'Call her in here. Now,' Freddie demanded.

He did as Freddie had asked and they waited in silence for Susan to join them. They didn't have to wait long until a soft tap on the door sounded and it opened to a round, friendly face.

'What's up? Oh.' She caught sight of Freddie and smiled. 'Hello again. Everything OK?' She frowned in concern. 'There wasn't a problem with your withdrawal, was there? I did count it twice…' Her voice faltered and her smile turned to a look of worry.

'What withdrawal?' Freddie asked, shaking his head in confusion.

'From the other day… For your house renovations,' she replied.

'You recognise me?' Freddie asked.

'Well, yes. I mean, my eyesight isn't what it used to be, but I tend to remember people.' She glanced at her husband and then back to Freddie.

'Is everything OK?' she asked.

Freddie studied her. She was in her late fifties and had a clear, open face. Either she was the best actress in the world, or she really thought she had seen him before. Freddie prided himself on being able to read people and even though the situation was absurd, he believed her reactions were genuine.

Freddie ran his hands through his hair in agitation. Whoever had taken his passport had also gone to great lengths to resemble him, so he wasn't sure he even had any grounds to fight the bank and get his money back through their insurance.

He pointed his finger at the bank manager. 'If I find out either of you had anything to do with this, I will come for you.'

Walking past a shocked Susan, Freddie stormed out of the back office, through the bank and out to the busy street. He growled under his breath as he marched to his car.

First this guy had broken into their home and now he'd stolen fifty grand. When Freddie found out who he was – and he would – he was going to regret even so much as thinking about it. This was one murder Freddie was looking forward to.

*

Anna entered the flat and paused. A crash sounded down the hall and then a muttered curse. She gently put the carton of milk she had been out to get down on the sideboard next to the door and tilted her head to listen. Her heart began to speed up and she swallowed. A door banged hard against a wall as someone threw it open with no caution. Had someone broken in again? Had she walked in on them trashing the flat? She flinched as someone suddenly bowled into view but then sagged in relief as she realised it was only Freddie.

'Christ, you scared the life out of me. What are you doing? I thought we were being burgled again.'

'No, we're not. Or at least you're not. I have been, but apparently by myself.' Freddie looked pissed off.

Anna frowned. 'What are you talking about?' she asked.

Freddie sighed and quickly explained everything that had happened so far. 'So now I'm stumped. It makes no sense. I can't work out what's happened.'

'Who on earth could it be?' Anna asked in shock.

'Well, it wasn't me. I was with you all afternoon, and even if I hadn't been, I'm pretty sure I would remember doing something like that. I don't get that drunk, Anna,' Freddie replied, stress colouring his tone.

'I wasn't suggesting it was you,' Anna replied, holding her hands up in surrender. She pursed her lips. She had no idea what else to say. She could understand why he was so irate; it was a lot of money to lose. But she didn't want to add any more fuel to the fire, so she stood in silence for a few moments. 'Come on.' Anna picked up the milk. 'I'll make you a cup of tea. You look like you need one.'

Freddie bit back the retort that he needed something a lot stronger than tea. It was the right suggestion – he needed to keep his head clear. There was so much going on right now, so many puzzles to solve, he couldn't afford to be anything other than mentally sharp. He tried to curb his temper. It wasn't Anna's fault; he shouldn't be short with her. He followed her into the kitchen and sat at the breakfast bar whilst she put on the kettle.

'It's just one thing after another at the moment,' he said.

'I know. Do you want to talk about it?' she asked.

'Not really.' Freddie stared into her eyes intensely until she looked away. Even despite all of this, the break-in, the money, Dale's murder, the one thing that was burning him up more than anything was knowing that Anna was still keeping secrets from him. Her secrets were like an invisible wedge between them and he couldn't shake off the feeling of dread. He needed to find out what she was hiding, and soon.

CHAPTER TWENTY-ONE

Paul walked down the cobbled path towards their Portakabin by the docks. A couple of the dockhands waved in greeting as he passed. Years they'd had this place. It was his brother's favourite venue to conduct business, though not somewhere they took clients. The club offices were the warm, inviting rooms they used for meetings. The Portakabin was no frills and starkly furnished, but the views over the river were pretty spectacular. It was Freddie's sanctuary, somewhere he frequented even more often when he was feeling stressed.

The bright sunlight glittered on the moody waters of the Thames and he breathed in deeply. He understood why Freddie liked it so much down here. It wasn't exactly fresh air, but there was a freedom in watching the life on the river and in feeling the breeze on your face.

Paul opened the door and smiled in greeting as he saw Freddie seated behind the desk.

'Alright, Paul, what's 'appening?' Freddie said.

'Not a lot, Fred. Just met with Fraser to get an update and it's not looking good.' He sighed and sat in the chair opposite Freddie. 'There's really not much to tell you.'

'Yeah, I'm hearing that a lot lately,' Freddie replied, resignation in his voice.

'I've seen to it that Jay's been sorted. The Old Bill had nothing on him; they were holding him on a thin excuse. Toby did his thing and made sure he was released. They're still hoping they'll find evidence from what I hear.'

'Which of course they won't, because he didn't do it,' Freddie added.

'Exactly. So that's sorted. There's no leads whatsoever on Dale's case, not a single print or trace of any DNA other than what Fraser said he'd expect to find. Handles have all been wiped clean so they ain't rookies.'

'Anything on who broke into my house?' Freddie asked. 'That is one fucker I need to find.' His voice turned hard. 'I won't rest until I have him in my grasp. No one breaks into my home, and then on top of that raids my fucking bank account. I mean, what is that cunt even thinking? I'm Freddie Tyler. What is he on, a death wish?'

'He must be, Fred,' Paul said, shaking his head. 'I just can't make sense of it. Do you have any ideas at all as to who it could be?'

'No. Well…' Freddie paused. 'Not exactly. I mean, things have been peaceful for a while. No one already in play would stand to profit from all this and no one new would have the knowledge to pull all this off.' He breathed out heavily. 'The only thing out of the ordinary right now is Gambino. He's rocked up this side of the pond, rolled out the red carpet then suddenly clammed up. No explanation, nothing. Now that's odd.' Freddie's gaze was unwavering as he waited for Paul to process this. He lit a cigarette and took a deep drag, before blowing the smoke out into the air. It curled upward.

'I can't see it,' Paul said eventually.

'Nah, I can't either,' Freddie admitted, shifting his gaze out of the window over to the river. 'But at this point, I think we have to consider every possibility. At the end of the day, he's the only wild card and he also has the know-how. I can't rule it out.'

There was another knock on the door and Freddie called for whoever it was to enter. Seamus came in with an eager grin and joined them, sitting down in the last available chair around the desk.

'Alright, Freddie, Paul.' He nodded at them each in turn.

'Hello, Seamus,' Paul greeted him back.

'You wanted to see me?' Seamus asked, shifting his attention to Freddie.

'Yeah, I've got a job for you.' Freddie eyed the young man in front of him. Every day he was proving more and more that he had been a good candidate to bring into the fold. Eager, loyal and hardworking with a stomach of steel when it came to even the dirtiest of jobs. He was exactly the sort of person Freddie needed around. And he had proven his trustworthiness time and time again. Freddie was ready to try him out with a bit more responsibility.

'One of our dealers is no longer around. Another man of ours called Jay will be picking up the slack, but I need you to help him out. You'll be picking up deliveries once a week from a warehouse – I'll give you the address – and meeting him with them at the Somers Town estate. You'll be helping him to cut and re-bag the product, before he takes it on to the appropriate people. I can't stress enough how important it is that you aren't stopped for any reason whilst you have the packages on you.' Freddie gave him a long, serious look.

'Of course. What is the product exactly? Is it the funny flour?' Seamus asked, in his melodic Irish accent. He was pretty sure they were talking about cocaine, but he wanted to be sure. He didn't want to show up talking about the wrong thing and look like an idiot.

'It is indeed, mate. Makes up the majority of our drugs trade these days.' Freddie picked up a pen and wrote something down on a scrap of paper. He handed it to Seamus. 'The top one is the address for the warehouse; the bottom is Jay's address and his phone number. Save the number, memorise the addresses and then burn that. Got it?'

'Got it,' Seamus confirmed. He folded it up and slipped it into the pocket of his jeans.

'Pick up the packages at 10 a.m. tomorrow, then take them straight over. Jay will be expecting you. Now, if something happens and you get caught—'

'I say nothin' at all, Mr Tyler,' Seamus interrupted. 'I don't know you and I don't know how those packages got in me bag. And then I call me da, which is a normal thing to do, who will then tip you the wink and sort me out a brief.' Seamus nodded in confirmation of his words.

The corner of Freddie's mouth turned up in a wry smile. 'Good man. That's the ticket.'

Freddie drove home distracted by a million questions chasing each other around his brain and was surprised when he saw he had reached his destination. He supposed he must have been on autopilot. Parking the car, he took the lift up to the top floor. He was taking an evening off from the clubs and had left them in the hands of their more than capable managers. Everything else could now wait until morning. Tanya and Tom were coming over for drinks and he wanted to enjoy pretending that he and Anna were just a normal couple with normal problems for once.

Freddie walked in and almost jumped out of his skin as Tanya screeched at him down the hall.

'Freddie! Get out! Close your eyes!' She ran towards him and twisted him round.

'What? What the hell is going on?' he asked, letting her turn him away, but not quite sure why.

'Quick, in the bedroom!' Tanya shouted back down the hallway in the direction she had come from. To Anna, Freddie assumed.

'I hate to burst your bubble, Tan, but I have actually seen her naked before you know, if it's her modesty you're trying to save,' he said drily.

'Yeah, I actually got that, Fred. It was a bit of a giveaway when you moved in together.' She rolled her eyes at him dramatically. 'Your birthday present arrived early – we were just having a look at it before Anna hides it from you.'

'What?' Freddie twisted out of Tanya's grasp. 'Let me see.'

'No! It's a surprise!' She stepped in his way again, with a face that told him she would stand for no nonsense. 'Go on, piss off. Tom's on the balcony, go chill out with him. We'll be out in a sec.' Tanya pushed him towards the lounge and disappeared back towards their bedroom.

Freddie shrugged and made his way out to the balcony to see Tom, as Tanya had so gracefully suggested. With everything going on lately, he'd forgotten it was his birthday coming up. Tom grinned at him as he stepped out.

'Alright, mate? It's safer out here,' Tom said with a chuckle. He had overheard the exchange.

'Yeah, seems like it,' Freddie replied, bemused. He took out his cigarettes and lit one, offering one to Tom. Tom took one and thanked Freddie, lighting up and leaning on the edge of the balcony next to him. The pair stared out across London.

Freddie loved standing on the balcony listening to the sounds of life buzzing away below him, the traffic and sirens, the quiet dull beat of music coming from somewhere. He could watch the twinkling lights from buildings and street lamps and the endless train of cars for hours. It soothed him, the same way the view at the docks did. He really didn't want to leave this place; the thought saddened him. But if it was the only way Anna would feel safe again then there was no choice. He blew out a trail of smoke and watched it curl away into the night air.

'How's things with you?' He turned his body towards Tom and studied his face. Although Tom had repeatedly expressed that he was fine, Freddie wanted to keep an eye on him to make sure that the knowledge and involvement he'd had so far wasn't going to turn him into a nervous wreck. It could easily happen. It had happened to many men before him and it would to many more in the future. Not everyone was cut out to cope with this life.

Tom nodded. 'Everything's good.' He knew Freddie was watching him. Everything really was fine. He had spent a lot of time coming to terms with the way things had gone down. All he was trying to do now was stay close and watch out for the next opportunity.

'Good.' Freddie gave a curt nod and turned back towards the view. 'Everything on schedule with the build?'

'As close as it can be,' replied Tom. 'I've spoken to Ralph about moving the opening a bit, but only by a couple of days, nothing major. We lost a little time with late material deliveries, but we've made most of it up.'

'Brilliant. That's good to know.' Freddie had a lot of plans for the businesses that were going to take root in the new complex. He and Ralph stood to make a lot of money, so long as everything ran smoothly. It was even a completely legal venture, all above board – if you overlooked the shortcuts on the building paperwork, of course.

'You can come in now,' Tanya's voice wafted through to them from the lounge. She was holding a bottle of champagne. 'Bubbles, boys?'

'Yeah, go on then,' Tom replied with a grin, and the two men stepped inside.

Anna and Tanya were standing with a young woman that Freddie hadn't seen before. He deduced that this must be Izobel, Anna's new friend. Anna had told him she would be inviting her this evening to meet them all. He smiled in greeting.

'Freddie, this is Izobel,' Anna introduced them with a warm smile.

'Ahh, yes, nice to meet you,' Freddie said pleasantly, as Tanya handed him a freshly poured glass of fizz. 'How's things?'

'Great, thank you,' Izobel replied.

'Anna mentioned you're new to the city. Where is it you're living?' Freddie asked, curious to learn more about this girl. He understood why Anna wanted to befriend her; he remembered when it was Anna who was the new girl on the block. Izobel seemed nice enough too, but he was still always wary of newcomers. He had to be.

'My flat is in Finsbury Park,' Izobel replied. 'It's not much, just one bedroom, but it's home for now.' She shrugged. 'It's a bit bare at the moment though. I was actually going to ask you' – she turned back to Anna – 'where can I go to buy some nice things for around the house? I want to make it more homely. I have the next couple of days off work, so I wanted to do some shopping.'

'Well, I guess it depends on what sort of stuff you want and your budget,' Anna said. 'There are a few places not too far from you. I tell you what, I'm not up to much tomorrow. I can come with you to look around if you like?'

'Oh, that would be fun,' Izobel exclaimed. 'Yes, let's do that. A girls' day.' She smiled happily.

'Brilliant. Tanya, are you free?' Anna asked.

'No, I've got too much on, sorry,' she replied.

'OK, just the two of us then.' Izobel clapped her hands together and raised her glass. 'I make a toast, to new friends and fun times.' Her eyes were bright as she looked at Anna.

'New friends and fun times,' everyone chanted.

Tanya sipped at her champagne and watched Izobel thoughtfully. She had been excited to meet her, this new friend of Anna's, but there was something about her she didn't like. She'd seen the look of annoyance flash across Izobel's face when Anna had asked her if she could join them. And when the girl had made the toast to new friends, she hadn't once looked at the rest of them. Tanya and Anna had many friends, both together and apart, but Tanya was getting the feeling that this new one wanted Anna all to herself. She filed this thought away to talk to Anna about later. It could wait for tonight.

CHAPTER TWENTY-TWO

Anna checked herself over in the mirror with a critical eye. She felt like crap so had made a big effort with her appearance in the hope it would make her feel better. Her thick, dark hair shone where she had styled it to perfection and her make-up was flawless. She puckered her red lips and checked that they hadn't smudged anywhere they shouldn't. Satisfied that she looked as good as she could, despite being thoroughly exhausted, she stood up straight and ran her hands down her dress.

The buzzer sounded and she skipped down the hallway to answer it.

'Hey, it's me! I have a taxi waiting, are you ready to go?' a voice crackled through the line.

'Yes, just about. I'll be down in a sec.' Anna quickly grabbed her handbag from the kitchen side, slipped on her shoes and travelled down to meet her new friend.

The lift doors opened and Izobel stood waiting with an excited grin.

'OK, let's go! I have so many ideas about what I want to find.'

'Well, let's get started.' Anna stepped into the black cab and gave the cabby the first destination. Izobel joined her, closed the car door and settled into the seat opposite as the cab pulled away. As the cab moved into the traffic, Izobel rummaged around in her large handbag and pulled out a bottle of something.

'I took the liberty of making something special.' She handed over the evil-looking green smoothie and Anna pulled a face.

'What is that?' she asked warily.

'I know what's wrong with you,' she said, lifting an eyebrow. 'I used to be a nurse. And of course, I'm a woman,' she added. 'This is a special recipe that my grandmother used to make for women in the village who suffered with morning sickness. They called her a miracle worker.'

Anna felt her heart skip a beat and grow cold. She squeezed the phone she was holding in one hand, hard. There was a heavy silence. 'How did you know?' she asked eventually. She hadn't told a soul except for Tanya, not even Freddie. Even Tanya only knew because she had been the one to suggest taking the test.

Izobel rolled her eyes. 'I'm not blind,' she said, laughing. She held the drink out to Anna. 'Seriously, try it. It doesn't taste amazing, admittedly. But it really does work. Just knock it back in one.'

'Really?' Anna wasn't sure, but then again she really did feel terrible. 'What's in it?'

'Mostly vegetables and herbs. Some egg. But it is the way it is cooked that releases all the vitamins to work in a way that helps to balance your extra hormones. It calms the stomach.' She nodded encouragingly. 'Go on, drink it all down so it can get to work. Then rest, and by the time we get to the shops you'll feel as good as new.'

Anna grimaced but decided to give the vile concoction a go. After all, what did she have to lose? The worst outcome was that it didn't stay down, and after a couple of close calls she now always travelled with a plastic bag, just in case. Closing her eyes she tipped the bottle and gulped it down quickly without stopping. The taste was horrendous, like rotten cabbage on a hot day, but she ignored that. Old family medicinal recipes were hardly going to come sugar-coated.

'There.' She passed the empty bottle back to Izobel and shuddered. 'Let's just hope it works.'

'Oh, it will,' Izobel said. 'Why don't you rest?' she offered, her tone soft. 'Close your eyes a while and I'll wake you up when we get there.'

Anna was about to protest that she felt fine, but suddenly she felt even more tired than she had before. A wave of exhausted nausea washed over her. For the hundredth time she wished she could have been one of those lucky women who carried babies easily; the ones who told everyone that pregnancy actually *gave* them energy instead of sucking it away, and who sailed through without a problem in the world. But that was not the case for her. She had been suffering more and more as the days went on. She was surprised no one else had noticed really, though Freddie had been so distracted lately she wasn't sure he'd even notice if she dyed her hair pink and tattooed her face. She rubbed her forehead and the cab span a little before her eyes. Perhaps she did need to close her eyes for a bit, like Izobel said. It was refreshing to be around someone that she didn't have to hide her true condition from.

She relaxed back in the wide seat and leaned against the tinted window. Closing her eyes, she could taste the bitter flavour of the drink still in her mouth. She needed water, a drink to make it go away. She tried to ask Izobel if she had one, but she suddenly wasn't able to get the words out.

She tried to open her mouth and then her eyes, but nothing happened. Everything felt so heavy. She tried once more half-heartedly, helpless against the weight of her own body, before she drifted silently into unconsciousness.

CHAPTER TWENTY-THREE

Freddie sat at the desk in his office at Club CoCo, listening to the dull boom of the music from the dance floor below. His gaze wandered over the plans in front of him once more. It was the latest design for the layout of the retail level of his new complex. He wasn't sure it was quite there yet. He put down the large whisky he had been holding and picked up a pen. He jotted down some notes on the plan, circling a couple of the shops he wasn't happy with.

His phone rang and he looked down at the screen. The caller ID showed that the call was coming from Club Anya. *Finally*, he thought. He picked up.

'There you are! What happened to your phone? I've been trying to get hold of you all afternoon,' Freddie said.

'It's me, not Anna,' Tanya replied. 'I was just ringing you to try and get hold of her, but it sounds like you're having the same problem.' Tanya's tone held a hint of annoyance. 'She was supposed to be here an hour ago. It's Carl's day off. I wouldn't usually mind, but I had plans tonight.'

'Oh.' Freddie frowned. 'No, she ain't with me. In fact I haven't seen her all day. She was going to meet me for a late lunch after her shopping trip with Izobel, but I haven't heard a dicky bird.'

'What?' Tanya asked sharply. 'That don't sound right.'

'No, it doesn't.'

The line went silent for a moment. Freddie felt a trickle of worry make its way down his spine. It wasn't like Anna to not be reachable. Even if she'd lost her phone she would have called him from another one by now, knowing he would be trying to get hold of her.

'Do you have Izobel's number?' Freddie asked.

'No,' Tanya replied. 'She wasn't exactly chomping at the bit to be my bestie – she was just all about Anna.'

Freddie cursed under his breath.

'Can you go check your place? She might be there, but I can't leave the club,' Tanya said.

'Yeah, I'll call ya.' Freddie ended the conversation and grabbed his jacket, his whisky and the floor plans forgotten.

*

Anna came round slowly and groaned. She put her hands up to her head. *Why does it hurt so much? How long have I been asleep*? She looked around and frowned. The room around her looked strangely similar to her bedroom at home, except that it wasn't. The bedspread was the same, and the curtains. There was a dressing table that even had the same brand of face cream she always used. And… *is that my hairbrush?*

Trying to shake off the thick fuzz still swirling in her brain, she stood up, staggering as she did so. She squeezed her eyes shut for a moment as the throbbing intensified, but shook it off. She needed to focus. She tried to remember how she got here. She had been in the cab on her way to the shops… Izobel was there. She had given her a drink… She froze. The drink! It must have been drugged. *Why would Izobel drug me?*

Anna's eyes darted around the room and widened as they settled on a camera in the top corner of one wall. A little red light flashed every couple of seconds. She was being watched. Her heart thudded against her chest and her breathing heightened. *What the hell is this?*

She tried the door, but it didn't budge. It was locked. Her heart began to hammer against her chest as she realised how bad the situation was. She ran to the window and tried to open it, but gasped and stood back as she caught sight of the view. There was nothing to see but miles and miles of fields and trees. *Where the hell am I? This isn't London.*

Anna moved away from the window and swallowed. She shook her head, trying to make sense of it all. Clearly she'd been drugged and kidnapped. And it had been so easy for them to do it too. How had it been so easy?

Izobel… She closed her eyes as she realised that her new 'friend' was no friend at all. Why the hell would she kidnap her? What had Anna ever done to her? Was this some sort of sick, twisted game? Who was she? Anna realised with a sinking feeling that she had let her guard down far too quickly with the girl. She'd felt sorry for her, had seen a bit of her old self in there. And now it appeared she was paying a heavy price for that lapse in judgement.

She jumped as a voice sounded from the camera that was watching her.

'Oh there's no way out; I wouldn't waste your time. You won't be going anywhere.'

'Shit,' she uttered as her breathing spiked. Stepping backward she moved towards the bed and sat on it, pulling her legs up and wrapping her arms around them.

Anna shook her head, trying to rid herself of the fuzz from the drugs. Her thoughts shot to the unborn child, sitting in her belly. What had the drugs done to him or her? Would they cause the baby damage? Her breaths were coming in short, sharp gasps now and she closed her eyes, trying to calm herself down. It wouldn't do her any good to let herself fall into a full-on panic attack. She needed her wits about her.

Anna shuddered as she looked around the strange room. She tried to think logically. There was a reason she was here and she needed to find out what it was. She just hoped that whatever the situation was, she would be able to either talk or pay her way out of it. She couldn't allow herself to think about the alternative. She didn't dare.

*

Freddie strode straight through Club Anya to the office at the back. His stance was rigid and his face held a thunderous expression. People swiftly moved out of his way. He walked in without knocking to find Paul and Bill already present with a worried-looking Tanya. Sammy walked in directly behind him. He had called them en route and told them to meet him there.

'What's going on?' Bill cut to the point.

'I don't know exactly. Anna didn't turn up to meet me earlier. I figured something must have come up, that she'd lost her phone or something. It's been ringing out all day. She didn't come to work tonight and she ain't at the flat either. I tried her mum and The Last Laugh – no one's seen her.'

'And there's no other reason at all that she might have gone off?' Paul questioned.

Freddie rounded on him. 'And what the fuck's that supposed to mean?'

Tanya stood up. 'Calm down, Freddie, he don't mean nothing. It's a reasonable question. No' – she turned her head and answered Paul – 'there's no other reason.'

'You got a tracker on her phone?' Sammy asked.

'No,' Freddie replied, rubbing the bridge of his nose. He was getting seriously worried now.

'I rang the hospitals, just in case,' Tanya interjected. 'There's no sign of her. Which I guess is a good thing.'

There was a knock on the door and Freddie opened it. Seamus walked in. He was sweating and breathing heavily and was dressed in a tracksuit.

'Sorry,' he panted between breaths, 'ran as fast as I could. I was in the ring.' He had been getting in some additional training in the evenings lately.

Freddie had to admit, he greatly respected the boy's determination. 'Sit down,' he said. Seamus did as he was told.

'Anna wouldn't just disappear and ignore her phone. She's not the type, not even if she had *reason*' – he shot a glare at Paul – 'to want to get away.'

Paul sighed quietly and ignored it. He hadn't meant his comment in the way that Freddie was taking it, but then he was sure Freddie knew that deep down. He was just looking for an excuse to take his frustration out on someone. And Paul could take that.

'Something's seriously wrong. I can't say for certain, but someone must have taken her. There's no other viable theory. So, we need to find out who, when and why. I think we can all safely assume it's linked to me. And when we do find whoever it is that's taken her I'm going to rain hell on the fucker until he wishes he had never been born, until he begs me for death.' Freddie clenched his fists and a dark, icy look flashed through his eyes.

Tanya saw it and shivered. She averted her gaze. Freddie was her friend and pretty much family, but he was the last person on earth she would ever dare to push too far. He was one dangerous creature to those who crossed him.

'Where do you want us to start?' Bill asked. This whole situation reminded him of a time four years before, when Anna had been kidnapped by a psychotic ex. They had worked together then to get her back. The difference this time, though, was that they had no clue where she was or who had taken her.

'Get word out to everyone we know, get all our men out searching and asking questions,' Freddie ordered.

Bill nodded and stood up. 'On it. I'll go now.'

'Sammy, go with him – you'll get round quicker. Seamus' – he turned to the boy as the others left the room – 'take the Tube down to Morden, then a taxi to the St Helier Tavern. Inside ask to speak to Ray Renshaw. Say I sent you. Tell him what's happened and that if he could look into things south of the river, I'll owe him.'

'Got it.' Seamus stood up.

'Oh,' Freddie added, 'keep your head up and your wits about you while you're there. It's a rough place and it's not our territory.'

'No problem. I can look after meself.' Seamus nodded and left without another word.

'Why don't we check over the flat again,' Paul suggested. 'See if there's anything there that could give us a clue. We can call Fraser on the way, see what he can do about looking into it.'

'Yeah, let's go. Tanya, keep trying her phone and stay by this one in case she tries to call you. I'll let you know if anything happens.'

'Yeah, of course.' Tanya's face was pale with worry, her usual smile missing.

Freddie marched back out with Paul in tow. As they walked, Paul glanced over at his brother. He had never seen Freddie so angry and shaken.

'Don't worry, we'll find her,' he said.

'Damn right we will,' Freddie responded. 'And then I can promise you' – he gritted his teeth – 'I'll murder whoever's done this.'

CHAPTER TWENTY-FOUR

Seamus stepped out of the taxi and looked up at the building in front of him. He closed the door and before it had even clicked properly shut, the driver screeched off like his life depended on it. Seamus shrugged. Perhaps it did. Freddie did say the pub was rough.

Dusting himself off, Seamus wished he'd had time to change into his normal clothes. He hated making bad first impressions and here he was standing in his sweaty gym gear. It would have to do. He tutted in annoyance and walked inside the pub.

Holding his head high, he scanned the room, looking for the people who seemed like they were in charge. As the door swung shut behind him, all conversations halted and even the barman stopped serving to stare as the new stranger walked into their midst.

Seamus grinned brightly at three men standing at the bar. 'Alright, lads? It's a fine day, is it not?' He moved to the bar and signalled to the stony-faced bartender. 'I'll have a Jack Daniels and Coke, when you have a second, fella,' he said, his Irish accent cheery in the silence. He leaned forward and waited casually.

The three men he had aimed his greeting at walked over and surrounded him.

'Don't you mean Guinness?' the largest one asked, his tone menacing. 'That's what your lot like, innit? You potato-loving pikeys.'

'Oh, no, I don't much like the stuff, meself,' Seamus replied casually. 'Prefer a drop of whisky. And actually I'm not a gypsy either. Although some of me cousins are,' he added.

'Oh, I dunno, what d'ya reckon, George?' the big bloke addressed the barman. 'I think he definitely needs a Guinness. The drink of his homeland. Maybe' – he grinned nastily as George handed him a pint of Guinness he happened to have already been pouring – 'if he don't want to drink the stuff, we should give him a little bath. He does look a bit dirty, don't he, boys?' He lifted the pint up and grabbed Seamus by the front of his T-shirt.

'I'd really rather you didn't,' Seamus replied. He didn't try to manoeuvre himself out of the other man's grasp, knowing that the move would just trigger an all-out brawl. 'It's just that I need to talk to Mr Renshaw and I don't really want to meet him looking any worse than I already do.' He pulled a face and held his hands out in a plea.

The big man quickly dropped him at the sound of Renshaw's name and placed the pint back down on the bar. He scowled.

'And what do you want to talk to Mr Renshaw about then, you little shit?' he growled.

'Well, that's for me to discuss with him, isn't it? I'm here on behalf of Freddie Tyler. D'ya think you could point me in the right direction?' Seamus straightened his T-shirt and tucked it back into his jogging bottoms.

A deep, craggy voice sounded from the back of the room, where a few tables were elevated away from the rest.

'He's over here, son.'

Seamus looked for the source of the voice and found a hard-looking middle-aged man staring back at him.

'So, what's my old pal Freddie doing sending you down here then?'

Seamus quickly walked away from the bar and over to Ray Renshaw. The noise in the pub began to bubble again as people resumed their conversations. As he approached the older man he tipped his head to show his respect.

'You are Mr Renshaw?' he double-checked, not wanting to waste any more time talking to the wrong person.

'In the flesh,' he replied.

'Great. May I sit down?'

'Knock yourself out,' Renshaw replied.

'Thank you.' Seamus perched on a stool and quickly told Ray Renshaw about Anna and repeated Freddie's request for help. Ray frowned and nodded, his expression serious.

'That's fucked up,' he said finally. 'Tell Freddie I'll get my boys asking questions and that if we hear anything I'll get word to him straight away through Club CoCo. And also' – he took a long drag on the cigarette he was smoking – 'when he does find her, if he needs manpower, he just needs to let me know.' He shook his head. 'It's not on. It's bad times indeed when someone crosses the line and takes a civilian. It can't be allowed.'

Seamus nodded in agreement. It was one of the most absolute rules of the underworld. If you had reason to, you could go after an enemy in whatever manner you wanted. You could gun them down, take their businesses, torture them until they begged for death – but never, under any circumstances, did you touch their family. Family – or 'civilians' as they were often referred to – were one hundred per cent off the table. No matter what. This was a law that no one in their world would accept being broken. Because if it became acceptable for one person, it could easily be their own family next. Freddie knew this, and that was why he knew he could count on Ray to step in and help him.

'Thank you, Mr Renshaw. I know Freddie will appreciate that.' He stood up. 'I'd best get back.'

'Yeah, you get off, lad.'

Seamus left the building as Ray Renshaw called his men over to start the search.

*

Anna sat in silence on the bed staring at the camera, a dark look on her face. After calming herself down the night before, she had methodically searched the room from top to bottom. It hadn't taken her long to realise that whoever had abducted her was also the person who had broken into their flat. A tub of her face cream, an old hairbrush she didn't always use and some of her jewellery were all spaced out neatly on the dressing table. When she saw her grandmother's ring she immediately put it on, a small spark of relief from been reunited with it briefly spearing through the worry and fear of the overall situation.

In the set of drawers there was an odd assortment of her clothes that she hadn't realised were missing. Among these had been a pair of yoga trousers and a thin, baggy summer jumper. She had changed into these, knowing that when she finally came across an opportunity to escape, she would get much further in these than in the dress she had arrived in. To her frustration there had not been any shoes, so she had settled for a pair of thick socks instead. She hoped they would protect her feet enough if she needed to run. Anna refused to allow her mind to wander to the possibility that she wouldn't escape.

She had tried to stay awake, but the mixture of exhaustion from her pregnancy and the drugs still in her system had finally got the better of her and she had fallen asleep at some point during the night. When she awoke there had been a tray laid just inside the door with some toast, cereal and orange juice on. The toast had been cold, but after a wary inspection Anna had eaten as much as she could whilst fighting her morning sickness. She needed to keep her strength up. Clearly, she had deduced, they planned to keep her decently nourished. So at some point someone would have to come back to take the tray and swap it for some lunch. There was no clock in the room so she had no idea what time it was, but she could tell it had been several hours. They should be coming soon. And when they did, she would be ready.

A fresh wave of nausea washed over her and she ran through to the small en suite she had discovered the night before. She hurled into the toilet, the contents of her stomach resurfacing violently. As she wiped the vomit from her mouth with tissue she heard a small noise. Her head whipped round as she focused in on it. Someone had opened the door. She scrambled up from her position on the floor and burst back into the bedroom.

Izobel's expression was startled; she clearly hadn't been expecting Anna to come out so quickly. She let go of the tray she had been setting down and turned to flee, but Anna was too fast. She ran across the small space and tackled Izobel to the ground before she could reach the door. The pair grappled as Anna tried to throw her to the side and get to the door but Izobel held on fast, stopping her. Anna grabbed Izobel's hair in her fist and screamed at her in frustration.

'Why are you doing this to me? What is this? What the hell is going on?'

Izobel tried to pull her hair back with one hand, whilst locking her arm around Anna's neck with her free arm. She screamed as Anna pulled harder.

'Answer me, goddamnit! Why are you doing this to me?' Anna growled.

'It isn't me!' Izobel squealed. 'I'm just doing a job.' Tears of pain began to fall down the younger woman's face but still they grappled, each getting nowhere, fighting on the floor. Anna tried squirming out of the headlock but couldn't escape. They rolled over and knocked the drawers as Anna tried to push away with her legs and Izobel responded by locking hers around Anna.

'What job?' Anna spat. 'What sort of sick, fucked-up job is this? Why would you even go along with this? What's wrong with you?'

'I just did, it's a job,' Izobel said through gritted teeth. Incensed, Anna yanked harder, beginning to rip chunks out of the woman's scalp.

'Oww!' Izobel screeched. 'OK, OK, I have no choice!' Izobel began to cry in earnest now. 'He has my mother. He'll kill her. I have to do as I'm told; I don't have a choice.' She sobbed deep, wracking sobs.

Anna paused and loosened her grip, surprised at the answer. Izobel was being blackmailed. That's why she was doing this to her. She was as much a prisoner in this whole thing as Anna was.

'Oh. I–I'm sorry,' she stammered, letting go. 'Who—' Before she could get her next question out, Izobel roughly shoved her away, taking the opportunity to slip out of her grasp. She jumped up onto her feet and shot back out of the room as fast as lightning, locking the door again behind her.

Anna sat up and rested against the foot of the bed in shock. Izobel was nothing but a puppet, whose strings were being pulled by someone else. She glanced up at the camera. Whoever was really behind this was most likely somewhere in the building too with God only knows how many other people. Even if she had been able to get round Izobel, what would she have been facing? Anna rubbed her forehead, stressed.

She needed to get more information somehow, before she could form a proper plan of escape. She stood up and faced the camera.

'Izobel, if you can see this, I'm sorry. I didn't know.' She shook her head and sighed. 'I won't do that again. If you come back, I won't touch you or try to run out. I hope you'll come back.' She gave the camera one last look and then turned away.

What on earth is going on here? And who the hell is 'he'?

CHAPTER TWENTY-FIVE

Tanya stared at the wall in a daze, the glass of neat vodka in her hand almost forgotten. It was nearly three in the morning and no matter how she tried, she just couldn't sleep. Tom had sat up with her at first, trying to comfort her or distract her, but she had sent him to bed. He was aching to sleep after a long day on site and there was no point both of them suffering.

She didn't know what to do, how to help. This was the second night that her best friend had been missing and she had never felt so useless. Her hands moved irritably on their own, her fingers rolling one of her rings around and around.

The door buzzer sounded, shattering the silence and she jumped, spilling the vodka down her front. She tutted as it soaked through her clothes but she ignored that, standing up and walking to the door. She already knew who it would be before she opened it.

Freddie leaned against the doorframe looking haggard and dishevelled. His eyes were bloodshot, indicating to Tanya that he had been getting about as much sleep as she had. She moved aside to let him in without a word.

Freddie made his way into the kitchen to where he knew the drinks would be and poured himself a large whisky. 'Thing is,' he said, his voice hoarse, 'I haven't touched a drop since she disappeared. Been keeping my head clear, my wits about me for when I would need them. But what are the chances that something's going to come up now, at this time of the morning, when everyone is asleep, eh?'

Tanya shook her head. 'None,' she whispered.

'Even the bastard that took her is probably getting some shut-eye,' he continued. 'But here I am, and I can't sleep. And I can't do anything. And I can't look at our home and her stuff anymore.' His voice began to shake and he stopped, clenching his jaw. The emotion on his face was raw.

Tanya sniffed and wiped away the tears that were silently falling down her face. She nodded and poured herself another drink. She knew exactly how he felt.

'The spare room's made up. Stay as long as you like,' Tanya said.

'Thanks,' Freddie replied. He walked through to the lounge where Tanya had been sitting before his arrival and sat down in an armchair.

Tanya grabbed the bottle of whisky he had poured his drink from and followed him through, placing it on the coffee table in front of him. *He might as well get blind drunk tonight,* she thought. *Like he said, nothing is going to happen.*

Tanya knew why he had come here. He could have gone to his mum's, or to Paul's house but he didn't want to have to put up a pretence. Mollie would have flustered around him and would have been unable to keep her thoughts to herself and Freddie would have ended up having to comfort her. Paul wouldn't have known what to do and the atmosphere would have become awkward and stilted. Freddie and Tanya were two of a kind in many ways. They dealt with things in a similar manner, and on this particular occasion they knew exactly how the other felt. Each of them loved Anna like she was a part of their own bodies, for different reasons.

Tanya curled back up at the end of the sofa, hugging the cushion to her. She drank deeply from her glass of vodka and the pair settled into a frustrated silence. It was going to be a long night, but at least they had each other for company. *And of course,* Tanya thought wryly, *misery does love company.*

*

The morning light crept through the slit in the curtains and Anna blinked the sleep out of her eyes. She rubbed her face and sat up, glancing towards the door. Again, breakfast had been left out before she awoke. Izobel had entered the room again the night before, warily, bringing her dinner. Anna had stayed across the room and tried to apologise again in person, but Izobel had quickly retreated without answer or eye contact. She was scared of a repeat performance, Anna guessed.

As always, a picture of Freddie came to the forefront of Anna's mind. She closed her eyes sadly. She missed him so much. She knew he would be going out of his mind right now with her gone. He would be turning over every stone in London trying to find her. Except, she wasn't in London. Would he know that? How could he possibly know? His last lead would be Izobel and she was here too. Anna's handbag and phone were not in the room, so she guessed her captor had probably disposed of those elsewhere. Anna knew she had to think of some way to get a message or at least a clue out to Freddie. But the question was, how?

So far she'd not been able to find out anything more about her situation. There were no clues around the room as to who had taken her and all that she could logically assume was that whoever had her clearly didn't want to harm her. They wouldn't have gone to such lengths to make her stay comfortable, breaking into her home to steal her personal home comforts. They were feeding her well too. So, on some level, her kidnapper cared about her. This worried her, perhaps more than if she had been carelessly shoved in some cold, bare cell.

If they had taken her to blackmail Freddie or Tanya for money, they wouldn't care so much about the details. They would be focused on the money and that would come to a swift conclusion. That would have been the best option that she could think of.

But she was pretty sure that this wasn't the case. Whoever had her was focusing intently on her. They even had that camera watching her every move outside the bathroom. This felt personal, but she couldn't think of anyone who would be this fixated on her. Other than Frank Gambino of course. But something told her this wasn't his style.

The memory of his threats, his vice-like grip upon her face, flashed through her mind. Surely if he had taken her, he'd want her to know it was him. His style was blunt and intimidating. He wouldn't take such personal care of her, filling the room with her home comforts. She couldn't see him hiding away behind a camera like a coward either.

But then again, she could be wrong. She didn't know Frank; perhaps this was a game. Perhaps there were more levels to the man than she had been giving him credit for. After all, the things he'd already put Freddie through hadn't exactly been in keeping with what she would expect from someone like him; digging up bodies and trying to get him arrested.

Anna rubbed her head, perplexed. Whoever it was, she kept asking herself the same question. What could they possibly want?

A whirring noise broke through her thoughts and Anna's eyes darted around the room until they settled on the source. It was coming from the camera. It was slowly turning from its normal angle to face her head-on. Anna felt the colour drain from her face as it came to a stop. An icy sensation trickled down her spine.

Its previous angle canvassed the whole room. It didn't need to move to get a good view of where she sat. There was only one reason it had been moved. It was to let her know that he was watching. Her kidnapper was flexing his muscles. Whoever was behind that screen wanted her to know that he was there.

CHAPTER TWENTY-SIX

James opened the front door and blinked at Mollie in surprise.

She smiled at him expectantly. 'Hello, love,' she said cheerily. There was an awkward pause. 'It was today, wasn't it? For making the lemon drizzle?' Mollie asked, her voice less certain.

'Yes, of course. Sorry, Mollie.' James moved aside to let her in, shaking his head with an apologetic smile. 'It is today. I'm just completely distracted with everything that's going on.' A thoughtful and perceptive man, James was very aware of how lonely Mollie felt these days. Whenever he could he tried to ask for her advice on things and invite her over, so that she still felt needed and included. He had completely forgotten that she was coming over today to teach him her family recipe for lemon drizzle cake.

'What do you mean? What's going on?' Mollie asked, shrugging off her coat and hanging it on a hook. She glanced sharply over to Paul who was tucking in his shirt as he crossed the room towards her.

'Oh, I'm sorry, I thought everyone knew—' James bit his lip and looked to Paul for direction.

'Well, apparently I'm not included in "everyone" these days, James.' Mollie folded her arms. 'Apparently once you move out you no longer have to bother telling your mother anything, according to my sons,' she huffed.

Paul sighed. 'Hi, Mum,' he said with a crooked smile. 'Look, I was going to pop over later and talk to you. I've just been busy with Freddie.'

'Well, that's lovely, ain't it!' Mollie exclaimed. 'Too busy to even keep your old mum in the loop. Too busy to swing by. Well, at least your James bothers with me, Paul. At least *someone* appreciates my company and expertise these days, eh!'

'Anna's missing,' he replied bluntly. He could have sugar-coated it, but it was easier to just stun Mollie off her soapbox rather than wait out the rant.

'What?' Mollie asked, taken aback.

'Two days ago she disappeared and we don't know why. Freddie's pretty sure she's been taken. We tried everywhere she might be and the hospitals already.'

'Have you called the police?' Mollie asked.

'You know we can't do that,' Paul replied, shaking his head. 'Freddie's got Fraser working it as an off-record case. He has access to all the systems that would be used if it was official but none of the red tape, so it's actually more efficient than calling it in anyway,' he reassured her.

Mollie didn't look convinced, but she held her tongue. Her sons' businesses were not something they discussed. She was well aware of who they were and what they did and she worried about them greatly. But she knew it wasn't her place to tell them she disagreed with it, so they had an unspoken agreement that it was never discussed.

Mollie stepped around James and put the bag of ingredients she was carrying down on the kitchen counter. She began to unpack it.

'How is Freddie holding up?' she asked. She wanted to run to her eldest son straight away, hold him in her arms and rock him better, but he was far too old for all of that. And if he had wanted his mother's comfort he would have come round before now. She swallowed down the disappointment that he hadn't. Now wasn't the time to focus on her own feelings.

'Not great,' Paul answered honestly. He kept to himself that Freddie was now staying at Tanya's. Mollie would find out soon enough and when she did she'd be spitting feathers. He didn't have time to calm her down today; Freddie was expecting him at the club.

'I've got to go, Mum,' he said, his tone apologetic. 'I promise I'll let you know when anything happens.' He kissed her on the top of the head and gave her a big bear hug before leaving. He winked at James on the way out, who returned a smile.

Mollie sighed as she watched her big, strapping middle son walk out. She knew they were all busy these days, but she still couldn't shake the feeling that her nest was emptier than she'd like it to be. Even Thea wasn't around as much anymore.

She turned back to James and beckoned him over. 'Come on, then, let's show you how a decent lemon drizzle is done,' she said, the worry not leaving her face.

James joined her. 'Sorry, Mollie, I should have checked you knew already.'

'No, it's OK,' she brushed it off. 'I just hope Freddie finds her soon. I can't imagine what he's going through.' She sniffed and blinked away the tears that were forming in her eyes. 'I can't believe someone would do this. I… well. Let's get on.' She cleared her throat.

James nodded and went to find a baking tin. Anna's disappearance was hanging like a black cloud over all of them.

*

Freddie put the phone down and turned his attention back to Bill, Paul and Seamus. They were in the main office at Club CoCo. Freddie was reluctant to go anywhere else, as this was the first place people would try to get hold of him with any news.

'What's Sammy said about Frank?' Freddie directed his question to Paul.

'That there's been no contact still,' he replied.

'I don't like this. Something's off. And when something's off at the same time as Anna goes missing…' Freddie trailed off meaningfully.

'You really think there's something in it?' Paul asked.

Freddie was silent for a moment as he considered his answer. 'I think it's wise to gain more information before accusing the Mafia of something like this, but I want it looked into as a priority. We can't afford to waste time.'

'OK, I'll get things moving.'

'So still nothing else?' Freddie asked, turning his attention to Bill.

Bill's expression was grave. 'I heard some rumblings about a South East crew wanting to gain more ground. They've been heard giving it large in a couple of pubs, talking about working more central and shouldering you to the side. That came from one of Ray Renshaw's guys.'

Freddie sat up straight, suddenly alert. 'You think it could be them? That they've taken Anna to blackmail me?'

Bill considered it. 'I'm not sure. They're small time, just kids. I don't think these lot would have the brainpower or the balls to pull it off. They're all as thick as two short planks from what I've heard.' He pulled a face.

'But maybe that's exactly why they have done it,' Freddie answered. 'This whole thing goes against rules that no one with a brain in this world would break.'

Bill nodded. He had to admit, Freddie had a point. 'They call themselves the Bexley boys, over in Bexleyheath. Other than that, there's not been a dicky bird. Everyone's shocked. Even those who don't like you are disgusted.'

Paul grunted in agreement. Everyone they had talked to had reacted in pretty much the same way.

'Right.' The light seemed to reignite in Freddie's eyes. 'Bill, can you meet Declan for me and sort out the issue he has with the last shipment. Seamus, I need you to collect the Soho protection fees. You've been around enough times with Paul to know what to do. It's all on you today, don't fuck it up. Paul, call Dean, tell him to tool up and meet us at Ruby Ten in twenty minutes.' Freddie stood up.

However thin the threat, this seemed like one of the only viable parties to have taken Anna. He hoped it *was* them, that he could get her back today and put an end to the nightmare they were all stuck in.

His expression darkened. 'Let's go pay those fuckers a little visit.'

CHAPTER TWENTY-SEVEN

Kai Carter leaned down over the pool table in the back room of the small rundown pub he was drinking in and took his shot. The dull beats of his currently favoured rap album sailed out of the small speaker set on the table behind him where his friends sat, and his head bopped along to the rhythm.

There was only a small section of the bar that opened into this room. Most people sat in the main part of the pub on the other side. That was partly why Kai liked it so much. It was private and they were pretty much free to do as they pleased. The landlord left them to it, wise enough to have worked out that so long as he caused them no trouble, they wouldn't cause him any in return.

'Oi, Gaz, roll me a spliff, yeah?' Kai called casually over his shoulder. Two girls sat at the opposite end of the pool table giggled and whispered behind their hands. Kai's grin broadened and he winked a dark brown eye at them, kissing his teeth.

'You ladies wanna play pool with me, yeah? Or is it my other set of balls you're interested in playing with?' He grabbed his crotch and started strutting over. His friends guffawed at his apparent wit and one of the girls blushed. He decided she would be the one for tonight's entertainment.

She looked about sixteen, which was the sort of age Kai liked them to be, with pert tits and a tiny skirt that barely covered her small behind. The heavy make-up she had applied didn't help to hide how young she was, but it showed him she was game.

She fluffed her hair back and played with the large gold hoops in her ears.

Kai reached the table and was about to make his move when the door burst open and three men entered. He rounded on them with another kiss of the teeth, annoyed at the interruption.

'Which one of you fuckers is Kai?' the first one demanded in an angry voice.

'I'm Kai,' he replied, puffing his chest out. 'And what's it to you?' The two members of his crew who were present had stood up and gathered behind him. It was now that he suddenly noted the big one was armed with a baseball bat. He swallowed, wondering who they were. *Have I got one of their daughters up the duff or something?* The one who had spoken stepped forward, right up into his face. There was not a flicker of fear, which surprised Kai. Usually their reputation meant people treated them with a natural wariness, but not this guy.

'Do you know who I am?' the man asked.

'No, I don't. Do you know who *I* am?' he retorted. The man grinned and it made Kai shiver involuntarily. It was a cold grin that didn't quite meet his hard eyes.

'Oh yes, I know exactly who you are. Sit down,' he commanded.

'I don't take fucking orders from you, blood, I— Argh!' Kai screamed as Paul took a hard swing to the back of his knees with the baseball bat, sending him to the floor.

On the rebound, Paul smashed it back into one of the men next to Kai, who had started forward to aid his leader. He fell to the floor next to Kai and moaned in pain, hugging his sides. The second man put his hands up in surrender and stepped back. Paul pointed to a chair in the corner of the room. He immediately scurried over to it and perched without a word.

The two young girls who had been eying Kai up like a piece of meat just minutes before screamed and ran out. Dean moved aside to let them through, then quietly pulled the door shut behind them. He nodded at the barman, who closed the shutter over the back bar, blocking it off out of sight of the main bar.

Freddie grabbed Kai's face in a vice-like grip, forcing him to look up. 'My name's Freddie. Freddie Tyler. I believe you've been discussing your plans for the redistribution of Central London control. And how's that going for ya so far? What your strategy?'

Kai's mouth flapped open and closed like a fish as he realised who Freddie was.

'No answer, mate? But you were so vocal about it before? Telling everyone who'd listen, wasn't that what we heard, Paul?' Freddie turned to his brother.

'It was indeed, Fred,' Paul answered in his deep, craggy voice.

Kai seemed to get his bearings and yanked himself backward out of Freddie's grasp. Freddie wiped his hand on his trousers and Kai's eyes darted back and forth between the men and the bar.

'You can't touch me,' he blustered. 'South London ain't your turf, it's Renshaw's.'

'Yes, it is Renshaw's. Which is why I had the manners to get the go-ahead from him on my way over. And he was more than happy to give me the green light. He ain't got time for shit-stains like you who go round shouting their mouths off and breaking rules.'

'What the fuck you on about?' Kai asked, his tone petulant.

Freddie lunged forward and punched the younger man hard in the stomach. As he doubled over, Freddie grasped the back of his tightly curled hair and slammed Kai's face into his knee. He both felt and heard the crack of the boy's nose exploding, before the cries of pain began. Dean quickly placed a wooden chair behind him and Freddie pushed Kai down into it.

'Where's Anna?' he roared, punching Kai's already bloody face with full force. Kai screamed out in agony.

'Who's Anna? I don't know an Anna, I swear!' he sobbed.

'You don't know an Anna, no? OK, maybe you ain't so good with names.' Freddie paced back and forth. 'Brunette. Attractive. Currently missing. She's been taken and I want her released. Now,' he snarled.

'Why would you think it's me?' Kai whined helplessly. His nose felt like a thousand knives were stabbing through it and he could taste the blood as it cascaded down over his mouth. His nose was definitely broken. All he wanted to do now was get to a hospital, but this crazed madman seemed to have other ideas.

Kai wasn't feeling so hot now. Ten minutes ago he was convinced that he was up there with the hardest men in London; now he wasn't so sure. Maybe his days of dealing weed on his estate didn't make him as big as he'd thought he was.

'Because, sunshine' – Freddie grabbed the baseball bat out of Paul's hand which made Kai whimper – 'you're the only fucker in London stupid enough to tell people you want to take me on. You're the only candidate. So, I'll ask you one last time before I consider letting Dean here take his tools out. Where. The fuck. Is she?'

'I swear to you, I don't know.' Kai shook his head and began to beg, all pretence of hardness forgotten. 'Please, I promise you. I have no idea what's going on. Please, you have to believe me.'

Freddie growled in frustration and, lifting the bat, he smashed it down on Kai's legs. Without stopping to hear anything more, Freddie threw the bat to one side and proceeded to beat ten bells out of the boy with his bare hands. Kai didn't fight back, just held his arms up to protect himself from the worst of Freddie's wrath.

Freddie's punches were hard and vicious, his boxing skills coming to the fore. He rained them down time and again until he was physically spent and Kai was a bloody mess on the floor.

Stepping away he pushed his hair back into place and straightened his jacket. He picked up the bat from where he had thrown it and pointed it at each of the three young men.

'I suggest you remember this the next time you think about mouthing off in a pub about other people's territories.' He kicked Kai in the back of the thigh and turned to walk out. 'And get him to a fucking hospital.'

Paul and Dean followed Freddie back through the pub to where they had parked the car outside. They got in and Paul pulled the car out of the car park.

As they drove Freddie took a packet of wipes out from the glove compartment that he kept for times such as these and wiped the blood off his swollen knuckles.

Paul glanced sideways at him. 'So, it's not them then,' he stated.

'No.' Freddie closed his eyes tiredly. 'But I guess that will serve as a fresh reminder of who we are to anyone thinking of trying to take us on. For a while, at least.'

Paul stared at the road and nodded. It would certainly do that.

CHAPTER TWENTY-EIGHT

'You need to get your house in fucking order or you're out, do you hear me?' Freddie ranted. 'Out.' He paced up and down behind his desk, staring at the man in front of him. It was Gavin, one of his longest-standing security guards.

Tonight, someone had been caught selling gear out of one of the toilet cubicles. The problem wasn't that gear was being sold – this was a club and drugs and clubs went hand in hand, the best of friends – but this particular gear wasn't from one of Freddie's dealers, and that was a no-no. No one was allowed to deal from one of Freddie's clubs unless they worked for him.

It was an unusual occurrence, because most dealers knew the score and didn't fancy pissing off the Tylers by going against their wishes. But tonight someone had decided to try their luck. As soon as the bouncers heard, they had dealt with the guy accordingly and now Gavin was reporting the incident to Freddie, as he knew his boss would want to know. However Gavin now stood wishing he'd sent his colleague Matt to deliver the news, as it seemed his boss was not taking it well.

Gavin stayed silent as Freddie ranted, knowing as they all did that he was climbing the walls in his search for Anna. That was the real reason for this reaction. They were seasoned bouncers and they did a good job. But short of body searching everyone who entered, there wasn't much they could do about chancers bringing drugs in. Gavin knew that Freddie was aware of this, under the anger.

He felt for his boss. He couldn't imagine how he would cope in Freddie's shoes. For once he didn't envy Freddie his seemingly perfect life. He wouldn't want to go through the nightmare Freddie was living for all the money in the world.

There was a knock at the door, cutting Freddie off.

'What?' he responded fiercely.

DI John Fraser practically fell through the door, panting as though he had been running. He leaned forward, supporting himself by placing his hands on his knees as he caught his breath. He shot a look at Gavin.

'We'll talk about this later,' Freddie said grudgingly to the bouncer. 'Now fuck off and do your job properly.'

'Yes, boss.' Gavin retreated, glad to be out of the line of fire. The door closed and Fraser stood up.

'I called in a favour with an ex-girlfriend. I was surprised it came off – it doesn't usually. She works in IT at the phone company.' He swallowed and stood up straight, starting to catch his breath. 'Going through the official lines we almost always get declined, but off-record is different. She must have been in a really good mood. She triangulated Anna's phone. I've got the current location.'

Freddie shot up like lightning and grabbed his jacket. 'Let's go,' he replied, his eyes lighting up in hope.

*

Anna stared up at the ceiling in the dark. The shadows danced around making shapes as the moonlight filtered through the leaves on the tree outside. She couldn't sleep. It was her third night in this strange place and she was still no nearer to finding out why she was here.

Her hand slipped onto her stomach protectively as she felt a slight bubbling sensation within her womb. The little life inside her was busy growing away with no idea of the threats and terrors the world outside held.

The memory of the last time she had been pregnant crept into her thoughts. She had been in a bad position then too, though a very different one to her situation now. She'd been trapped in an abusive relationship with a complete monster. He had beaten her half to death and in doing so had caused her to violently miscarry. The doctors had told her she might struggle to carry a child again, due to the damage he had caused. Yet here she was, growing hers and Freddie's child inside her against all odds.

She closed her eyes as a wave of guilt flooded through her. Freddie still had no idea that she was pregnant. When she had found out it had been a huge shock – they had been so careful.

She hadn't been able to find the right words or the right time to tell Freddie. If she was being honest with herself, she hadn't wanted to tell him either. Because the moment she said it out loud and he knew, then it would be real. Whatever the outcome, whatever they decided to do, things would change forever between them.

It wasn't that Anna didn't want children; she did – one day. But she hadn't planned on that day arriving so soon. It was the worst time possible for this to happen. She and Tanya were riding high at the moment – their second club had just opened and they had so much more planned over the next few years. She was building up her empire and it took all of her energy and time. She couldn't just drop the ball to have a baby right now.

And even if she did manage to do that, what sort of mother was she going to make? She had no idea what she was doing. And what sort of environment would she be bringing this child into? A house with hidden guns and fake passports just in case they needed to go on the run? It wasn't exactly the safe, homely place she had imagined bringing her baby home to.

And how would Freddie feel about becoming a father, so out of the blue? She knew that he also wanted children someday, but again, she doubted he meant now. He might be devastated. Or he could be ecstatic. Family meant everything to him, and of course it wouldn't interrupt his life anywhere near as much as it would hers. He would still be able to come and go as he pleased, run his businesses and carry on whilst she was tied up at home with the day-to-day care of their child.

That thought terrified her. What would it mean for her? She heard so many new mothers talk about how they had lost their identities. And what would it do to her and Freddie's relationship? He had always admired her fierce independence and drive. How would he feel about her when she was at home all the time, asking for his help and looking like crap after weeks of no sleep? Would he still have the same level of respect for her? Or would he be disappointed that she was nothing special after all?

These thoughts whirled around in her mind one after the other, but another set of questions pushed forward. What if it was the best thing that ever happened to her? It might not be the right time, but children were a gift. There were so many people out there who would kill to have a child, but weren't able to fall pregnant. What about the feeling of unconditional love she would feel when she held him or her in her arms for the first time? And what about the amazing person this baby would grow into one day?

Suddenly her arms ached to hold her baby and a feeling of longing replaced the fear.

Anna was confused and frightened of the unknown, but deep down she knew that in her heart of hearts she wanted this baby. The question still remained though: would Freddie feel the same?

She sat up in bed and made a sound of frustration. She wished she could turn her brain off. It was as if the isolation and stress had sent it into hyperdrive.

Why hadn't she found the courage to tell him before she was taken? At least now that would be one question she knew the answer to. But then again, that might not matter anymore. For all she knew she might be dead soon. She shuddered at the thought and wrapped her arms around her stomach protectively. Izobel knew about the baby. Which meant that her kidnapper knew about her baby. And that was a dangerous problem. Neither of them were safe anymore.

She stood up and paced back and forth angrily in the dark. Grasping the sides of her head with her hands she pulled on her hair. She needed to get out of here. For her sanity as well as to get her baby to safety. The frustration burst out of her like an explosion as she finally snapped.

'Let me out of here,' she screamed at the dark corner where the camera sat, still and silent. 'Let me out of here now, do you hear me?' She ran over and beat her hands against the wall underneath it as hot tears began to fall down her face. 'Let me out, let me out.' Her loud, hysterical cries echoed down the hallway as she repeated herself over and over again for what seemed like hours. She raged and cried until her throat began hoarse and her body sagged in defeat. No one replied; nobody came.

CHAPTER TWENTY-NINE

Fraser pulled the car up at the side of a dark country lane. They had stopped briefly en route to pick up Paul, in case they needed the extra manpower. None of them had any clue what they might find when they arrived and Freddie always liked to be as prepared as possible. It seemed that this had been unnecessary though, as they were sitting in the middle of nowhere.

Fraser cut the engine. He turned the headlights back on as an afterthought, realising that no light was coming from anywhere else. They all looked around but there was nothing to see. There were no houses in sight, no street lamps or shops. Just wide-open countryside and a few collections of trees. Either side of the road there was a shallow ditch that met the bottom of the low hedges bordering the fields. The fields rolled up into hills and off out of sight all around them.

Freddie opened the door and stepped out, with the others following behind. He frowned and turned slowly, searching for something, anything that might indicate where Anna's phone was.

'How accurate is that location?' Freddie asked.

'To within quarter of a mile,' Fraser responded. 'Or at least that's what I'm told.'

'And how do they track it? Does it have to still be on?'

'From what I understand, no. As long as the phone still has the SIM in it, they can track where it last was before the signal died.'

'I see.' Freddie pulled his phone out and dialled the number. It connected straight to voicemail. He had been expecting as much, but he had to try. Putting it back in his pocket he noticed Paul wading through the twigs and grass in one of the shallow side ditches. He had the torch on his phone pointed at the ground.

'What are you thinking, Paul?' he asked.

'Well, if it was me...' Paul stopped to look at something, then continued his slow walk. 'If I had kidnapped someone, I'd want to get rid of the phone somewhere like this too, the side of a quiet road where no one would come across it. I'd drive along and throw it out of the window into the ditch, en route. If we can find the phone, we can work out what direction he was driving in. It's not much, but it's a start.'

'I think we can safely assume they were coming from London,' Fraser said.

'Not necessarily,' Paul replied. 'If this was the way they took her, yeah. But if this was a detour designed to throw us off, it might be from the other direction.'

'Worth looking, whilst we're out here,' Freddie said, ignoring Fraser. He turned his torch on and jumped into the opposite ditch. He started scanning the undergrowth, careful not to miss anything.

'Fair enough. I'll go the other way and circle back,' Fraser said.

The three men searched in silence, walking further and further away from the car. Ten minutes passed, then fifteen and no one found anything. Eventually Freddie turned and began to walk back to the car.

'Paul, there's no point. It's dark and overgrown and it could be anywhere in a quarter of a mile.' He shrugged, defeated. 'It was always going to be a long shot.' He huffed in exasperation.

Paul and Fraser walked back towards him.

'Well, at least we know it's around here somewhere,' Fraser commented.

'Yeah and what fucking good has that done me?' Freddie snapped. He rounded on the other man. 'What does this give us, eh? We're in the middle of fucking nowhere, with no more to go on than we did before. Why haven't you found anything yet, Fraser?' Freddie's voice rose as his anger bubbled to the surface. He squared up to him. 'What do I even fucking pay you for?'

Paul intervened. 'Let's not lose our heads, yeah? It's a stressful time; we've got to stay on track. Come on, let's just get back.'

Freddie walked away and took a deep breath.

He wasn't sure what he had been expecting. It wasn't like she was going to be sitting there on the side of the road with her phone in her hand, waving at him as he came round the corner. A pang of longing shot through him. He missed Anna so much and he was going crazy with all the terrible thoughts of what could be happening to her right now running through his head. He hated himself for the fact that each terrible thought was a genuine possibility, due to who he was. It was most likely that she had been taken because of him somehow. He just wished he knew who or why. He felt so useless. His job was to protect the ones he loved and he had failed.

Freddie got into the car and waited as the others followed suit. Fraser started the engine.

'Let's drive on ahead a bit before we leave. Just see what's about. There might be something, you never know,' Fraser suggested.

The car continued down the road and they all kept their eyes peeled for something that might give them a clue. Suddenly Fraser pulled the car to a halt and made a sound of exasperation. They had reached a crossroads.

There were three possible roads to take and from where they sat, Freddie could see another turn-off up ahead. He groaned in defeat. They had no chance of working out where they had gone from here. He wondered if that was part of the reason they had dumped the phone before they got here.

'Fuck!' He punched the dashboard and then ran his hands down his face. He sighed and slumped, but then suddenly sat forward, frowning, and tilted his head.

'What is it?' Fraser asked, alert.

'I don't know. It's just… I think I've been here before. I recognise this junction. But I can't remember why.'

'Well, it's not that far out of London,' Fraser offered. 'Perhaps on your way through to somewhere? Or a traffic diversion?'

'Yeah, maybe.' Freddie stared at the road a little longer. 'OK, let's go back,' he said reluctantly.

They pulled into the car park at the back of Club CoCo, which was silent and in darkness. The club closed at two and it was now past three.

Freddie pulled out the keys to open the back door and was focused on finding the right one when Paul noticed the plastic bag hanging from the handle. He frowned.

'What's this?' He opened it and pulled out a beige rolled-up jacket.

'That's Anna's,' Freddie said.

'What the…' Paul snatched his hand away from the garment. It was covered in something dark and sticky, but he couldn't make out what it was in the darkness. Freddie pulled his phone out and turned the torch on, shining it onto his brother's hands.

As his mind registered what he was looking at, Freddie gasped. He twisted round and punched the back door with rage. He cursed and closed his eyes.

The sticky substance coming off the jacket was a deep crimson colour that Freddie was all too familiar with. Someone had delivered Anna's jacket to them, covered in blood.

CHAPTER THIRTY

'Please, Izobel, talk to me?' Anna pleaded as the young woman came to collect the breakfast tray and deliver the lunch one. It was the same every day. She said the bare minimum and stayed only long enough to do what she had to do. 'Will you at least sit with me a while?' Anna begged. 'I'm going crazy in here by myself, all day every day. If you can't tell me anything, fine, but at least give me some company?'

Anna knew how desperate she sounded but she didn't care. She really was climbing the walls. Consumed by the need to escape but having come up with no way to do so, she was driving herself insane. She'd run through every possibility as to who her abductor could be, but without any new information she was still going round in circles. There was nothing to even take her mind off the situation. No television, no books, no internet, nothing. Just the never-ending silence within the four walls of her little prison and the occasional twitch of the camera in the corner, letting her know that he was still there.

Izobel bit her lip as she considered it. Anna's hope rose – perhaps she would stay a while.

'Say you'll stay? We can… I don't know, talk, play a game, anything.'

Izobel glanced worriedly at the camera and quickly shook her head.

'I can't,' she said, her voice quivering. Before Anna could try to change her mind, she turned and left the room, locking the door once more.

Anna's shoulders slumped and she walked wearily over to collect the lunch tray. She set it down on the bed and studied the contents. It was a fresh chicken and bacon salad, with a probiotic yoghurt and a banana for afterwards. Whoever it was out there, they seemed strangely intent on keeping her healthy. She picked up the banana with disinterest, her frustration beginning to bubble over.

As something inside her snapped, she pulled her arm back and launched the banana at the door. 'I don't want a *fucking* banana and I don't want a *fucking* yoghurt!' She stood up. 'I want to see *you*, the one hiding behind your camera like the pathetic creature you are. Do you get off on it? Do you? Watching me locked up like this? What the hell is your game, huh?' she screamed at the camera, all her fury exploding out. 'What have I ever done to you, you scumbag? Come out here,' she shouted, her eyes burning. 'Come on, come out – I dare you. I dare you to come in here and face me like a man, you spineless, sick, twisted piece of shit.'

She waited for some sort of response, any response, but all stayed silent around her. She stood still, her angry breathing ragged and hard in the quiet. Eventually the camera moved a few degrees to the left and then back again. It repeated the motion again and Anna realised in furious disbelief that the person on the other end of the feed was shaking the camera's head. They were telling her that they wouldn't come through. She began to shake with rage.

'That's it!' she screeched like a banshee. Stomping over to the dressing table she grasped hold of the hairbrush, the chunkiest thing to hand in the minimalist room. Dragging the chair over to the corner with the camera, she stood on it and began smashing the handle into the camera lens again and again until the glass broke. With that done, she grasped the chunky contraption with both hands and yanked it back and forth, trying to pull it off the wall. It held fast though and she could see it had been bolted on. It would take more than that to get it off. Still undeterred, she pushed it to the side and checked the back. Several wires ran out, into a small hole in the wall.

Bingo, she thought. Wires she could work with. One at a time she plucked them out easily, breaking their connection. The little red dot at the front finally stopped flashing and she smiled. She had done it. He couldn't watch her anymore, and if he wanted to fix his camera, he would have no choice but to enter the room.

Stepping down, Anna replaced the chair and sat back in her usual position on the bed, facing the door. She would sit and wait for him, whoever he was, to arrive. She smoothed down her hair and the front of her top. She needed to be in control and therefore had to appear cool and collected. She took a deep breath and psyched herself up.

Minutes passed with no sign of life. She counted off the seconds to pass the time. Eventually she heard a heavy tread come down the hallway. She held her breath as the footsteps stopped outside the door and the key turned in the lock.

The door opened wide and the man behind the camera stepped into the room. Anna's eyes widened and her jaw dropped. She breathed in sharply and then let out a long breath as her mind finally made the connections. She nodded slowly and then shook her head as she finally found her voice.

'You,' she said, her tone falling flat with defeat and resignation. 'It's you.'

CHAPTER THIRTY-ONE

Freddie's phone rang and he closed his eyes anxiously as he saw who it was. Swallowing hard, he took the call and tried to brighten up his voice.

'Leslie, hi, how are you?'

'I'm OK, thanks, Freddie, but I can't seem to get hold of Anna. Her number has been going through to voicemail for days. Has something happened with her phone?'

Freddie could hear the worry in her voice, the undertone of anxiety. It was understandable, considering the things Anna had been through in her past. He knew Leslie Davis called every couple of days just for a chat and to check everything was going well in her daughter's life. It would be bringing back old ghosts now that she couldn't get hold of her.

Freddie quickly thought over his options. His natural instinct was to tell Leslie the truth. He liked and respected her, and he didn't like to lie to family. But then he thought about what Anna would want him to do, and he knew that he would have to hide the truth this time. She wouldn't want her parents to suffer unnecessarily. Hopefully he would find her soon and get her home and the Davises would be none the wiser. And even if the worst came to the worst and he had to give them the bad news, he could at least spare them the sleepless nights and the hell of not knowing beforehand.

'Yeah, sorry, she lost her phone a few days ago. We've been so busy we haven't had time to get a new one yet. She did say you might call and that if you did to tell you not to worry.' Freddie leaned his head forward onto his free hand as he talked.

'Oh, OK then.' Leslie sounded relieved. 'Is she there with you now?'

'No, sorry. I'm out of town at the moment, had to sort out some business,' he lied. 'I won't be back for a few days. And I felt bad leaving Anna, so I surprised her with a spa retreat. She's gone with Thea for a week. Total relaxation. She's been so stressed lately with the extra work, I figured it would do her some good to get away.'

'Oh, how lovely.' Freddie heard the smile in Leslie's tone. 'That's so thoughtful, Freddie. And you're right, that's exactly what she needs. I think she's taken on a bit too much with that second club, you know. She looked very peaky the last time we met up. I've been a bit worried about her, to be honest.'

You and me both, Freddie thought wryly. 'Yeah, it has been taking its toll.'

'Well, hopefully it gets easier soon once she's got more of a routine in place there,' Leslie said. 'Anyway, I'll leave you to it – you must be busy. If you speak to her, tell her we love her lots and to call us when she sorts out the new phone.'

'I will do, don't you worry. Speak to you soon, take care.'

Freddie ended the call and covered his face with his hands. He prayed to God that the next conversation he had with Leslie wasn't to tell her that Anna was coming home in a body bag.

*

Tanya marched down the road with purpose. Her stiletto heels tapped out a rhythm on the concrete slabs of the pavement and her hips swung from side to side encased in a tight leather knee-length skirt. Heads turned, watching her appreciatively as she walked. Her bright red lips matched her gauzy blouse and her glossy locks curled around her shoulders. She was dressed to kill.

Putting on a front for the rest of the world was the only way she knew how to fight whatever she was feeling. And right now she was feeling completely lost.

Anna was more than just a friend and business partner; she was family, the only family she had. Tanya had left home and everyone she was tied to by blood a long time ago. Her father had died when she was young and her brothers had moved out and on with their own lives when she was still small, as they were much older than she was. They never had much time for the scrawny kid left at home and eventually they stopped seeing her at all. After that, she was just left with Rosie, her gin-soaked mother, for company. And that had been no easy ride. Her mother had hated her and taunted her cruelly each and every day of her life. Her real life, as she thought of it, had only really begun the day she ran away for a fresh start. And she only gained family again the day she met Anna. But now Anna was gone and no one seemed to have a clue where or why.

Unlocking the front door of The Last Laugh, she stepped into the building and closed it up again behind her. Turning to look around, she pursed her lips. It was doing well on paper, turning a decent profit. Not quite as much as Club Anya was, but still very good for what it was. Still, Tanya didn't enjoy the running of it at all. The vibe was completely different and the acts were much more difficult to handle.

The girls at Club Anya were easy to talk to. They were all on the same level. Perhaps it was because she used to be in their shoes and understood how they felt about things. Perhaps that was why they showed her respect and trusted what she had to say. But here, it was like the comedians spoke a different language altogether and they were often rude and difficult. She had to bite her tongue and manage them gently, and that wasn't something that came easily to Tanya.

Tanya's phone began to ring, the shrill noise echoing through the empty club. She pulled it out of her bag and looked at the screen. Breathing out heavily she let it go through to voicemail before putting it away. It was Tom. She couldn't face talking to him right now. He kept asking her if she was OK and going out of his way to do nice little things for her, to let her know he was there. She appreciated the thought, but she couldn't bear answering the question again right now.

No, she wasn't OK. And she wasn't going to be until Anna came home. For the first time since they had got together, she couldn't bear to be around Tom. She couldn't bear to be around anyone. Except Freddie. He was the one person who knew exactly how she felt and who didn't try to make it all better. She was glad he was still staying with them.

A clanking sound came from the door that led through to the green room, like a glass bottle being knocked along the floor. In a flash, Tanya yanked up her skirt and whipped out the small knife she kept in a purpose-made garter. It was something she had only purchased and started wearing the year before, after she had been backed into a corner by a stalker, who surprisingly had ended up becoming a good friend. That friendship aside, though, Tanya had firmly decided that she would never be caught off-guard again. This was the first time she had reason to use the knife and was immensely glad she had it with her.

She held the blade out with a steady hand, all senses alert. No one knew yet why Anna had been taken. Was it her kidnapper in the green room? Had he come for her too? If he had, she was ready. Narrowing her eyes she felt a strange, angry resoluteness flow through her body. She hoped it was him. She needed this. She needed a release, someone to take her frustrations out on and who better than the man who was causing her all the stress in the first place?

Tanya glanced at the bar. If she edged that way she would move into view of the green room. But as long as she was quick enough, she should be able to grab a bottle of something before he got to her. A second weapon would be useful.

A shadow began to creep over the floor and she realised it was too late. Whoever it was, he was coming through already. She flexed her muscles and prepared herself for what was coming. His body came into view and she began to lunge, before quickly pulling herself up short.

He staggered forward, shirt untucked and stained, rubbing his eyes and groaning.

'Christ, your phone makes a bloody noise. Don't you have volume control?' The irate voice belonged to Drew Black, one of Tanya's resident comedians. She dropped the arm holding the knife to her side and let out a whoosh of breath.

'What the hell, Drew?' she complained, in an accusatory tone. 'I thought you were… oh, it doesn't matter. What are you *doing* here?'

'Oh, well, there was this party, it got crazy…' His lazy drawl had a false tone to it and Tanya raised an eyebrow. He caught the look and sighed, slumping his shoulders. 'I had a fight with my wife and left my wallet at home, so I couldn't book anywhere to stay. The back window was ajar, so I managed to get in. And then… Well, I owe you a bottle of rum.' He had the grace to look a little embarrassed and Tanya rolled her eyes.

'This ain't a flippin' hotel, Drew,' she said, but her tone was softening.

'It's not a dark alley either, love,' he replied, motioning towards the knife still in her hand. 'What exactly did you think was going to go down here?'

Tanya looked at the weapon in her hand. 'Doesn't matter,' she said dismissively. She pulled her skirt up and placed it back into its holder. Drew gave a quiet whistle of surprise and lifted his eyebrows. He leaned back against one of the tables.

'So what now?' he asked.

'Well, are you going to sort your shit out with your wife any time soon?' Tanya asked.

'Probably not. Apparently she doesn't want to stay married to an alcoholic and I don't want to stay married without being one. So, she's decided we're getting a divorce.

Tanya sighed. She really didn't need to be taking on other people's problems, but it seemed like she wasn't being given much choice.

'Right.' She rubbed her forehead. 'There's a bedsit upstairs that's empty right now. It's not much, but it's furnished and comfortable. If you want it, it's yours.'

'Really?' Drew stood up. 'Wow, that would be perfect, thank you. Seriously, thanks. That's helped me out a lot.'

'It's fine,' Tanya replied dismissively. 'Now for Christ's sake, please go and get yourself cleaned up. You're supposed to be on in three hours.'

'Yes, I am indeed. I'll catch you later then.' Drew disappeared.

Tanya headed for her office sighing wearily, hoping she still had a decent amount of cherry vodka in her personal stash. She was going to need it tonight. Still, she felt a tad better for helping Drew. If she couldn't help her best friend, at least she had been able to help someone.

Closing the door she sat down heavily in her chair and opened the top drawer in the desk. She pulled out the nearly empty bottle of vodka and poured some into a glass that already sat on the desk. As she put the vodka back, she paused and her hand hovered above the small leather pouch next to it. Her personal cocaine stash.

She used it from time to time when she was super busy, just to give her a little edge, or for fun at the occasional party. She was a recreational user and could take it or leave it. But lately she had been relying on it more and more, as sleep was still playing hard to get. She knew she had been hitting it hard and should pull back a bit, but at the moment it was the only thing getting her through. She reached in and pulled it out. *In for a penny, in for a pound,* she thought as she cut her first line of the night.

CHAPTER THIRTY-TWO

Anna strained her ears, waiting for him to return, half hoping he would and half hoping he wouldn't. She still couldn't believe it was him. He was the last person she would ever have imagined to be her kidnapper. Why would he want to take her? It made no sense.

He had stood there earlier staring at her for about a minute, just letting her see him, letting it sink in. Then he had left, without a word. She hadn't known what to say.

It had been hours, but she knew he would come back. He had to. Aside from anything else, he clearly wanted to watch her and he couldn't do that from out there anymore. Not now that she had destroyed his link to the camera.

Finally, the sound of footsteps came through the door and she straightened her back, holding her head high. Her heart thundered against her chest and she swallowed hard as he opened the door.

'Hello,' she said, her calm voice not betraying the fear and wariness underneath.

'Anna,' he replied cordially. There was a strange silence as once again he just stood staring at her.

Anna felt a chill run up her back but she tried to suppress the shudder. She didn't want him to know how afraid she truly was. And she *was* afraid. She knew exactly what sort of person he was and now, being held by him in this way, that knowledge terrified her.

She still had no idea why he had taken her or kept her locked up like this. None of it made sense. *Surely he's got nothing to gain?* she thought. *Surely he must know that by now?*

'Does Freddie know?' Anna kept her tone light and conversational.

He took a step forward, further into the room. 'No, not yet. He will soon though,' he replied.

'I see.' Anna's heart fell. She was hoping Freddie might know, that it would only be a matter of time before he found her. 'Look, you must realise by now that you have nothing to gain by taking me. I'm guessing that this was all done without much forethought,' she said carefully. 'I can understand that in your world mistakes like this can happen. I'm sure we can all come to the agreement that this has been one big misunderstanding.' She swallowed. 'Why don't we start again and go grab a coffee. I'm sure we can work something out.'

'No, I'm afraid that's not possible.' He shook his head. 'This was all planned, Anna. There's been no misunderstanding.' He walked into the room and sat down on the chair by the dresser, facing her.

Anna's heart plummeted and her blood turned to ice in her veins. This was bad. Very, very bad.

'You see, things are about to change in London,' he explained. 'Soon Freddie will be facing a lengthy stretch in prison and Central London will need a strong leader to take his place. One like me, perhaps.'

Anna shook her head in disbelief. 'What? Why would Freddie be going to jail? And what makes you think London would just roll over and accept you in his place? That position has to be earned. You don't just waltz in and sit down on someone else's throne.'

He gave her a sympathetic look. 'You don't see it yet. But that's OK. That doesn't matter now. What matters is the future and that's exactly what I'm building for us. We just have to wait until Freddie's finally inside and then we can settle back down, start over.'

'What?' Anna breathed. 'What do you mean, *we*?'

'I mean you and me, Anna. Don't think I haven't noticed the connection between us. It's been there since we met. And besides, I've seen you with Freddie. You're a good partner to have around. You're intelligent and you understand the way of things. You're feisty too. I find that actually I like that in you. When everything goes down, I don't want you getting dragged down with him. So, for now you'll stay here with me, and then when it's all over, we can start a new life. You, me and even the little one you're growing in there.' He pointed to her stomach. 'Oh, I know all about that. It's OK – I wish it no harm. I'll keep you both safe. So long as you cause me no trouble.' His eyes bored into Anna intently and she felt her skin crawl. Turning on his heel, he left the room and locked it after him.

Anna stood up stunned, reeling from the madness she had just heard. Surely he couldn't be serious? How crazy was he exactly? She shivered as the enormity of the situation hit her. She hoped that Freddie and his men would work out who had taken her soon. She wasn't sure how safe she was after all.

CHAPTER THIRTY-THREE

Freddie woke up with a start and groaned. He gripped his head as if trying to hold it still. He felt as though a herd of angry rhinos were stampeding through his skull. After finding Anna's jacket he had tried to keep it together and had succeeded in putting on a brave face the following day. But sleep evaded him again the next night as his mind screamed out all of the possible scenarios that ended in her jacket becoming drenched in blood. He had driven around for hours, trying to think of something, anything that he hadn't already thought of. But there was nothing. In the end he'd come back to Tanya's and drunk himself into oblivion.

Although he drank a lot in general, getting off-his-face drunk wasn't a usual occurrence for him. He liked to keep his wits about him, but last night all he had wanted to do was forget and slip into some sort of sleep, even if it was broken and fitful, for just a few hours. Now, though, he was beginning to regret that decision. He felt awful. *Serves me right, I guess,* he thought.

Dragging himself upright, he waited for the room to stop spinning before he stood up. He reached into the gym bag at the bottom of the bed and pulled out a pair of tracksuit bottoms and a white T-shirt. He slowly shrugged these on and made his way out to the living room, where he could hear voices.

Tanya glanced over and looked him up and down. 'Christ, you look like shit. I'll get you a coffee.' She walked into the kitchenette that sat to the side of the lounge and turned on the coffee machine.

Freddie thanked her and greeted Fraser, who appeared to have just arrived. Freddie figured it was his arrival that had woken him up.

'What's going on then? Any news?' Freddie's voice was hoarse. He cleared his throat and sat down on the sofa.

'I have got some news, yes,' Fraser began, 'and it's good.'

'You've found her?' Freddie's expression lifted in hope.

'No, not quite that good, sorry,' Fraser answered apologetically. 'But I can tell you this – the blood on Anna's jacket isn't hers. It's male, but whose it is beyond that we can't tell. Whoever he is doesn't have a record – the DNA isn't on the system.'

'So what does that mean?' Freddie frowned as he tried to understand why Anna's jacket would be covered in some guy's blood.

'It could be his blood, though I would say that's unlikely. Why would he hand us that lead? It's more likely that he's taken someone else too. Perhaps the guy's hurt and Anna's tried to put pressure on a wound with her jacket to stem the bleeding. There could be a number of reasons as to how the blood got on the jacket. I think what's more obvious is why it was left on the door. Whoever has her wanted you to think it was her blood. They're trying to taunt you, drive you crazy.'

'It's working,' Freddie said.

'Yes, I know.' Fraser took a sip of his coffee.

Tanya looked over to the hall as Tom poked his head around the doorframe.

'I'm off. I'll see you later, Tan.' His tone was awkward but he gave her a warm smile. She tried to return it. 'Hope you find something more today, Freddie. Good luck, mate.' Tom waved and disappeared.

Freddie shot Tanya a questioning look, having noticed the strain in the interaction. She shook her head slightly and turned her attention back to Fraser.

'Whoever this is they're trying to play a weird game with you, Freddie. With no ransom demand, no calls or texts, this is totally out of my field. I don't know what to make of it. At this stage in any investigation I'd bring in a profiler. Of course, that's a bit tricky in this case, seeing as this is all off the books.' Fraser sat back and waited to see what Freddie thought.

Freddie bit his lip. So far Anna's disappearance had not been officially reported to the police. He had Fraser running an investigation, using all of the officers on Freddie's payroll as his team. They had access to all the technology and databases they needed and were doing everything any team could do, so there had been no need to make it official. This worked well for Freddie, as it meant that everyone on the team already knew who he was and that he was the most likely reason for the abduction. There was no need for any fresh-faced, do-good officer to go looking too closely into his businesses.

Now though, if Fraser needed to bring someone in, that complicated things. He didn't have any profilers on his payroll and wasn't sure he wanted to be under the scrutiny of one either.

'How much would that help, in the grand scheme of things? Is it the difference between finding her or not?' Freddie asked.

'It could be, yes,' Fraser answered. 'My gut is telling me that we're dealing with a nut job. We've been focusing on Anna, but there's been a lot going wrong lately that doesn't add up, and I don't think it's coincidence.' He counted them out on his fingers. 'Viktor Morina, Dale Matthews, the break-in, the money, Anna… I think these might all be the same guy. I think someone is out to get you, big time.' He took a deep breath, his expression serious. 'And if that's the case, this isn't a normal abduction. If we are dealing with a nutcase, then a profiler could be all we have to help us work out where or how to get him.'

Freddie rubbed his head, stressed. He wished he wasn't so hungover. 'How closely can you look at Frank Gambino without it being noticed?' he asked.

'Pretty closely. There's been a watch on him since he entered the UK; he got flagged at the airport.' If Fraser was surprised by the question he didn't show it.

'See if you can find out where he's been around the times everything's been happening. But subtly. I don't know who he has on payroll over here.' Freddie wasn't stupid enough to think Gambino didn't have his fingers in the law-enforcement pie of London. He had men everywhere.

'Fuck it,' Tanya muttered. She knelt down by the coffee table and pulled a small pouch out of her pocket. Taking a small mirror out from under the table, she placed it in front of her and emptied the contents of the pouch onto it. She deftly cut herself a line and then a second one to the side. Snorting the first, she offered the mirror to Freddie. He blinked, surprised.

'Bit early, ain't it, Tan?' he asked.

'Oh, you feeling fresh and full of beans then, mate?' she asked sarcastically.

Freddie was surprised at how sharp her response was. Though she had a point, he acknowledged. He took the mirror. Just like getting drunk, it wasn't a regular habit of his, but it would give him the kick he needed this morning. He sniffed the white powder up neatly, before handing the mirror back to Tanya. Neither offered Fraser a line, knowing full well that he was happy to ignore it but wouldn't touch the stuff himself. Random drugs tests put paid to any ideas he might have had of trying it.

'So, going back to the profiler, what do you think we should do?' Freddie asked Fraser. 'I can't exactly report it and hand over everything we've found so far without getting you struck off, or myself banged up for not reporting it sooner.'

'I've been thinking about that and I've got an idea. It will cost you and it's still a bit risky, but I think it's the best option we've got.'

'Go on,' Freddie said.

'I know a freelance profiler who's available at the moment. She's good. I can't approach her myself for obvious reasons, but I have a friend who used to be on the force. He's a private investigator now and not above taking things that he shouldn't, for a price.' He drank some more coffee and put the mug down on the coffee table. 'We can get him to invite her onto the case, say that he's running it and that the client details are private. That's the easy part. The hard part will be getting her to take the job. It's classed as "misprision of felony" to know of a kidnap and not report it to the police. She may well tell him that she'll have nothing to do with it. And worst case…'

'Worst case she reports it herself and we're all screwed,' Freddie finished.

'Pretty much,' Fraser answered.

'Do you think she would? How well do you know her?' Freddie asked.

Fraser thought about it before he answered. 'I worked two cases with her, but I don't know her much on a personal level. She kept her head down and got on with things. If I had to bet, I'd say she's likely to decline but she won't get involved by reporting it.'

'So we just have to convince her she needs to take it,' Freddie said.

'That would be the plan. If we can pull it off. I think it's worth a shot,' Fraser said honestly.

Freddie nodded slowly. 'How soon could you have the scenario set up?'

'In an hour,' Fraser responded.

'Do it,' Freddie replied. His lips formed a hard line. They were running out of options and at this point in time, slim though the chances of pulling it off were, this idea was the only one they had.

CHAPTER THIRTY-FOUR

Paul ended his call with Marco, their cocaine supplier, and slipped the phone back into the inner pocket of his dark-grey suit jacket. He leaned over the small balcony of his flat and sighed heavily.

James walked up to stand beside him, his hands wrapped around a mug of coffee, and gave him a sad smile. 'Are you OK?' he asked, knowing that he wasn't.

'Nah, not really. Freddie's losing the plot over Anna. And I can understand that. I'd feel the same if it were you.' Paul nudged James fondly and James squeezed his arm.

'I know you would,' James said.

'It's not just that though. Freddie's dropped the reins on the business.' The worry lines on Paul's brow deepened. 'I've been picking up the slack as much as I can, but people are starting to notice. You know, a year ago there were three of us running things. And now it's mostly just me and there are only so many hours in the day.' Paul sighed again heavily. 'And on top of that, there are a couple of people that don't want to deal with me. So, Freddie sorts them out usually, but he's so preoccupied that I'm going to have to step in and I'm just not looking forward to that.'

'What do you mean?' It was James's turn to frown. 'Why wouldn't they want to deal with you? There's nothing you can't do that Freddie can. What's the issue?'

Paul turned to face James and chewed his cheek. He didn't want to upset his partner and he knew that his next words would. But he wasn't going to lie to him either. 'Some of the people we're in business with are very old school. They don't understand some of my life choices.' He put it as gently as he could. In truth, some big issues had arisen when he had come out the year before. He and Freddie had known that this would be the case and had been prepared for it.

Most people didn't bat an eyelid about the fact he was gay. But sadly some of the older faces that they worked with were very set in their ways. It didn't matter that he wasn't the first – Ronnie Kray had been one of the first men in their position to be publicly known as homosexual and there had been others – there were still people in their world who refused to accept it.

'You've got to be joking…' James's expression turned from surprise to anger. 'Are you serious?'

'Yeah, I am. And it's fine, it don't affect anything. It's just a ballache, that's all.' Paul dismissed it casually.

He had never told James how Freddie had had to fight to keep a lot of business and how he had beaten one man nearly to death to send a message to the rest of their world that in his presence homophobia would not be tolerated. It had been a tense time for the Tylers. With an empire like theirs, in the dark, cut-throat shadows of the underworld, all it took was a couple of bricks to be moved and it could all fall down in an instant. But they had shown a strong united front and although they had to rejig their responsibilities slightly to avoid any fallout, everything had settled back down pretty quickly.

'So, who are they then? Can't you just tell them to piss off if they have a problem?' James was annoyed. He had lived with this sort of bullshit for years when he was younger, but it wasn't a problem much anymore. Not in the multicultural, modern freedom of London. He was furious that it was causing a problem now, to his Paul. Paul didn't deserve that. 'What is it with these people? I mean, Christ, having a problem with someone because they're gay is like having a problem because they're black, or Jewish, or a woman!'

Paul nodded his agreement but didn't respond. It wouldn't help the situation to tell James that these people were also well known for all of those things: racism, sexism, the lot. They weren't the nicest of people, but in the underworld you had to work with all sorts.

'Are they important? Can't you just not work with them?' James asked.

Paul hid a smile. Life was always so black and white to James. 'No, they spend a lot of money with us. They used to be much bigger players, but these days they're semi-retired. They own a couple of clubs on the East side and run some small illegal enterprises from within. We supply them with the right sort of men for security and run the drugs through the clubs. We also supply their spirits. They would be a big client to lose, overall.'

'When do you need to go see them?' James asked.

'Tonight,' Paul answered.

'OK. Which clubs are they, anyway?'

'Jui over in Shoreditch and Roar on Brick Lane. I'm meeting them at Roar at ten. It will be fine. The meeting will be short and sweet and I'll be home by eleven hopefully.'

James pursed his lips and dropped it. 'OK, well, I said I'd pop and see if Tanya needed a hand tonight now that Anna isn't about, so I might not be back. I'll let you know.' James looked at his watch. 'Oh crap, I'd better go, I'm late.' He leaned up and kissed Paul on the cheek. 'See you later.'

James strode back inside to grab his jacket and set off. He nodded to himself firmly as a plan began to form in his mind. Paul always had his back – now it was time to return the favour.

CHAPTER THIRTY-FIVE

Freddie watched as the door opened and a tall, slim woman with a deep tan and light brown hair that fanned out around her shoulders entered the room. Against Fraser's advice he had decided to be present for the meeting. They had one shot at getting Helen Romano to agree to work this case; Freddie had to make sure that everything possible was done to swing her their way.

Dan Jones, Fraser's private-investigator friend, stood up and shook her hand.

'Helen, thank you so much for coming to talk to us at such short notice.' Dan's whitened teeth glared out from his wide smile and his voice boomed around the room.

He reminded Freddie of a used-car salesman and he'd taken an instant dislike to the man, but Fraser said he was good and could be trusted, which was all that mattered.

'No problem. I understand it's an urgent situation?' Helen questioned, sitting down and crossing her slender legs. She turned her attention to Freddie.

'Yes, very urgent,' Freddie answered with a polite smile of greeting. The action felt alien and his cheeks twitched. He hadn't smiled much lately.

Dan sat back in his seat and took over. 'Here's the situation…' He told Helen everything they had discussed so far, reeling off all the facts and timelines that Fraser had prepped him with, only leaving out the true nature of Freddie's businesses and the matter of all the bodies turning up. When he had finished, he clasped his hands on the table and waited.

Freddie watched Helen's face as Dan spoke. She kept her expression neutral as she made notes in a small pad, but he could almost see the cogs in her brain beginning to turn, beginning to analyse the situation. He needed to know what she was thinking. Furthermore, he needed her to take the case.

Her lips pressed into a firm line and her eyes dipped down. She took a deep breath.

'Listen, this needs to go to the police. You've known this long that she's been taken – if something were to happen to her you could already be charged with—'

'Misprision of felony, I know,' Freddie finished. She turned to him and Freddie leaned towards her. 'Listen, please…' Freddie took a deep breath. Her light brown gaze held his own, open to hearing what he had to say. Freddie had no idea whether what he was about to say was the right thing, or whether it was the worst idea he had ever had, but he made the decision to be honest. To a point, at least.

'I can't take this to the police. Who I am and what I do don't matter right now, but they will most likely cause me to be detained, and if I'm busy fighting that, I can't be focused on helping Anna. And I need to be able to do that. I'm running out of time. She's been gone for five days. She'll be scared and alone. I already have a team of people working on this who have access to everything the police do, though please don't ask me how as I won't be able to tell you.'

Freddie's gaze bored into hers intensely. 'I know that this situation is not a normal one. But we need to understand this man on a level that we're not equipped to do. It could mean the difference between Anna coming home alive…' Freddie swallowed the lump that had caught in his throat. 'All I need is for you to look at the case, look at what we have and tell me what you think. That's all I'm asking for.'

Freddie slid a small bag out from under his chair and unzipped it. Inside there was a thick stack of twenty-pound notes. 'I know you can't have this job on your record. In here is three times what you would charge for an average full-length case. It's yours if you help me.'

There was a silence as Freddie and Dan waited to see what Helen would say. She studied Freddie as she sat and he fought the urge to evade the soul-piercing scrutiny. Helen eventually looked away and down at the notes she had taken as Dan had run through everything.

Finally she spoke. 'I don't know exactly what's going on here. Dan, you've clearly had no involvement with this case so far – I can tell by the way you delivered the information.' She held her hand up to stem his protest. 'Please, I have a Masters in Psychology; I read people for a living.' She turned to Freddie, biting her lip in thought. 'I think I get the gist of the basic situation with regard to you, Freddie.'

Freddie could see Helen warring with herself. His hopes began to lift. She hadn't dismissed it out of hand. He pressed forward.

'I know you're fighting your conscience on this one. It's not an official case and you usually stand by the law, but this is an unusual situation. Doing things this way is the best chance Anna has of us finding her, of there being no delays or setbacks. Please. All I need is your professional opinion.'

Helen pushed her hair back and closed her eyes. There was a tense few moments where Freddie began to think he had lost her, but then she nodded.

'OK,' she said heavily. She took a deep breath and stood up. She paced back and forth slowly as she talked. 'The biggest motivator for someone to kidnap an adult victim is control. Whatever other reasons that may have triggered it – money, politics, sexual intentions – it all boils down to an in-built need for absolute control. Control of the situation, or of the person or geographical area they are holding. Kidnappers also have a lack of empathy. It's how they're able to go through with it. I'd say that someone who embodies this distinct lack of empathy and need for control, along with the cool, logical thought process involved in a complex kidnapping like this, is most likely a psychopath. The abduction was well planned and the organisation meticulous. If you're sure that it was the same person who broke in, leaving no fingerprints and who's been methodically trying to trip you up professionally, then this all adds to that theory.'

Freddie cast his eyes away as she studied him, unnerved by her professional skills. It was as though she was reading his thoughts when she spoke again. 'It's OK, Mr Tyler – I'm not interested in probing any further into your personal life than I have to.'

Freddie cleared his throat and straightened his jacket. 'So you think he's a psycho, that much isn't exactly a surprise. What else?'

'The jacket isn't in keeping with his normal style. Obviously it was meant to taunt you, but that's odd in itself. There's been no ransom demand, so it wasn't sent to hurry you up. If it's game play that this person likes, they would have sent some version of a set of rules. There would be a task of some sort, or a goal they require you to fulfil. This would serve as a motivator for you to go along with it. This person wants to hurt you with no particular agenda, but despite that, they don't want to hurt Anna.'

Freddie's head shot around at the last sentence. 'What do you mean?' he asked.

'If they wanted to hurt her or if they were even indifferent to her, they would have spilled her own blood on the jacket. They wouldn't need to kill her, just cut her. A psychopath wouldn't care about spilling a little of Anna's blood – it would be the logical first choice and much easier than spilling someone else's. There's something stopping him. More than just a need to keep her alive. He has an emotional connection.'

'But I thought psychos didn't feel emotion?' Freddie said.

'Not at the same level as the rest of us, but yes, they do. They feel things on a sort of lower frequency. So they can go around doing things mainly uninhibited by things like fear, guilt, remorse, self-doubt… but when things don't go as planned, they can feel genuine anger and resentment. One of the core personality traits in a psychopath is narcissism. They often feel greatly entitled and self-righteous. It can overpower everything else, consume them almost.'

She took a breath and sat back down in her chair. 'Not all psychopaths are bad people – there are a lot of decent, well-functioning psychopaths out there. They're all around us, actually. But in this situation, we can assume that we are looking at one who sports some of the darker personality traits.'

'How does this knowledge help us work out how to find her?' Freddie's tone was short. He was getting tired of the analysis. He didn't care how the inner mind of the arsehole who had taken Anna worked; all he cared about was getting her back.

'Right, so, humans are creatures of habit. Non-psychotic people tend to form those habits following emotional triggers. For example, if you had good customer service in a sandwich shop one day and the warm colour on the wall made you feel at home, you'd be likely to go back there again and again, forming a habit. A psychopath has the same in-built tendencies to be drawn back to places they know, but for more logical reasons. For example, they will habitually visit a sandwich shop because it is seven paces closer to work than the next. They will remember somewhere because it made their lives run more efficiently, not because of a past emotional response. So, wherever he's taken her will likely be somewhere he knows, which would be efficient in holding someone hostage and all that this entails.'

'But we don't have a clue who he is, so how could we work out what's emotional or efficient for him in the first place?' Freddie was perplexed.

Helen shrugged. 'You asked for my professional opinion based on very little information. That's all I've got for you.'

Freddie stared across the room at Dan, who had remained silent throughout the exchange. He didn't see much hope in the other man's eyes either.

'OK,' he said, his voice barely more than a whisper. 'Thank you, Helen. I appreciate your time.'

Helen nodded soberly and stood up to leave. Freddie held the bag with the money out towards her but she shook her head. 'No, keep it. I've not been able to give you much to go on and I can't take your money for a ten-minute conversation. I just hope you know what you're doing.' She gave Freddie a long, serious look. 'Because if you don't…'

'I know. Anna will be dead,' Freddie said.

'No, I don't think she will. Like I said, he doesn't want to hurt her. But that might not be a good thing, Freddie. We have no clue what he has in store for her.' She watched as Freddie flinched. 'Good luck,' she said as she left the room.

Helen walked out the door subdued and vowed firmly to herself never to speak of their interaction. Whatever the outcome, some things were just better left buried.

CHAPTER THIRTY-SIX

Paul walked past the bouncers on the door of Roar with a nod. They nodded back respectfully, unclipping the rope for him to pass without question. They knew who he was. He was one of the bosses.

Bouncers who could keep their mouths shut when it counted and were loyal to the right people were rare and in demand, so Freddie and Paul had spent years building up a security firm full of only the best. Now, all the other clubs that served as fronts for their owners' more nefarious businesses hired their security through them. They didn't need to worry about the level of loyalty they were getting when it came from the Tylers.

Paul made his way through the throng of people on the dance floor to the end of the bar where a small raised, cordoned-off platform held one table with four men seated around it. The two men in the middle were around sixty and were not ageing gracefully. Both rounder than their frames should really allow around the middle, one was bald with jowls that hung low, making him resemble a bulldog, and the other sported numerous scars across one side of his face and a thin comb-over, as he desperately displayed his last few strands of hair. Chunky gold rings adorned their fingers and matching chains glinted up through the open tops of their designer shirts.

Business partners and lifelong friends, they looked every inch the hard, has-been gangsters that they were. Now, their businesses were smaller than in the days when they had thrived under the permission of Vince and Big Dom, but they still did well enough for themselves and used the two clubs for money laundering.

Paul ignored the two other men there. They were no one he knew, clearly just guests of the proprietors for the evening. As he approached, the one with the comb-over curled his lip and gave him the hard eye. Paul walked into their private area without waiting for permission. He knew he was unlikely to get it. Keeping a cool expression he approached the table.

'Ron, Jimmy.' He nodded in greeting.

Ron looked him up and down, the curl not leaving his lip. 'Where's Freddie?' he finally asked.

'Busy,' Paul responded.

Ron turned and exchanged a look with Jimmy. 'We only conduct business with him,' he replied rudely.

'Well, this month you'll have to settle for me. Like I said, he's busy,' Paul repeated, his tone clipped.

Jimmy leaned forward, anger in his expression. 'We don't deal with faggots in 'ere, boy. So sling your 'ook and tell your brother to get his arse down here if he still wants to continue our agreement.'

Paul silently boiled with fury, but he kept it contained. It wouldn't do him or Freddie any favours to publicly fall out with some of the old-schoolers. He smiled coldly and stepped forward so that he towered above them.

'I'd watch your tone if I were you,' he said quietly.

'Why's that then, nancy boy?' Ron jeered. 'Gonna set your brother on us like you did to Tim Clancy last year?' The pair laughed.

'Nah,' Paul replied, 'I'll just wipe the fucking floor with you, before asking your – sorry, *my* – security guards to clear up the mess.'

Both men fell silent for a second. Jimmy suddenly began to leap forward, but Ron stopped him with his arm. His eyes narrowed.

'There's your money, Tyler,' he spat, kicking a full bag across the floor towards him. 'Take it and fuck off.'

Paul picked up the bag and smiled. 'That weren't so hard, was it? Now, before I go, we got your message about upping the vodka. We'll start sending the additional load next month, from the fourth. You'll need to send an extra guy to the pick-up point from then on.' Without waiting for an answer, Paul turned on his heel and left.

He didn't notice James sitting on the end bar stool, with his back to them all, listening.

James watched Paul retreat and anger flowed through his veins. It had taken all his strength not to walk over and punch those idiots in the face.

'Sandra,' Ron barked at the barmaid from behind him. 'Get us a bottle of whisky. Now!'

James saw Sandra purse her lips and shoot her boss a hateful glare. As she looked away, she clocked James watching her and her expression turned immediately to one of guilt. Her eyes darted back and forth, as if working out if James knew her employer.

James laughed lightly. 'Boss giving you a hard time tonight, sweetheart?' he asked with a sympathetic smile.

She visibly relaxed. 'He can be a little… difficult, shall we say!'

'Oh, tell me about it, my boss is a total arse,' James replied, rolling his eyes. 'Bless you, though, you look so stressed. And that's not good for anyone. How about after you've got him his whisky, you pour yourself a drink and tell me all about it…'

*

Tanya poured herself another vodka and stared out the window. It had been another long, hard day running both the clubs and worrying about Anna non-stop. She had no idea how she was still functioning; she felt like an absolute mess inside. She had stayed behind well after closing at the comedy club and had a few drinks with Drew. He was actually quite good company, to her surprise. She was aware that he was an alcoholic, but she didn't care. He worked his shows and didn't cause any problems. He was clearly a functioning alcoholic and Tanya didn't have the energy or the will to go around saving people from themselves. At least he was one person who didn't shoot her loaded looks whenever she took the edge off.

She knew she was drinking and self-medicating too much at the moment, but she wasn't about to change that. She'd have a detox when Anna was home safe and sound again. When she could finally breathe without anxiety piercing her heart.

It was nearly two in the morning, but she didn't want to go to bed. She knew she wouldn't sleep well, and aside from that, Tom was here again. In fact he hadn't gone home since Anna disappeared and it was irritating her beyond belief. She had purposely not asked him to move in with her so that she could keep her space and independence. But since Anna had gone, it was like he didn't want to leave her alone.

In the back of her mind Tanya knew that this was a normal reaction from someone who loved you, but this in itself was new to her. She had spent her whole life looking after herself and getting by without love and without anyone carrying her through the hard times. It was difficult to change her natural reactions now, especially at a time like this.

Tanya rubbed her head. The stress of Tom continuously trying to help her was just getting too much. She stared out of the window, unseeing. Sipping her vodka, she rolled her neck around, trying to ease the knot that had formed.

A noise sounded behind her and she tensed, knowing exactly who it was. She turned to find Tom standing at the doorway, bleary-eyed with messy bed-hair. His chiselled face was covered in short stubble, just the way she liked it. She raked her eyes up and down his impressive physique. He wore nothing but a pair of boxers, his tanned, muscular body on show. Her eyes rested on the tattooed sleeve on his right arm. The patterns curled around his biceps.

The sight of her handsome partner standing there in all his glory like this would usually have excited her. In normal circumstances she wouldn't be able to keep her hands off him – she'd feel a heady mixture of lust and love and would have dragged him off to the bedroom within seconds.

But tonight she felt nothing. She felt cold and empty and flooded with a dark anxiety that someone like Tom couldn't possibly understand. She watched his eyes flicker towards the vodka in her hand. He didn't say anything, but she could tell what he was thinking. A stab of irritation shot through her and her anxiety increased.

She couldn't do this, she realised. She couldn't be around him anymore, not at the moment.

'Tan, you coming to bed?' Tom asked. He held a hand out to her.

Tanya stepped back and breathed heavily. 'No, not right now,' she replied, her voice hard.

Tom frowned slightly. 'It's nearly two in the morning – you must be knackered. Come on, I'll rub your back?' He gave her a tentative half-smile.

Tanya closed her eyes. 'Tom, I can't do this.'

Tom paused before he answered. 'I know it's been tough on you, this whole Anna thing. No one wants to have to deal with this, but it's happened. And you *will* get through it, I promise you.'

'No, not that, *this*,' Tanya answered firmly. 'You. I can't be around you at the moment. I can't come home and pretend I'm OK and act like the things you do and say make things any better, because they don't.' Tanya put her glass down and ran her hands through her hair. 'I know you mean well, but I just can't do this right now. I need you to give me some space. I need you to back off for a bit.'

'What?' Tom recoiled as though he had been stung. 'What do you mean? I'm just trying to be there for you—'

'Exactly!' she cut him off. 'I can't deal with that on top of everything else right now, OK?' Tanya ranted, letting it all out. 'I'm not some sad little girl who needs you to pet her better. I don't need you. I have never needed you. You're with me because I *want* you to be, not because I need someone around. Your job isn't to save me and shelter me from shit – I can look after myself. And right now, that's what I need to do. I need space to look after myself and get through this.'

There was a heavy silence as they faced each other across the room. Tanya hated herself for hurting Tom, but she had no choice, she was suffocating. 'Listen, just… go back to bed and then tomorrow go and stay back at your place for a while. Just let me figure things out for a bit,' Tanya said wearily.

Tom made a sound of disbelief and shook his head, the pain he was feeling evident in his face. 'Nah, I'm good,' he shot back. 'I'll go now. I'm not staying where I'm not wanted.' He stared at her for a second before continuing. 'You know what, Tanya, I haven't been trying to help you through this because I think you need me. I know better than anyone how strong and fierce and independent you are. I've been there for you because I care, and that's what people who care about each other do. I don't think that I'm making it better, or saving you. I'm just showing you support. Clearly, though, just like everyone else around here, you don't appreciate what you've got in me.' He shook his head and left the room.

Tanya heard him pull his clothes on in the bedroom and a minute later he reappeared. He stared at her from the doorway, misery etched onto his face.

'No? Nothing?' he asked.

Tanya clenched her jaw to stop her tears from falling in front of him. It hurt her to do this, but her need to be left to her own devices was too strong to ignore. She crossed her arms, hugging herself and cast her eyes to the floor.

Tom didn't say any more. His pride prevented him from begging her to keep him. She had made herself clear and he would just have to deal with that. He left the flat, slamming the door shut angrily behind him.

Tanya waited until she heard the lift doors close before she crumpled to the floor and cried uncontrollably.

CHAPTER THIRTY-SEVEN

He pressed a button on one of the laptops in front of him and the screen flickered to life. There she was again, Anna. He felt immediately soothed. He'd finally installed the new camera today, after it arrived by post this morning. He had felt irritated when she'd smashed up his camera. It meant that he had no choice but to show himself and that had not been part of the plan. Perhaps it was for the best though, he figured. After all, now that she knew who he was and his plan for the future, he had a shot at Stockholm syndrome.

He'd read about a few cases, during his research into past kidnappings, of captives who had ended up falling for their captor. Apparently it had been coined as a psychological condition that causes captives to form mental alliances with their captors, developing emotions such as trust and affection as a form of survival.

It was fairly simple, when he thought it through. He just had to keep her contained long enough for it to happen naturally. The baby she was carrying would help hurry things along too, he reckoned. Expectant mothers had an even stronger natural instinct for survival than normal.

The door to the room he used as his office opened and one of his men came in, carrying a coffee. He placed it on his boss's desk and waited.

'You can go and sit downstairs with Izobel,' he said. 'I don't need anything else at the moment.' He waited until the other man had left before turning back to the screen.

He didn't enjoy having to suffer other people around him so much, but he needed them at the moment. He wasn't so arrogant as to think he could pull absolutely everything off all by himself. He'd needed Diego's help for a lot of the grunt work, especially at the beginning.

Finding the exact location of Viktor's body in that field again hadn't been easy in the dark. They had dug several holes before finally reaching him. The stench had been almost unbearable, he recalled. He was thankful for the thick plastic sheeting in which Viktor had been buried, as he and Diego carried Viktor out to the side of the road. That wasn't a job that would have been easy alone.

Izobel had been worth taking along for the ride too. He'd told her to befriend Anna in any way she could, knowing that he would need someone to lure her away at some point. She had come up trumps on that front.

Despite having these two working for him, there had been some things he had needed to do himself. Breaking into the flat to collect some of Anna's personal things was one of them. He had walked around studying the way they lived, careful to only take things that wouldn't be noticed, including the gym bag he had later used when he'd withdrawn Freddie's money.

That hadn't been hard at all really. He had swiped Freddie's passport to show as ID and styled himself after the other man. The dim old woman behind the counter had been as blind as a bat, not looking too closely as he flattered her with meaningless compliments.

Dale Matthews he'd taken care of himself too. He had enjoyed snuffing out that reprobate, slitting his throat as he slept. It was almost calming, watching the blood pour out from the wound in his neck as he gargled, trying to cling on to life. It had been a risk, going onto the Somers Town estate – he could easily have been noticed. But he was careful to go in the very early hours of the morning when everyone would be asleep, even the party animals.

With a hoodie on and a scarf over his mouth just to make sure, he had slipped in and out without seeing a soul.

Again, though, it had been Diego stationed in a car opposite the building who had waited for Freddie to arrive before tipping off the police.

His mind tuned back to the present as the Anna on screen stood up from sitting on the bed and wandered across to the window. She placed her forehead on the glass and looked out across the endless fields. He studied her, the sad droop of her shoulders and her tired stance. He knew she was desperate to get out of the room. He rubbed his chin thoughtfully.

He stood up and, as he walked out of the room, touched the cool metal of the handgun in his pocket, confirming its presence. It was his insurance policy. He didn't want to kill Anna, but he was a logical man. If she tried to cause trouble now and betray him, he could always teach her a little lesson. Flesh wounds were painful, but they always healed.

CHAPTER THIRTY-EIGHT

Freddie walked through the small side door of Club Anya and through the bar area. Carl was changing over the optics and turned to greet him.

'Alright, Freddie, how's it going?' he asked. 'Any news?'

'Nah, not yet I'm afraid, Carl,' Freddie answered, pausing to talk to the older man.

'No, course not,' Carl said glumly. 'Tanya would have said when she came in, I guess.'

'Yeah, she here, actually?' Freddie pointed his thumb towards the back office in question.

'Yeah, came in not long ago. She er—' Carl glanced towards the office and lowered his voice. 'She's not looking too good. She didn't want to talk, so I didn't push, but… well anyway, she's in there.' He turned back round as Freddie walked off to the office. He hoped that Freddie would be able to get through to Tanya. She was usually chatty and full of life, and even when trouble hit she would be at the bar pouring her heart out to him. But not today. He had never seen her so withdrawn. It was worrying him greatly. He shook his head sadly. With Anna gone and Tanya a mess, nothing seemed right with the world.

Freddie walked straight into the office without stopping. Tanya jumped in her seat at the desk, taken by surprise.

'Freddie,' she exclaimed. 'God, you gave me a right fright. What you doing?'

'How you doing, Tan?' Freddie asked, sitting opposite her.

'What? I'm fine thanks, you?' she asked, bemused.

'No, you're not,' Freddie responded. 'I just got off the phone with Tom.'

'Oh, for fuck's sake,' Tanya cried, rolling her eyes. 'Are you serious? He got his new mate to come talk to me? How bloody pathetic. Don't go there, Freddie. It's no one else's business what goes on in my relationships.' Tanya's back was well and truly up. She was fuming.

'He didn't send me to speak to you, Tanya, and honestly I'm not here to fight his corner. I'm here because you're family and I've been watching you go downhill since Anna was taken. I'm worried about you.'

'I'm fine,' Tanya replied crisply.

'No, you're not, Tanya. Look at yourself – go on, go look in the mirror.' When she didn't move, Freddie stood up, grasped her by the elbow and walked her to the mirror by the door.

As Tanya looked at herself she knew exactly what Freddie could see. The bags under her eyes, the grey tinge to her skin, the limp hair that was never usually seen without style and volume, and above all, the haunted, stressed expression that hadn't left her face in a week. She shrugged him off and sat back down at the desk.

'So, what? I look tired and I haven't dolled myself up. You ain't exactly looking so perfect yourself, mate,' she said caustically. Tanya pulled open the top drawer and took out her stash of cocaine and a small mirror.

'It's not just that, Tanya. I know you're stressed – we all are. But just look at what you're doing.' He pointed at the line she was cutting. 'It's barely lunchtime and you're coking up. It was with morning coffee yesterday. You're relying on it, and that ain't you.'

'Freddie, we all dabble, yourself included, so please don't start playing the saint now.' Tanya snorted the line and tidied it all away neatly again. Irritated, she left her chair and walked over to sit on the sofa.

'Of course we do, but there's a difference between the occasional dabble and a gram a day. Yeah' – he nodded as she glanced up at his face – 'my dealers talk to me, Tanya. I know how much you've been ordering.'

There was a silence, as Tanya didn't bother to deny it.

'And now suddenly you're pushing away the first person you've ever been happy with. You're telling him to leave you alone, so that… well, why? So that you can drink and coke yourself to death in peace?' Freddie held out his hands. 'Come on, Tanya, that isn't you. I know you aren't dealing with Anna's abduction well, but do you really think she'd want to see you like this? I can tell you for a fact, it would break her heart if she was watching you right now.'

They stared at each other hard for a moment, until Tanya crumbled in front of Freddie's eyes. She fought the sobs that were forcing their way through until eventually they won. The tears bubbled over and she covered her face as she began to cry.

More than a little surprised, Freddie got up from his seat and sat beside her, pulling her into him for a hug. He'd never seen Tanya break down like this before. In fact he doubted anyone had. She cried it out for a minute against his chest, before pulling herself back, taking a deep breath and wiping her eyes with her hands.

'Fuck.' Her face turned crimson in embarrassment. 'Christ, you know how to make a girl cry, don't ya? It's just because I'm tired, by the way,' she said defensively.

She sighed. 'Look, I know I'm overdoing it a bit at the moment, but that really is just to get me through working both clubs on my own, on no sleep. It ain't healthy, I know. And once she's back and I can sleep knowing nothing bad is happening to her, I'll pack it back in. But right now I need the kick.'

Freddie nodded. He believed her. He knew junkies and he knew people who just needed an extra boost from time to time, and Tanya was definitely the latter.

'I know, Tan. But what sort of friend would I be if I didn't check up on that, eh? And seriously, you need to think hard on things with Tom. Because I've never known you so settled.'

'That's the thing, though, innit?' Tanya sniffed and wiped her blotchy face again with the sleeve of her thin summer cardigan. 'Settled ain't necessarily happy. And it's not exactly *me*, is it? I mean…' She blew out her cheeks. 'Tom is amazing. He's the perfect man and he loves me. And I do love him too. But… you know, I was damaged a long time ago. I learned to live without all that and on my own two feet, and I like that. I like knowing that whatever happens, I've got my own back. And I like not knowing what's round the corner, who I'll meet next, what adventure is still in store. I'm not built to be a… I don't know, "nice girlfriend" – the steady little woman. Like, he does the same thing every day, you know? He works the same hours, has the same evening routine and I can always tell what he's thinking. There are no surprises.'

'A lot of people would call that a good thing,' Freddie offered.

'Exactly! There's something seriously wrong with me – I'm damaged.' Tanya laughed. 'I look at something good like that, and it fills me with dread. I just want to get away. I've ignored that so far, but then Anna got taken and I feel like my arm has been ripped off.' Grief rippled across her features. 'And Tom just wants to be there for me. *All* the time, in *every* way. And I just feel like I can't breathe. It's not even his fault. He's not doing anything wrong, or going over the top with it, it's me. I'm the problem. I don't know…' She slumped back on the sofa. 'I think that after all the years of opening up to the wrong men, the bad boys, I'm just too far gone to be content in a normal, healthy relationship.'

Freddie lay back on the sofa next to her and sighed. He wanted to tell her that she was wrong, but the truth was he didn't know if she was. Tanya had been fiercely independent and headstrong for all the years he had known her. She had grown from the wide-eyed new girl in town to underworld star, to successful business owner in her own right – all through her own determination and without the help of any man. She hadn't had many relationships over the years, but the ones she'd had had been thrilling, fast and a total car crash. She had left with her heart and soul crushed every time. And Freddie knew that better than most, being the first man to have crushed it, many years before.

He hadn't realised how much he had hurt her at the time. They had been young – he a local up-and-coming face and she a stripper at one of the racier clubs on the circuit. It had been a bit of fun, until she'd started getting ideas about relationships and the future. He'd dropped her quickly, moving straight on to the next girl. He hadn't even thought about her again until he'd met Anna a couple of years later and discovered they were business partners.

Now, here they were, four years later and they were practically family. He felt heavy remorse at the part he'd played in damaging her and wished he'd let her down in a kinder manner and with more respect. Hindsight was often a curse. He glanced at her and gave her a sad smile, which she returned.

'I'll be fine. Let's just focus on getting Anna back and then I'll think about it all with a clear head.'

'Yeah, let's do that,' Freddie replied.

Tanya glanced sideways at him. 'Have you got any idea yet who has her?'

'Not a clue, that's the problem.' He pinched his nose.

'Other than that Carter boy, have you had any more proper leads?' she asked.

'Not really.'

'But you've considered Frank Gambino. I heard you say so to Fraser. I think there may be something in that,' Tanya said quietly.

Freddie's eyes locked onto Tanya's. 'What do you know about Frank Gambino?' he asked, his tone sharp.

'Not much, but… there was something Anna hadn't told you. I wouldn't usually pass on things that aren't my business, but in the circumstances…' She trailed off. She felt guilty betraying Anna's trust but this was more important. It might be the information Freddie needed to find her. 'He tried to blackmail her into selling him Club Anya.'

'What?' Freddie was shocked.

'He's been dangling your casino in front of her, offering her an exchange. Our club for permission to build your casino. He got pretty shitty when she told him to piss off.'

'Why wouldn't she tell me that?' Freddie was annoyed. At least now though he knew why she had been acting so shifty before she was taken.

Tanya shrugged. 'I don't know. But what I do know is that he didn't take kindly to how things went down.'

'Why didn't you tell me this before, Tanya?' Freddie asked in exasperation.

'To be honest, I knew he was already on the suspect list. I didn't see much reason to shit stir.'

'Well, it didn't fully make sense before, but it bloody does now,' Freddie exclaimed, standing up. 'Christ, what else has she been keeping from me?'

It hadn't been meant as a genuine question, but when Freddie saw Tanya's guilty face he realised that there was indeed something else. He paused and the look he gave her made her blood run cold.

'You need to tell me whatever else it is I don't know, right now,' he said, his voice hard and authoritative. 'I mean it, Tanya. I have always respected Anna's right to privacy but right now nothing is more important than getting her back and to do that I need full transparency.'

'You might want to sit down,' Tanya said heavily. She squirmed in her seat. She couldn't believe she was about to do this. She prayed Anna would forgive her.

'I don't want to sit down, Tanya. Tell me now.' Freddie's voice rose with every syllable. It was something bad, he was sure of it. He needed to know what it was; the suspense was physically painful.

Tanya ran her hands over her strained face. Her voice came out as barely more than a whisper as she revealed Anna's deepest secret.

'She's pregnant.'

CHAPTER THIRTY-NINE

He walked into Anna's room and smiled at her. *The smile of a predator*, she thought. Her dark blue eyes stared back at him warily.

'I thought you might fancy a little walk. Get out of the room for a bit,' he stated.

Anna's eyes darted towards the hallway behind him and back to his face. He could see the suggestion both appealed to her and worried her simultaneously.

'I'll give you a little tour of the house and then leave you with Izobel in the kitchen for a bit, if you like,' he continued. 'She's always cooking something; maybe you could give her a hand. Or just chill out with a cuppa, whatever you fancy.'

'Whatever I fancy?' Anna laughed humourlessly. 'OK, I fancy a trip into London, a large gin and tonic and maybe some sushi. But I somehow doubt that's going to happen.' She smiled pleasantly, as if they were exchanging normal conversation.

He ignored her jibes and lifted his eyebrows in question. 'So, are you coming?' he asked.

Anna narrowed her gaze coolly but stood up and began to cross the room.

'Ah.' He held his hand up to stop her. 'Please take off your socks.'

'What?' Anna asked, her tone incredulous.

'Not that you'll get much opportunity to run, but this should deter you from trying.'

Anna made an indignant sound and rolled her eyes, but she did as he asked. As she pulled them off she muttered expletives under her breath. They were the thickest ones that were available and she had them on for exactly that reason. She'd seen the ground outside – it was uneven and rocky, sharp pebbles strewn around where they'd been kicked up from the sides of the track. Her feet would be ripped to shreds within minutes if she ran barefoot.

Following him out of the door she tried to memorise the layout of the house and look for anything that might be of use later. Her room was almost at the end of the hallway and he took her to see the last room first.

'This is where Izobel is staying,' he said casually, as though he were showing her around his own home. The room was neutral and slightly old-fashioned, like her own. The furniture was sparse, nothing much to see.

They moved back past her room and into another almost directly opposite. 'This is Diego's room,' he said.

Anna looked at him in surprise. She hadn't heard anyone else mentioned so far, nor heard noises or voices around the house, so she had begun to assume that perhaps it was just the three of them.

They carried on, past the top of the stairs. There was a split second where Anna considered pushing him down them. She was right behind him, all she had to do was reach out… but she thought better of it. It would be unlikely to do much more than bruise him and then what would she do? This Diego guy was somewhere in the house and even if she got around him, she'd be running around in the middle of nowhere with bare feet. Not the best plan she'd ever had.

'This is my room.' They had stopped outside a closed door and he didn't open it. He pointed to the adjacent door. 'That is my office. Both are out of bounds unless you're invited. And you will be,' he added in a softer tone, 'just as soon as I can trust you. As soon as I know you're with me.'

Anna raised her eyebrows. It would be a cold day in hell before she'd join forces with him.

'Oh, give it time,' he said, reading her expression. He walked back through the hallway and made his way downstairs.

Anna followed, looking at the pictures on the walls as she walked. There were photos of a couple, some in black and white, where they looked very young and then the pair grew older as the pictures changed to full colour. Some of the photos showed a third person who she guessed to be their son, growing from a baby into a young man. She wondered where they were now. Did he know them? They hadn't been home in at least the seven days she had been here.

'Whose house is this?' she asked, as they reached the bottom step.

'Mine,' he answered.

'Then who are these people? Where did they go, leaving all their belongings and memories behind?' She gestured at the wall. He didn't answer her. She swallowed. *I need to get out of here*.

They walked into a large, warm, farmhouse kitchen where Izobel stood cutting up potatoes. She physically jumped when he walked in, Anna noticed.

'I'll leave you with Izobel for one hour, then I'll take you back up.' He stepped towards her and leaned in with a menacing look. 'Don't do anything stupid, or there won't be a next time. Got it?'

Anna nodded, not trusting herself to speak. She looked away and tried not to shiver. Looking at him was like staring into the eyes of the devil.

He turned away and, walking over to Izobel, took the knife she was using to cut the potatoes. He walked out without a further word and Izobel shook her head, plopping the rest of the uncut potatoes in the pan of cold water so that they wouldn't brown in the air.

Anna listened to him walk back upstairs and shut himself in the office. 'Izobel, who's Diego?' she asked urgently. She didn't have a lot of time, only one hour to figure something out.

'My brother,' Izobel answered wearily.

'Where is he?' Anna questioned, looking around for signs of life.

'Gone into town to get a few things.'

'Oh, OK.' That was interesting. It was only two of them she would have to get past. She eyed the younger girl. Izobel was watching her warily, not eager for a repeat of their last scuffle. Anna tried another tactic.

'You could just let me go,' she whispered. 'If you help me get out, you can pretend I knocked you out. It wouldn't be your fault.'

'I can't take the risk,' Izobel replied.

'Please, Izobel, do the right thing,' Anna pleaded.

'What is the right thing for you is not necessarily the right thing for me, Anna,' Izobel shot back. 'I told you before – he has my mother. That is why we are both here. We have to do as he says and when it is over we can go home and our mother will be safe. But if we don't do as he says, she will be killed and we won't even have the money for a ticket home. So I am doing *the right thing* for my family. I have no choice. Neither does Diego.'

Anna rubbed her head. 'Where is he holding her?' she asked, sitting down in the wing-backed armchair by the hearth. 'I know you're scared of him, but Freddie can help you. If you get a message out to him, give him the details, he can get your mother back safely. Then we can all get back home to normality. He'll deal with *him*,' she added, her voice darkening.

Izobel sighed again. 'That would be a great plan if we knew where my mother was, or if she was even in this country. But he took her from our home in Mexico. Two men with guns dragged her from her bed and took her away in a van. He told us she would be kept safe until we had done our job, then returned home. I have no idea where they took her.'

Anna nodded and dropped the subject. She knew that no amount of persuasion was going to convince her to put her mother's life in danger. Anna could understand that. She looked around the kitchen. There had to be something she could use to help herself. There was a phone attached to the wall, but on closer inspection she could see the cord had been cut. There were no pokers in the hearth either; he must have removed them. Standing up casually, she wandered over to the drawers near the sink.

Izobel spoke as she opened the top one. 'He already took everything out. That knife I was using on the potatoes was the last knife in here.'

Anna slammed the drawer shut. She quickly checked the others just to be sure, but Izobel was telling the truth. There was nothing of use in there, just a couple of forks and spoons and a whisk. She wasn't going to get far with those.

'Can I go outside?' Anna asked.

'No,' Izobel replied. 'He had me lock the door. I do have the key,' she said, 'but I'd really rather you didn't try to fight me for it.' She pulled a face.

Anna sat back down. There was no point jumping into anything right now. She was determined to get out of here and she wasn't going to let anyone get in her way. But she needed a good plan first. And now she knew who was here and the layout of the house, she could finally begin to strategise. She nodded to herself as Izobel filled the kettle.

He was clever, she'd give him that. But then he'd never been up against her before. Relaxing his hold and allowing her this extra freedom had been a big mistake. Even under normal circumstances Anna would fight to get out of here, but now that she had another life to protect She was more determined to get back home and to Freddie than ever.

CHAPTER FORTY

James walked through the busy back streets of Soho with two large cappuccinos in hand. He smiled as he looked around him. He loved it here – the bright colours, the sounds of the day starting up, the buzz of people on their way to work and shops opening up for trade. He sidestepped out of the way of a busy-looking woman hurrying in the opposite direction.

Stopping outside a door with no number or name, he pressed the buzzer and waited. It was a while until the door finally creaked open, revealing a tall, slender man with blonde highlighted hair and big blue eyes that any woman would kill to have. His long lashes flicked up and down as he blinked in the morning light.

James grinned. 'Good morning, sunshine.'

'Oh my God, if it isn't James Waters himself! What are you doing here?' The excited screech turned into a tone of sarcastic accusation as he continued. 'At ten in the morning, what on earth would possess you to wake me up at such an ungodly hour, you heathen?'

James laughed. 'I'm sorry, Nathan, I thought you might be getting up soon. I've brought coffee.' He held out the peace offering, knowing this would likely get him forgiven for waking up his old friend.

It worked – Nathan flashed him a dazzling smile. 'Well, in that case, you may enter.' He stepped aside and James walked into the building.

Inside, the walls were a deep burgundy, low-level spotlights highlighting the path through to the bottom of the stairs. James followed Nathan up to the second floor and into a cosy lounge. Nathan flopped onto one end of the sofa, pulling his dressing gown around him more securely. James handed him the coffee and he sipped at it gratefully.

'So, how are you?' James asked.

'I'm fab, other than a slight hangover. Big party last night. Business is good. Moving to this place was a great decision. It's true what they say, location really is everything.' He paused to light a cigarette. 'Want one?' he offered.

'No, I'm good thanks,' James replied.

'So yeah, you know Soho. So many reprobates loitering at the end of the night, looking for a suck or a fuck.'

Nathan was a male prostitute and enjoyed his chosen profession greatly. He had been one of the first people James had met after he came out. Nothing romantic had ever come of their meeting and James had declined his professional services, but the pair had become great friends.

These days he didn't see his friend as much, but they stayed in touch and caught up now and then.

'So, what about you? How's things going with that boyfriend of yours?' Nathan asked.

'Oh, it's going great,' James answered with a warm smile. 'You should come over to the new place sometime for dinner. Sadie too. We haven't done a dinner party in ages.'

Sadie was another good friend of theirs, who James knew would still be asleep upstairs right now. A Russian beauty, she and Nathan had set up this flat together. Due to the natural differences in their clients' needs they were never in competition with each other, so it worked well.

'That sounds like a plan; we'll get something in the diary. Now' – Nathan tilted his head and arched an eyebrow – 'I know you didn't come here and interrupt my beauty sleep for a bit of small talk over coffee. So, what's up?'

A slow smile crept over James's face. 'You're right, I didn't. I've got a little problem that I need to resolve. I have a plan to do it, if I can enlist both you and Sadie. I'll pay you well for it, but on top of that' – he chuckled – 'I think this is going to be something you're going to greatly enjoy.'

Later that night, James hurried down the road to meet Paul. He had a spring in his step, excitement bubbling under the surface now that his plan was in motion. He took a deep breath and cleared his face of all expression as he walked up to Paul and Thea.

Paul looked smart in his favourite suit and crisp white shirt. James smiled as a feeling of love for the man swelled through his heart.

Paul turned as he saw James approach. 'Ah, here you are. Was just about to call you.'

'Sorry, got caught up. How are you, Thea?' He leaned in to hug her warmly in greeting.

'All the better for seeing you, sunshine,' she replied happily. 'Shall we go grab our seats?'

'Yeah, let's head in,' Paul said. The three of them made their way inside.

Tonight was Seamus's debut fight, the first one in an official league. The tickets had completely sold out and the gymnasium was full to the brim. Vendors had their stalls around the edges, selling popcorn and hotdogs and drinks. Betting stands were placed every few metres and the queues were long at all of them.

Paul smiled at the sight. All the bookies on site were their own, so they stood to make a large amount of money tonight. Seamus had been told to win this fight at all costs, as the other man was marked as the favourite. Paul knew Seamus would have no problem winning. He might be new to the scene, but the boy was a born boxer. He was the fastest, lightest fighter Paul had ever seen. Luckily for them, the rest of the world didn't know that yet.

He led the small party to the front row, where their seats had been reserved. He was excited to watch this fight. With everything that had been going on lately it would make a nice change to just relax and enjoy something for once. He had James and Thea with him too, which just made it all the more pleasurable.

'I've never been to a boxing match before,' James admitted. 'How violent is it really? I mean, it's an official match so they don't let them get properly hurt and stuff, do they?'

Paul and Thea looked at each other and tried to hold their laughter in. It probably wasn't going to be something James would enjoy. They had tried to tell him this gently, but he had insisted he wanted to try it at least once.

'Nah, yeah, it's er… it's not that bad,' Paul replied, scratching the back of his neck.

The lights went down and a man jumped up into the ring with a microphone. His voice boomed out as he introduced himself and began to warm up the crowd.

'Oh, I should have put a bet on,' James said in dismay. 'Oh well, never mind.'

Paul looked around the room at the buzzing crowds and was surprised to see Frank Gambino and two of his men at the other side of the ring, a few rows back. Frank was looking in his direction, no expression on his face. Paul smiled and gestured for them to join him in the front row but Frank didn't seem to notice, instead looking up into the ring. Paul lowered his hand. Frank must not have seen him.

It wasn't too long before the fighters were brought into the ring, the crowds around them going wild with excitement. Seamus winked at Paul as he passed and they each took their corners.

The match started and the first round finished without much action. Each fighter was testing the other out and holding back their energy for later. Paul tensed his shoulders when the real fighting began in the third round. He watched every move Seamus made with a critical eye, cheering him on when he was up and praying silently when he was down.

James went to get drinks and snacks for everyone as the third round ended. Paul nodded encouragingly at Seamus as he retreated to his corner to take a gulp of the drink someone handed him and wipe the sweat from his face with a towel.

The air seemed charged with electricity and the crowd worked themselves into a frenzy when in the sixth round it looked as though Seamus was going to be beaten. But he pulled himself round and came back with full force, drawing the energy from somewhere.

The seventh round began and Paul had to remind himself to breathe. He gripped the side of the chair until his knuckles turned white, but he didn't notice that. He couldn't tear his eyes from the ring.

'Come on, Seamus,' he muttered under his breath. This was going to be a big payday for the Tylers when he won. There was no way he could lose. Paul had lived and breathed boxing since he could walk. He knew what he was looking at and Seamus was the most flawless rough diamond he'd ever come across.

Seamus was backed into a corner, sweat dripping from every inch of his skin, his hair plastered flat to his head and blood running down his face from a gash on his forehead. His opponent didn't look much better, but he had the upper hand, pummelling away at Seamus's sides.

With a roar, Seamus pushed forward and sidestepped the next punch. The other man stumbled, not expecting the move. Seamus was about to take full advantage of this when suddenly he paused. He locked eyes with Paul, a look of confusion on his face. His body began to convulse and his opponent took a step back, looking to the ref for guidance.

Paul stood up and called out to the ref. Seamus's body convulsed harder and seemed to go into full spasm before he contorted into a strange position and fell to the floor. The ref and on-site medic climbed into the ring and the medic immediately forced Seamus into the recovery position. Seamus's opponent was sent to the corner and a hush settled over the previously excited crowd. Paul watched as Seamus's eyes rolled back into his head and his mouth began to foam. It was all happening so fast, he couldn't understand what was happening.

'Shit, what's wrong with him?' Paul asked the medic, leaning into the ring. He didn't move any closer, knowing they would need the space to investigate. The other medic suddenly flew past him with a stretcher.

'We don't know yet,' he said as they quickly rolled him onto the stretcher. 'We just need to get him out of here and get him stable.'

'Of course.' Paul stepped back to give them more room as they rushed Seamus out of the ring and away from the hundreds of watching eyes. He ran his hands through his hair and looked around at the crowd whose mood was swiftly changing from shocked to pissed off.

It didn't matter to them that someone was hurt; all they cared about was their entertainment and their bets. *Their bets.* Paul closed his eyes as this thought registered in his head. Seamus was his first and most important priority now, but the realisation of what this meant to them on a business level still hit him like a punch to the stomach. Their big payday was most definitely off.

Paul turned to Thea and James, who were still sitting behind him wearing worried expressions. 'I've got to go find out what's happened. I'll go to hospital with him so just head home. I'll see you later.'

James nodded in reply and stood up to leave.

'Call us when you know how he is,' Thea said as she followed James out.

The angry crowd began to jeer and moan, bitching to each other about being done over. As Paul looked around, his eyes settled back on Gambino. He stood across the ring, facing him. He was definitely making eye contact now, with a cold hard smile on his face. Paul blinked in shock.

With chilling certainty Paul realised that Frank had just poisoned Seamus. His mind shot back to the man handing Seamus his drink after the last round. It had been one of Gambino's men. He hadn't taken notice at the time – why would he? But now he was sure. His hands balled into fists at his side as white-hot rage filled his veins.

Why would Frank do this? Why would he poison an innocent boy and go out of his way to cause them such professional trouble? If he had done this to them, what else was he guilty of? Paul's thoughts raced around his head as his angry heartbeat pounded in his ears. *How dare Frank Gambino go after us? He's going to pay…* he thought darkly.

Frank tilted his head in a deliberate nod to him and then turned and walked out, his two men in tow. It took all of Paul's strength not to launch across the room at him there and then, but he knew that would be a bad idea. He needed Freddie.

This wasn't a fight between two men. This was a full-on act of war.

CHAPTER FORTY-ONE

Anna woke up from her dream and immediately wished that she hadn't. It had felt so real. She had dreamed that she was back at home with Freddie. They had been laughing and joking over dinner, discussing names for the baby.

A tear slipped out and slid down the side of her face as she pictured it. He had run his hand down her stomach to rest on her small bump. It still didn't look much more than a little bit of excess fat, but that didn't matter. They knew what was inside. Their little creation, growing away, safe and sound.

It had been eight days. She had kept track by marking small lines in the wood of the window ledge, with her nail. She didn't want to lose track of the days, which would be easy in this house with no phones or internet or any of the usual things she relied on.

The door creaked open and Izobel popped her head round. 'Do you want to sit downstairs with me for breakfast today? He said you can.'

Anna sat up and nodded. Izobel disappeared, leaving the door open. Anna pulled her long summer jumper top from the chair and put it on over the vest top and leggings she had been sleeping in each night. Knowing he was watching prevented her from wearing any less.

She walked down to the kitchen and took her place at the worn oak table in the middle. Izobel had already placed a plate of toast and scrambled egg down for her, alongside a mug of tea and a glass of orange juice.

'Thank you. You don't have to do this though, you know. I can make it,' Anna said.

'Looking after you is part of my job,' Izobel said, her eyes flicking over towards the open door to the hall. 'And besides' – she sat down opposite Anna with her own cup of tea – 'it gives me something to do.' She shrugged. 'I don't want to be here any more than you do. It keeps my mind occupied.'

'Fair enough,' Anna answered. She could understand that. She wished she had something to distract herself with too. 'Perhaps I could help you with the cooking?' she asked.

'Sure,' Izobel replied. She gave her a small smile.

Anna tried the egg and picked up her toast. The egg was full of flavour and today she found herself enjoying it. She hadn't felt quite so sick the last couple of days. Perhaps the awful period of morning sickness was finally coming to an end. She could only hope.

Footsteps sounded behind them and they both looked up expectantly. He walked in, followed by another, smaller man. Anna could see he was Izobel's brother, Diego, straight away. They had the same warm, almond-shaped eyes and the same full mouth. She watched as Diego shot Izobel a look of concern, like he was checking that she was OK. She nodded almost imperceptibly.

'Diego, take the shopping list from Izobel and drive into town to get what she needs. Be back by lunchtime,' he ordered.

Diego did as he was asked, squeezing his sister's shoulder on the way out.

As he poured himself a coffee Anna took a deep breath. She had come up with an idea. It was a weak one and he would probably shoot her down straight away, but it was worth a try.

'Listen,' she said, clearing her throat. 'I need to talk to you about something.'

'Oh?' He turned and faced her, leaning backward against the kitchen side.

'You know that I'm pregnant and you've obviously made an effort to ensure I'm comfortable here, but nothing seems to have been arranged for the next stage,' she said.

'What do you mean?' he asked.

'Well, I'll need a midwife,' she replied. 'I need someone to help me through this pregnancy and of course to get through labour when the time comes. Ideally I should have already met with someone; they need to know everything that happens, and be with me on the journey. I can't do this on my own, you know. And no offence' – she glanced at Izobel – 'but Izobel is not equipped to assist me. She's barely more than a child herself.'

She saw Izobel raise her eyebrows and quickly raised her hand slightly to warn her to stay quiet. Izobel took the hint. Anna silently prayed that he didn't know Izobel used to be a nurse. If he did, she had even less hope than she thought.

He stared at Anna, a look of cold amusement on his face. She stared him out, maintaining eye contact, refusing to look away. She suppressed a shudder at the dark blankness she saw beneath the surface. He reminded her of a snake, waiting to strike.

It was obvious that he had seen straight through her feeble attempt at getting out, but she held her head high anyway, as if waiting for an answer.

Eventually his cold grin widened and he answered her. 'You're right. You can't go through this alone. I know just how to solve this.' He walked over to Anna, bent down and put his face close to her ear. 'Ask and you shall receive. Let that be the lesson learned today, eh?'

Anna fought against her natural instinct to cringe away and forced herself to stay still whilst he was so close. Chuckling softly, he walked back out of the kitchen and disappeared upstairs. Anna shuddered violently as soon as he was gone. She wasn't quite sure what had just happened.

'What on earth does he mean by that?' she wondered aloud.

Izobel shook her head, her eyes wide and the colour draining from her face. She was truly scared of the man, Anna realised.

'I don't know,' Izobel whispered shakily, 'but whatever it is, I don't think it's going to be good.'

*

Freddie, Paul and Sammy stood by the service entrance at the back door of the hotel. The weak afternoon sun was finally giving in to the early evening and they had received the text to tell them that Gambino had finally returned to his hotel room. They had been trying to track him down all day, after the diabolical move he had pulled the night before. More than ever now, Freddie was certain he had been behind all the screwed-up shit that had been happening lately. And that he had Anna.

At this point Freddie no longer cared that Gambino was a Mafia boss. Whilst he was happy to respect him and remember his place when it came to everyday business, all of that went out the window when it came to Anna's life. It didn't matter who Frank was anymore – family came first and no one fucked with Freddie Tyler's family and got away with it.

Bill gave Freddie the nod from the van and Freddie didn't hesitate a second longer. Bill had hacked into the cameras and had paused the service feeds and the feed from the seventh floor where Gambino currently resided.

Pulling the ski masks down over their faces, the three men ran up the back stairwell to Gambino's floor. Freddie took the safety catch off his gun and heard the others do the same. It was rare for Freddie to take out his gun; firepower was something he only resorted to when absolutely necessary. Any intelligent criminal knew that it was often smaller charges such as being caught with a firearm that ended up screwing them over. But Freddie wasn't taking any chances with Frank today. It was worth the risk.

They crept to the outside of his door and Freddie put his ear to it. He could hear their voices just inside. He nodded at Sammy and moved back as his friend took a running start and barged the door in with his broad shoulders. The door was not thick or particularly strong so it only took the one attempt.

As soon as he broke through, the two brothers ran inside. Gambino's two men drew their own weapons straight away and one took a shot. Paul dodged it by inches and returned fire. He hit the other man's shoulder and he spun backward to the floor, crying out in pain.

Gambino's second man held up his gun a second too late as Freddie shot him straight between the eyes without hesitation. Gambino ran to the desk where he'd just taken his gun out of his jacket. He grabbed it and quickly turned it on Freddie. About to pull the trigger he was taken by surprise as Sammy rugby-tackled him to the floor. He dropped the gun and it fell with a clatter, a few feet out of his reach.

Paul walked over to the man he'd shot in the shoulder.

'Please.' He held his hands up in surrender, his eyes flickering over to his boss.

'Sorry. No witnesses.' Paul lifted his hand and put a bullet in his head. He took no pleasure in it, but Freddie had been explicit about this job. There could be no one left to report the true story back to the rest of the Mafia. They needed to be able to shift the blame away from them when this was all done, or none of them would ever be safe again.

'You motherfuckers, you'll die for this!' Gambino roared and strained against Sammy's vice-like grip. He twisted and bucked but to no avail. He was a big man, but Sammy was bigger, and for the first time in his life Frank had no backup. He roared again in frustration and stopped struggling, trying to think of another tactic to get out of the position he was in. He was furious, but he tried to calm down and think logically. He had clearly underestimated this little London gang. He'd pegged them as a bunch of wide boys, playing with a few illicit businesses and prancing around just pretending to be something more. Clearly he had been wrong. The look in Freddie's eyes told him he was facing a cold hard killer. This was not what he had been expecting.

He seethed. 'Look, guys, I think we need to talk,' he said through gritted teeth.

'I think we're way past talking now, Frank, you jumped-up piece of shit. I don't know how you do it over there in America but I'll tell you now, we have rules here in London. And you've broken one too many.'

Freddie grabbed Frank by the scruff of his shirt and Sammy hoisted him up by his other arm. They began to drag him towards the door and he pushed back, trying to break free. Freddie stopped, cocked his gun and pushed it into Frank's forehead.

'I don't have time for you to fuck around, so you've got two choices. You either walk out that door and come with us, or I shoot you in the head right now. Choose.'

They had only been inside a couple of minutes, but Freddie knew that despite the silencers they would still have made enough noise to worry the guests in the neighbouring rooms. There would be concerned calls to reception going through by now and he had to get Frank out of here before anyone arrived to check things out. Luckily the will to survive was a strong motivator and, holding his hands up in surrender, Frank walked forward without another word.

Picking up Frank's gun, Freddie glanced around the room to make sure they'd left nothing behind, before he followed the rest of them out and closed the hotel door behind him.

CHAPTER FORTY-TWO

Tanya stared at the invoices in front of her until her vision blurred and each one split into two. She rubbed her eyes and reached down towards the drawer. She paused and sighed. Freddie was right – she was hitting it too hard at the moment. And that wasn't the person she wanted to be. It wouldn't be the person Anna would want her to be either, especially when she was running both their businesses. She pulled her hand back and decided to call it a night. She was so exhausted that she couldn't function anymore. She needed to sleep and just shut off from everything. The invoices weren't urgent.

Her phone beeped and she looked at the screen. She bit her cherry-red bottom lip as she read the message. It was from Tom.

I left some van keys at yours. Are you home? I need them. Tom

She opened it up and tapped out a quick response.

Just finishing up some stuff at The Last Laugh. I'll be home in half an hour or so. You can meet me then or I can drop them round tomorrow. Tan

She sent the message and stood up, arching her aching back. She hated being seated behind a desk; she could never understand why Anna preferred working in the office. She'd much rather be out the front running around. Her phone beeped again.

Need them for the morning so I'll meet you there. Tom

Tanya sighed. She wished she didn't have to go and face him right now. She was still so confused about how she actually felt. She hadn't yet worked out whether she was just reacting out of her own natural self-destruction because she was tired and going crazy, or whether she really didn't want to be with Tom. She'd thought about it over and over but she just kept going round in circles.

She did love Tom. She fancied him like crazy too. What she couldn't work out was whether she could be happy in a normal, everyday relationship. It wasn't Tom; the fault lay with her. Maybe she wasn't meant to be with anyone, long-term. Maybe she was destined to live a sad, lonely life, pushing away everyone who dared to come close as she grew into a hard, bitter old woman. Perhaps she'd die cold and alone on the hallway floor after falling down the stairs and breaking a hip. No one would know, because there would be no one to visit and check up on her. No one would care. Tanya's eyes widened as her thoughts began to terrorise her. She shook it off and picked up her handbag. Now was not the best time to depress herself further than she already was.

Double-checking the front entrance was firmly locked, Tanya walked through to the back and flicked off the main lights. She made her way down the hallway and out of the fire exit that opened into the side alley. The door closed behind her with a bang and the motion-sensor light above the door came on. She picked up her phone and dialled through to Club Anya. She had forgotten to ask Carl if he could open up the next day.

Distracted, Tanya was about to walk out to the main street when a sound behind her made her pause. She turned and stared into the darkness, towards the small car park behind the club. There was someone standing just outside the perimeter of the light's circular beam. She squinted, trying to make out who it was.

'What… Shit, Izobel, is that you?' she asked in disbelief. 'Oh my God, where have you been? Where's Anna?' Tanya started walking quickly towards her, scared that the girl was going to disappear.

Izobel backed up further into the dark car park. As Tanya drew closer she could see the misery etched into her small face.

'Izobel?' Tanya softened her voice.

'I'm sorry…' Izobel turned away.

'What for? Where's Anna, Izobel? What have you done?' Tanya's voice rose and she tried to grasp Izobel's arm, but suddenly someone grabbed her from behind. She screamed in shock. He was holding the tops of her arms, dragging her backward.

Self-preservation kicking in, she shoved her elbow back hard in an attempt to wind him. She heard a grunt of pain and although he didn't let go, he loosened his grip just enough that she could bend down to try to grab her knife. Just as her fingers reached it, he recovered and yanked her back up.

Tanya wasn't ready to give up just yet, though. She lifted her right foot and stamped down on the man's foot as hard as she could with her sharp stiletto. He howled in pain and bent to the side, still just managing to keep one arm around her in a vice-like grip. She used his movement to bend with him and this time she managed to get a decent grip on the small blade. With a crow of triumph she pulled it out and tried to twist round so that she could hold it. Before she could do anything though, his hand clamped a thick cloth down over her nose and mouth.

A strange, cloying smell filled her nostrils and she panicked. She tried to breathe, to scream, anything, but suddenly everything seemed to slow down.

She felt the knife slip from her fingers and heard it clatter to the ground. Her arms went limp and everything in her vision seemed to be moving away. She tried to speak, to ask Izobel to help her, but nothing came out.

Tanya's legs gave way and she felt herself falling down towards the concrete. She waited for it to hit her, to feel the pain, but the collision never came. She lost consciousness before she hit the ground.

*

Freddie secured the ropes around Frank's wrists and tugged at them to make sure they were uncomfortably tight. Satisfied that he wouldn't be moving from the wooden kitchen chair he was tied to any time soon, Freddie stood up straight and walked a few paces away.

They had taken him to an old unused barn Freddie and Paul owned, a few miles out of London. They had bought the field it was situated on from a retiring farmer a few years back for cash, and had registered it under a company that would be hard to trace to them should it ever be looked into.

Sammy had laid out the plastic sheeting underneath and Paul had helped Freddie tie Gambino to the chair, whilst he tried to reason with them to no avail. None of them engaged in conversation with him. They knew not to, until Freddie was ready to start.

The old barn was eerie in the darkness, the only light coming from a weak bulb hanging down from the ceiling above Frank's head.

'Freddie, you'll all die for this, you know that, right?' Frank said, his voice still hard despite the fear he must have been feeling at the predicament he was in.

'Nothing's going to happen to me, Frank, not to any of us. No one knows you're here. No one ever will. Your men are dead and you obviously hadn't been expecting us when we arrived, so I doubt you discussed us with anybody either.' Freddie took off the zipped black jumper he had been wearing and laid it on the old, worn trestle table he'd dragged over from the side of the barn. He was now in nothing but a white vest and his black jeans. He didn't mind getting blood on the vest. He would just burn it afterwards.

'What are you doing, Freddie? All this for a little warning? Don't you think that's a bit much? The boy isn't dead, for Christ's sake, I checked,' Frank said.

'You poisoned one of my men. That isn't something I take lightly. But on top of that, you fucked with my life and kidnapped Anna. She's pregnant, Frank. Did you know that?' Freddie's face hardened and his eyes shot icy daggers at the man in the chair. 'So, you're going to tell me where she is and how I can get to her and if you do that I'll do the decent thing and put a bullet in your mouth the second I have her back safe. Or' – his tone darkened – 'if you don't tell me where she is right this second, I'm going to torture you until you're nothing but a pile of bloody flesh on the floor, in more pain than you can possibly imagine.' He picked up a crowbar from the table, where Sammy had been laying out the tools.

'What are you talking about?' Frank asked, his brows furrowing into a look of confusion.

'Don't play that game with me,' Freddie replied in disgust. He lifted the crowbar up and smashed it down onto Frank's left knee.

Frank roared in agony as it shattered the bone. The veins in his neck popped out as he strained against his shackles.

'I'm not playing anything,' he yelled. 'I don't know what you're talking about!'

'I'm talking about Anna Davis,' Freddie yelled back. 'You remember her, Frank, the one you tried to blackmail into selling the club to you.'

'Aw, now come on, that doesn't mean I kidnapped her, for crying out loud,' Frank exclaimed.

'Bit of a fucking coincidence though, don't you think? You come riding into town like a fucking cowboy, blackmail Anna, poison Seamus, but when Anna goes missing you had nothing to do with it? I ain't buying it. I'll ask you again. Where is she?'

'And I'll tell you again, this is the first I've heard of it,' Frank seethed.

Freddie lifted the crowbar and smashed it down on the other knee. Frank cried out like a wild animal as the pain exploded through his leg.

'Where is she?' Freddie screamed, his face red with rage and spittle flying out of his mouth.

'I don't know,' Frank cried.

Freddie punched him in the face. 'Where is she?' His face contorted with rage and anguish. Frank snapped his head back round, licking the blood from his bottom lip. 'I don't know, you fucking psycho!'

Freddie punched him again, harder this time. Frank's head lolled and for a moment Freddie wondered if he had knocked him out, but eventually he straightened up again. Blood streamed out of his mouth, down his chin and onto his shirt.

'Where is she?' Freddie's shout was hoarse, as he kept repeating himself again and again.

Paul could see he was cracking up and looked away for fear that Freddie would see the pity he felt for his brother. Freddie was usually cool and calm, even in situations like this, but now he was venting every raw emotion that was tearing him up inside.

'You're going to fucking die for this.' Frank shook his bloody head from side to side as he panted through the pain he was in.

Freddie went to the table and picked up a can of gasoline. He walked back to Gambino and took off the cap. Frank's eyes widened as he realised what Freddie was going to do.

'What the fuck are you doing?' He looked over to Bill and Sammy, who stood together to the side helplessly. 'What is he doing? This is madness,' he shouted. 'Help me, for fuck's sake! Stop him doing this!'

'Where is she, Frank?' Freddie asked once more, his voice flat. He doused Frank in the gasoline, walking around him in a slow circle, making sure he covered him completely before pouring the last of the can over his head.

'I don't have your girlfriend, Freddie. I don't know who does,' Frank spluttered, his tone panicked.

Freddie stared hard at Frank, searching his face for the truth. Deep fear radiated from the other man and his usual hard mask was finally stripped back. Freddie had seen men in this position many times before. This was the point that they knew they were out of options. Without doubt they were about to die. Nothing else mattered but survival now. If he did know anything about Anna's disappearance, he would be singing like a canary.

Freddie felt the disappointment rush through him like a tidal wave. This had been his only lead. He had been so sure it was Frank, but now they were back to square one and no closer to finding Anna. The pain in his heart intensified; it felt as though it was being ripped in two.

'OK. I believe you. No one would be stupid enough to keep lying at this point,' Freddie replied in a dead voice. 'But you'll still die for what you did to Seamus. You fucked with the wrong firm.'

Frank let out a feral roar. 'Do you not understand who I am?'

Freddie laughed, the smirk not reaching his eyes. 'Oh yeah, I know exactly who you are, Frank. The problem here was that *you* never understood who *I* am. That was your big mistake. You never fuck with anyone you don't know, Frank. Perhaps they should have taught you that back home.'

Ignoring Frank's enraged cries Freddie lit a match. With one last look into Frank's eyes he flicked it to the ground at the other man's feet.

Paul walked over and stood by Freddie's side. They watched in silence as Frank was engulfed by the flames. They watched while he screamed and rutted against his fate. They watched as he finally fell silent and until there was nothing left.

*

'Wake up, please, Tanya, wake up…' Tanya could hear Anna's voice somewhere in the distance. *Am I dreaming? I must be…*

'Come on, please…' Anna sounded upset and stressed. *Why is Anna upset with me? Have I done something wrong?*

She tried to drift back into the comforting nothingness, but someone kept shaking her, jarring her away from it.

'What are you doing?' Tanya mumbled, as she started to come round. 'What's going on? Christ, my head…' She moved her hands up to hold her head. She had the worst headache she'd ever encountered. *What did I drink? But wait, I hadn't been drinking, had I?*

With sharp clarity the memory of what happened suddenly came back to her and she sat up fast – too fast. She quickly closed her eyes until the additional pain from the swift movement faded.

'Oh, thank God, you're OK,' Anna started to sob in relief and hugged her friend.

Carefully opening her eyes, Tanya looked around. She felt disorientated and fuzzy. *What did they knock me out with?* It was dark, night-time still. The only light was coming from a big lamp in the corner of the room. She was sitting on a bed in a room she didn't recognise and Anna was next to her, clinging on to her arm as if she'd never let go. *Anna!*

'Oh my God, Anna,' she exclaimed, grabbing hold of her friend. She touched her friend's hair and face, as if she couldn't quite believe she was real. 'Are you OK? Where are we? What happened?' The questions came tumbling out, one on top of the other.

Anna sat back and regained her composure. She had been terrified when she had been woken up to Tanya being dumped on the bed next to her, out cold. For a second she had thought her to be dead, until she realised her best friend was still breathing. She took a deep breath and updated Tanya on everything she knew so far.

'Fuck me,' Tanya said in shock, when Anna got to the end of her tale. 'I don't believe it. This is seriously fucked up.' She ran her hands through her thick, red hair as all the information sunk in.

'Why has he taken me? That doesn't make any sense,' Tanya said with a frown.

Anna's face dropped. 'Oh, Tanya, I'm so sorry,' she said, her voice full of emotion. 'It's my fault he took you.' She took a heavy breath. 'Like I said, I've been trying to work out an escape but so far haven't found a decent opportunity.' She glanced at the camera and lowered her voice. She didn't think it had sound, but she couldn't be sure. 'I told him I needed to see a midwife, that I'd need someone to help me through the pregnancy and labour. I figured he'd say no but thought it was worth a try. I just needed to try to get in front of someone, anyone, to get a message out. But then he went and took you and brought you here to me,' Anna said in distress, 'saying that he'd delivered me someone to help me through it all and that I should be grateful to him. It's punishment for trying to outwit him. God, Tanya, I'm so sorry…' Anna placed her head in her hands.

Tanya pulled her hands back down and grasped them in her own. 'No, mate, it's not your fault. You couldn't have known he'd do that. What a sadistic fuck, Jesus…' She shook her head angrily. 'Right. It's going to be OK. We're going to get out of this – together.' Tanya's tone was determined, despite the deep worry that had settled in her stomach. 'There's two of us now. Whatever happens, we're going to get ourselves out of here. No matter what.'

CHAPTER FORTY-THREE

Mollie opened the front door in her dressing gown and blinked in surprise. 'Carl! Hello, love. What you doing here?'

'Is Freddie here?' Carl asked, his voice awkward. 'Sorry, Mollie, it's just… well it's urgent.'

'Of course, come in. He's upstairs still asleep. Go on through to the kitchen; I've just made a pot of coffee. I'll get Freddie now.'

Carl walked through to the kitchen and rubbed his tired eyes. He hadn't slept a wink. When the phone had rung the night before he had thought it was an accidental dial at first. There hadn't been anyone at the other end. He'd been about to put it down when he heard Tanya's voice. She'd said Izobel's name and Carl's attention had instantly focused. He'd listened and heard the struggle before there was a crunching sound and the line had gone dead. He'd tried calling back and had even driven over to The Last Laugh, but it was all closed up and he couldn't see any sign of her inside. He'd stayed up worrying all night and eventually decided he needed to tell Freddie.

Thea walked through the kitchen door and greeted Carl with a warm smile. 'Carl, how you doing? I haven't seen you in ages. How's things?'

'They've been better, actually. I got a weird call from Tanya late last night. I could hear some sort of scuffle then the line went dead. I haven't been able to get through to her since.'

'Oh God.' Thea's smile was replaced by a concerned frown. Her fears immediately caught up with Carl's. 'Do you think…' She trailed off, not wanting to finish her question.

Freddie came through the door, pulling a dressing gown around his boxers and bare chest. His expression was dark. 'What do you mean you can't get through to her?' he asked, having caught the conversation on his way through.

'Freddie!' The relief in Carl's voice was palpable. He was so glad to have found him. Freddie would know what to do. 'I've been trying to call you.'

'Yeah, I've just seen. I was sleeping,' Freddie replied. He hadn't been asleep long, having spent most of the night cleaning up Frank's body and destroying all the last remnants of evidence. He was physically and mentally spent. The memory of the flames licking up Frank's skin was still at the forefront of his mind. He tried to push it back and focus on what Carl had to say.

'Yeah, I figured. Listen, I called back and texted her after the call but there was nothing. I even went over to the flat.'

Freddie acknowledged this with a nod.

'I waited for two hours, but there was still nothing. So I grabbed the spare keys she keeps at work and let myself in, thought maybe she'd got back and just passed out. I wouldn't usually ever do that, but with everything that's happened with Anna…' He trailed off and Freddie acknowledged it with a nod. 'But the flat was empty. Oh yeah, that reminds me – I thought you were staying still? She hasn't thrown you out as well as Tom, has she?'

Thea's eyebrows shot up at Carl's words. No one else had heard of this falling-out yet, so this was news to her. She pursed her lips and set about pouring the coffee. It was none of her business, no matter how curious she was as to what had happened.

'Nah, I just… with everything going on, I thought I'd give her some space for a couple of days. Still can't face going home without Anna there, so I came here,' Freddie explained.

'Where you should be,' Mollie said, bustling in, having got dressed quickly now that they had a guest. 'You should have come home to your family in the first place, when you needed people around you,' she scolded. 'Not bunked up at Tanya's. But you're here now, so that's all that matters.'

Freddie rolled his eyes before he turned his attention back to Carl.

'Right. You say you've tried The Last Laugh?' he asked.

'Locked up, no sign of life,' Carl replied. 'I'm really worried, Fred; there's something really wrong here. And I'm pretty sure I heard her say the name Izobel.'

Freddie drew in a sharp breath.

'Do you still have the spare keys?' Freddie asked.

'Yeah, brought them with me. I thought you might ask.'

'OK, let's go and check the CCTV footage. That's going to be the best place to start. Drink your coffee; I'll get dressed.'

He disappeared and Carl sat down heavily at the table.

'Here you go, love.' Mollie passed him the mug of steaming black coffee that Thea had poured. 'It'll be OK. There's probably a perfectly simple explanation. She'll have locked herself in the club and dropped her phone out the window, or something silly like that. Don't worry.'

Carl accepted the coffee gratefully, exhausted from being up all night. He turned away and sipped at it.

Mollie and Thea exchanged worried looks. This was how it had started with Anna. It looked as though they had a serial kidnapper on their hands.

An hour later Freddie and Carl sat in silence in the back office at The Last Laugh with the CCTV footage. Freddie fast-forwarded through the minutes around the time of Tanya's call to Carl, focusing on the side door. They knew this was where she would have come out after locking up. There was a flicker of light and he quickly rewound to a few seconds before. Pressing play, he sat back and they both waited.

The door opened, triggering the outside light and they watched as Tanya stepped outside, did something on her phone and started to walk towards the main street before she paused and turned around.

They both leaned forward, trying to get as much information out of the grainy image as possible. There was some movement in the darkness just beyond the light, but the quality of the footage didn't allow them to see any detail.

Tanya's head bobbed around as though she was speaking, before she suddenly darted forward out of the light into the car park at the back of the club.

'There,' Carl said. 'What just happened?'

'I don't know.' Freddie frowned at the screen. 'Just keep watching.'

They both squinted, trying to make out what was happening but it was all going on just outside the lit area. There were some blurry flashes of pale clothing and they could just make out a pair of trainers darting around as though the owner was in a scuffle. A minute or so later, the trainers moved out of sight and there was nothing more on the screen.

They sat in silence for a moment, hoping that something more might show up, but nothing did.

'Do they have a camera on the entrance to the car park?' Freddie asked. The road into the small car park ran between two shops.

He flicked through the different screens and couldn't see anything.

'No.' Carl shook his head. 'Just around and inside the actual building.'

Freddie bit his lip. 'Let's go look around outside, see if we can find anything. It's only been a few hours; no one would have been through there yet.'

They made their way outside and into the car park. Carl clocked one of Tanya's shoes lying on its side on the ground. He picked it up and showed it to Freddie with a grim look.

Freddie walked around the area with slow, deliberate steps. The ground was concrete, worn away in places with age, with a thin layer of pebbles that had been brought in to fill the potholes. His eyes scanned every crevice, aware he could easily miss something.

About five feet away from the shoe, something glinted in the early morning sun and he bent down to pick it up. It was a small blade with a simple handle. He recognised it as Tanya's immediately. She had shown them all when she'd first bought it, trying to convince Anna to get one too. Anna had refused, stating that she'd rather not accidentally stab herself every five seconds.

He turned it over in his hand. She must have managed to pull it out in the struggle but not had a chance to use it. There was no sign of blood on the blade. He stood up and walked back to Carl, holding it out for the other man to see.

'This was hers. Come on. We need to lock up again and call Fraser. The guys on my payroll are already working flat out to find Anna. We need to tell them what's happened,' Freddie said.

They walked back inside and through the long hallway towards the bar to lock up. They were reaching the end of the hallway when they heard someone curse in the bar just beyond the door. They froze and Freddie held his hand up to tell Carl to stay quiet. He crept forward and as he got to the doorway jumped towards the man near the bar, brandishing Tanya's knife.

'Who the fuck are you?' he demanded, his tone deadly.

The man jumped and held his hands up in surrender.

'Er, I'm Drew. I live upstairs. Why do you have Tanya's knife? And honestly, why does it always end up being pointed at me?' he asked, his eyes rolling dramatically.

'You live upstairs?' Freddie paused, half dropping the blade but still wary.

'Yes, I'm one of the comedians here. Tanya let me move into the bedsit when my wife kicked me out,' he explained. 'I was only down here to grab a bottle of whisky, which I always pay for, by the way. It's been a fine arrangement with Tanya, but I stubbed my damn toe on this table.' He motioned towards the table next to him with his hand. 'And then you guys came in. That's where I'm at, right now. So, who are you?' he came back at them, folding his arms.

Freddie dropped the blade into his pocket and stepped forward, holding his hand out to Drew. 'Sorry, mate, there's been a lot going on through the night, wasn't sure whether you were friend or foe.'

Drew shook Freddie's proffered hand.

'I'm Freddie; this is Carl. He runs their other club. Listen, what side is your bedsit on? Does it look out the front or back?'

'Back. What do you mean there's been a lot going on through the night?' Drew asked.

Freddie was reluctant to divulge everything. The last thing he needed was a concerned employee calling the Old Bill. He skirted the question. 'Did you hear anything in the night at all? There was just some trouble out back – we're looking into it.'

'Now you mention it, yes. About half ten a car came into the car park and just sat there with the engine running for ages. It irritated me, because I usually like to keep the window open, but the noise was coming from right underneath. I figured it was some drug dealer or whatever.' He shrugged dismissively. 'It's not uncommon. But they didn't leave, so I closed the window against the noise after about half an hour of it.'

'Did you see the car?' Carl asked.

'Yes, it was' – he frowned, recalling the details – 'dark blue I think, but it was dark so that might not be fully accurate. It was an old Jaguar. Not in the healthiest condition by the sound of it.'

'I'm guessing you didn't catch the reg,' Freddie said. He already knew the answer but he had to be sure.

'No, I had no reason to look. I only glanced at it briefly, or rather I glared at it, when I closed the window. Then I went to bed so no idea when it left, I'm afraid.'

'OK, thanks for that,' Freddie said with a nod. 'We'll just lock back up and leave you to it.'

'Sorry I couldn't be more help,' Drew offered.

'No, you have been, mate.'

Freddie locked the door and made his way back out to his car. It wasn't much, but it was something and that was better than nothing. Maybe Fraser could tap into the local CCTV and have a look for the car. After all, old blue Jaguars weren't that common on the roads.

For the first time in the nine days since Anna had been taken, Freddie felt a sliver of hope.

CHAPTER FORTY-FOUR

Sadie Petrov had been in the game for eleven years, since she had first arrived in England at the tender age of seventeen. She had thrived in the glamorous underworld of London, among the rich and dangerous. A natural beauty, she knew exactly how to use it. With her dark hair and piercingly bright green eyes, she stood out in a crowd. These qualities were enhanced by a body she worked very hard at the gym for and naturally large breasts. All of which meant she was never short of clients.

Tonight she had dressed to kill in a strapless corset top and leather miniskirt, ready to do the job James had asked of her and Nathan. She was excited about it. It wasn't her usual game, but when she heard the reasons why James wanted to pull the plan off, she had agreed in an instant. She couldn't stand prejudiced scum like Ron and Jimmy. She was more than happy to help them get their comeuppance.

She pushed her boobs out further as she approached the bouncers on the door of Roar and nibbled her full bottom lip seductively. Giving her an appreciative once-over, the doorman lifted the rope and let her straight through, much to the loud annoyance of all the people in the queue.

Ignoring all the looks she was getting, Sadie made a beeline for the end of the bar where she had been told the VIP area was and where she knew her two marks would be. Spotting them, she stopped by the bar and turned to face the dance floor, leaning back on her elbows. She waited for them to notice her.

James had relayed all the information he had managed to get out of his conversation with the unhappy barmaid. Apparently the two men owned an apartment above the club, where they often took young, attractive girls. Girls who threw themselves at them in the hope that they would gain some money and status from being a new accessory to an old face. The two dirty sods liked to enjoy the girls together, sometimes just the one and sometimes in an orgy. Their long-suffering wives had no clue, of course. Or if they did, they kept their mouths shut and ignored it.

It wasn't long before the bouncer by the VIP rope approached her.

'Er, miss? The two gentlemen over there wondered if you wanted to join them for a drink. They're the owners of this club.'

Sadie turned and flashed them a brilliant smile. 'That would be lovely,' she replied in her rich Russian accent. She still hadn't lost it even after all these years.

She stepped up to the table where the two old men were waiting. One of them handed her a glass of champagne.

'Well, hello, darlin',' he said, with a shark-like smile. 'Thanks for joining us.'

'Oh, it's my pleasure. Thank you for the invite,' she replied, sitting down and crossing her long, tanned legs. His eyes roamed over her hungrily.

'I'm Ron; this is Jimmy. What's your name then?' he said.

'I'm Alexa.' She held her hand out and he kissed it.

'Well, Alexa, what's a pretty girl like you doing in here all on your own?'

It was a loaded question. Sadie knew he was asking if she was a working girl or not. James had warned her to pretend she wasn't. They never slept with prostitutes; they were too tight and apparently had enough stupid young women with big ideas to choose from without having to pay for it.

'Well, I was supposed to meet with a friend tonight, but he cancelled.' She shrugged. 'So I decided to come anyway. It was better than staying home all alone. It gets so… lonely.' She ran her hand up her thigh and gave Ron a smouldering stare as she said it. Then she broke it off and smiled at Jimmy. 'Are you boys having a good night?'

'We are now,' Jimmy replied with a chuckle. 'Where's your accent from?'

'Russia. I moved over here a few years ago. Less cold,' she replied with a light laugh.

'Oh yeah?' Jimmy said. The men exchanged glances. 'So tell us, Alexa, what do you girls do over there to keep warm at night, when it's so cold?'

Sadie let a slow smile spread across her face. 'Oh, we do lots of things. But never alone. It's always best to share body heat, when it gets really bad.'

'Perhaps you could show us how that's done, Alexa,' Ron replied. He was practically drooling as he spoke.

Sadie pretended to consider it. 'Well, I guess I don't have the company I was expecting to have tonight. And two is always better than one… OK. I will show you how the Russians do things. But to start, you must drink vodka, not champagne. I shall go and get it.' She stood up to go and order the shots.

'Don't worry about that,' Jimmy said. 'I'll have some brought over. Just—'

'No.' She cut him off and wagged her finger. 'In Russia, it is the women who serve their men. You want Russian, you will get Russian. Sit. I will bring it back.' She winked and walked to a spot halfway down the bar to order the shots.

As soon as they came she glanced back at the men. They were chatting and laughing excitedly, their heads together. She grinned and shook her head. Old men like them were idiots. Checking that no one was paying attention, she slipped the two small tabs out of the waistband of her skirt and dropped them in two of the shots. Picking up a stirrer that had been discarded on the bar top, she quickly mixed them around until the tabs had dissolved. Careful to ensure she knew which one was hers, she carried them back and handed the other two out.

She lifted her glass. 'Cheers. Here is to embracing new cultures,' she said.

'To new cultures,' the two men replied in unison before downing their shots. Sadie allowed herself a smug smile. It was going to be a very funny night.

Twenty minutes later, Sadie and the two men were comfortably settled into the upstairs flat. Sadie had stripteased to buy some time and was down to just her underwear and heels. She could see Ron was beginning to feel the effects of the pill, but he was still trying to fight them.

'Now you both get undressed. I want you naked, now,' she ordered in her deepest, sexiest voice. They immediately obliged, ripping off their clothes, not in the slightest bit shy. Jimmy sported a raging hard-on, but Ron was only about halfway there. Sadie guessed the drug had hit his system a lot faster than Jimmy's. Everyone was different. Still, it shouldn't be long before they were both out cold.

The men approached her and Ron started fondling her breasts from behind, whilst Jimmy grabbed her waist and started kissing her. Ignoring his evil-smelling breath, Sadie got into her role and kissed him back, grinding against Ron.

Suddenly she pushed them both away and stepped to the side. 'I want you to lie on the bed. I have a sexy surprise in store for the both of you. Go on, lie down.' She waited whilst they did as she asked.

'You sexy minx, come on – come and play,' Jimmy called.

'Oh, I will. But first, I'm going downstairs to get some ice. Wait here. Don't start without me.' She blew a kiss and shimmied back into her top and skirt.

Leaving the front door to the flat on the latch, she walked downstairs to the doorway that led out to the street just beside the front door to the club. Nathan was waiting just outside, a plastic bag in his hand. She greeted him and stepped out beside him. She lit a cigarette and sucked in the smoke, relaxing as the nicotine hit her system.

'Is that what I think it is?' she asked, pointing towards the bag. He nodded. They exchanged a look and both burst into silent laughter.

'They not out yet?' Nathan asked.

Sadie looked at her watch. 'Getting there but I'd give it five more minutes to be sure.'

'You definitely gave them enough?' he checked.

'Definitely,' she confirmed. 'Gave them the highest dose. They'll be out like babies.'

'Clearly you have little experience with babies,' Nathan replied with a snort. 'Because they don't sleep much at all.'

'Well, I'm glad I don't have any then. I like my sleep,' she replied. Sadie stubbed out the cigarette and flicked it away. 'Come on, let's see how they're doing. Stay behind in the hall when we go in, just till I'm sure.'

They crept back up the stairs to the flat and Sadie closed the front door behind them.

'I'm back, boys, but without the ice, I'm afraid,' she called out as she walked in. 'The bar is really busy—' She trailed off and grinned broadly as she entered the bedroom. Both men were sparked out naked on the king-size bed. She poked her head back out to the hallway. 'Come, they're asleep.'

Nathan came in and got straight to work. Stripping off his clothes, he handed the digital camera to Sadie. She laughed as he dropped his boxers and saw that he had an erection.

'Really? This excites you that much?' She snorted.

'Don't be silly,' he replied. 'I took Viagra earlier. I wanted the pictures to look as real as possible. I'll deal with this' – he pointed down – 'afterwards.'

He approached the bed and prodded Ron with his finger. The man grunted slightly but didn't move or wake. With a grin, Nathan pushed him over onto his front. Jumping in between the other man's legs, he positioned himself so that it looked as though they were doing the deed. Sadie snapped away. After several fake positions, they repeated the process with Jimmy.

'Go on,' Nathan said, 'pass me it.'

Sadie giggled and pulled the Russian hat out of the bag. 'I can't believe you brought this – you crack me up!'

Nathan put it on and posed with the men a few more times before he threw it back. 'OK,' he said, 'now for the finale.'

With a little help from Sadie, Nathan positioned himself in the middle of the two men, with Ron spooning him and Jimmy's hand placed on his face as though in affection. Nathan closed his eyes and posed as though he was asleep with them. As soon as Sadie got the last shot, he stood up to put his clothes back on.

'I can't wait till they see these pictures. I wish I could be a fly on the wall, see their faces,' he said, his tone full of glee. 'But I think it's safe to say you and I should stay well away from this neck of the woods for a while.' He shrugged his top back on and wrapped his arm around Sadie's shoulders as they walked back out of the flat.

'Who likes it around here anyway?' she answered, wrapping her arm around his waist. 'I love our little corner of Soho. Fuck everywhere else.'

'Me too, my darling,' Nathan said with a warm smile, 'me too.'

CHAPTER FORTY-FIVE

The door to the bedroom opened and Tanya flew forward, ready to scratch their kidnapper's eyes out, but she stopped short and started backing up as she caught sight of the gun in his hand.

'You fucking arsehole,' she spat as he pointed it at her.

'Nice to see you too, Tanya. Feisty as your welcome has been,' he replied, his expression amused. 'I thought I might need this with you around. Now let's just get some things straight.' He lowered the gun now that Tanya was sitting back beside Anna. 'You are my guest for the foreseeable future. You're here to help Anna with her pregnancy.' He smirked at Anna as he said this. 'Because apparently she can't cope alone. I'm armed, so is my associate Diego and neither of us will hesitate to shoot you if you play up. We are in the middle of nowhere, there are no other people or buildings for miles, so an escape attempt would be pointless.'

He reeled all of this off as if he were relaying a shopping list. 'You will be allowed downstairs for a short time each day, so long as you cause no trouble. If there are any problems you'll be confined to this room and life can be made much less comfortable. Are we clear?' He paused and waited for an answer.

'Crystal,' Tanya growled through gritted teeth.

'Good,' he said with a nod. 'In that case, feel free to make your way downstairs for lunch.' He moved aside and waited until the two women filed out past him. Tanya shot him a scathing look as she went by, but she said nothing more.

'Oh, one more thing,' he said. They paused. His dark eyes glinted coldly. 'In case you were still thinking about trying to leave, you should know that I've buried several pressure-triggered bombs in the ground around the house. If you did somehow get through the doors and past our guns, there is a high chance of you being blown to smithereens. So I really wouldn't risk it if I were you, girls.'

Tanya let out a slow breath and narrowed her eyes at him hatefully. Anna felt her heart sink. This was unexpected. How were they supposed to get away now? She swallowed her disappointment and looked away.

Pushing past him, Anna held her tongue and led Tanya down to the big, cosy kitchen where Izobel was laying out their lunch on the table. Tanya paused just inside the door as she caught sight of the girl, anger colouring her face.

'Tan, come on, you know she had no choice.' Anna laid her hand on Tanya's arm. She had told Tanya all about Izobel and Diego's predicament, but naturally Tanya still harboured some resentment.

There was a tense few seconds as Tanya warred with herself. Izobel cast her eyes down and focused on straightening the cutlery. Eventually Tanya took a deep breath and walked forward to take her seat at the table.

Anna breathed a sigh of relief. There was no point Tanya arguing with Izobel, even though she did understand how her friend felt. She had felt the same when she had first arrived, but it wouldn't get them anywhere now.

'This looks lovely, Izobel, thanks,' Anna said, sitting down opposite Tanya.

'It's wild mushroom stroganoff with jasmine rice. I used to cook it for my mother a lot, back home. It was one of her favourites.' Izobel shot a wary look at Tanya.

Tanya took a bite and raised her eyebrows in surprise. 'Wow, that's really good,' she said.

'Thank you,' Izobel replied softly. She turned back to the sink and continued washing up the pans.

'Leave that,' Tanya called out to her. 'We can wash up after we've eaten. It's the least we can do, after you've done all the cooking.'

Anna shot her a suspicious look. Although she was glad Tanya had chosen to ignore Izobel's involvement in her abduction for the sake of peace, she hadn't actually expected her to be friendly. She was up to something.

'Oh, well… thank you.' Izobel reluctantly put the pan down. She would rather have done the washing up herself; it kept her busy. But she didn't want to offend Tanya when she had reached out with such a kind offer.

'No problem at all,' Tanya replied, a determined glint in her eye. Anna caught the look and pursed her lips. No doubt she would find out what Tanya was up to soon enough.

They ate the rest of their lunch in silence and then Tanya and Anna cleared away the dirty crockery. Anna filled the sink up with hot water and soap and began cleaning. Tanya picked up the towel and dried each item as Anna passed it to her, before finding the correct place to put things away.

Izobel hovered awkwardly for a few minutes before excusing herself to the toilet. 'But just to remind you,' she added hesitantly, 'the door is locked, OK? I won't be long.' She disappeared, after shooting them one last worried look.

'What's all this about?' Anna whispered, holding up the plate she'd been cleaning. 'Not that I mind, but I know you. This isn't just a ploy to be nice.'

Tanya checked behind her, to make sure Izobel was gone. Seeing that they were alone, she reached into her bra and pulled out a fork. She showed Anna and then stowed it back safely out of sight.

'We need this to jimmy the lock in the bedroom. I didn't want her to notice it was gone. I've got a plan,' Tanya said excitedly. 'First thing in the morning, we get the bedroom door open and come down here. He can't be watching all the time – we have to hope he's still asleep or getting ready for the day. If he catches us, then… well, the plan failed. But it's worth trying and there's no point waiting.'

'But what then?' Anna asked.

'Then we come down here, jimmy the kitchen door the same way we did the bedroom and get outside. You see that big barn over there.' Tanya pointed out the kitchen window. 'I'd bet my last Rolo that there's a vehicle of some kind in there. There are track marks worn into the ground – look – right up to it.'

'But what about the bombs? Tanya, I've seen what they've done to soldiers, they're seriously bad news,' Anna whispered seriously.

Worry and fear flashed across Tanya's face. 'I know, but what else can we do?'

'We can't risk it, we have to stay put,' Anna replied, glancing at the door. Izobel could return at any second. 'Freddie will find us.'

'Anna.' Tanya gripped her arm. 'We can't stay here. Freddie isn't going to find us here – we're in the middle of nowhere. He has all his men and every pig on his payroll working on this and they haven't even established that you're out of London.' She stared out of the window. 'We're not safe in here with him, Anna. Of the two evils, I'd rather take the risk. He's buried the bombs to deter us from leaving, I get that. But they won't be completely hidden. If we get out there and we're careful we can see where the ground has been disturbed and steer clear.' Looking back at Anna, determination coloured her face. 'We can do this, Anna. We can get out of here. We have to try. For the baby, as well as ourselves.'

Anna felt her heart quicken with hope. Could they do it? Could they pull this off and get out of here alive?

'You really think we can do this?' she whispered.

'Yes. We're getting out of here, Anna,' Tanya said firmly. 'We are *not* giving in and losing ourselves to something like this. Not us. Not ever.'

CHAPTER FORTY-SIX

James waited in the kitchen with two glasses of wine in hand as Paul came through the door.

'Hello, love. Good day so far?' He handed the wine to Paul and chinked the glasses together.

Paul laughed. 'Yeah, not bad. What's the occasion?' He motioned towards the wine before sipping it appreciatively. 'Mm, this is nice.'

'I have a surprise for you.' With a wicked grin, James picked up a brown A4 envelope and handed it to Paul.

With a smile and a slight frown, Paul opened it and pulled out the crisp, freshly printed pictures. As he registered what he was looking at, he nearly spat out his wine. Spluttering, he put the glass down and flicked through the pile, his eyes wide.

'What the…' He stared at James. 'What are these? I don't understand.'

James squeezed his arm and winked. 'I heard the things they said to you… I heard them treat you as though you were shit on their shoe, just because you're not like them, and it made me so angry that I decided to get my own back. No one treats my boyfriend like that and gets away with it. Homophobic arseholes,' he added. 'So I called some old friends.' James pushed his dark hair back off his forehead.

'I can see that.' Paul guffawed. 'Nathan looks as though he's having a lot of fun here. Did he, er…?' Paul lifted an eyebrow in question.

'Oh, God, no.' James shook his head. 'No, this is all posed. Nothing actually happened. But of course' – he giggled – 'they don't know that.'

Paul threw his head back and laughed long and hard. 'Oh, James. You jammy dodger, this is pure evil,' he said, tears of amusement running from his eyes. 'You never cease to surprise me.' He shook his head and smiled at the other man fondly. 'Christ… I may just have to bring you into the family business yet. Your skills are wasted in your job.'

'Well, now that's an interesting thought and one we should definitely discuss. But for now, here's what I think you should do…'

Later that night, Paul marched through club Roar. He signalled to the bouncer to make way for him as he approached the VIP area, and the rope was swiftly pulled back. He stepped up and greeted the two old faces with a wide grin.

'Hello, Ron, Jimmy. Having a good night?' He could see they were, with two young blondes sat beside them holding glasses of champagne.

The two men looked furious as he interrupted their evening.

'What the fuck do you think you're doing here?' Ron shouted, with a hateful expression. 'I told you once, boy, your kind ain't—'

'Welcome,' Paul finished, 'yeah, I heard that. Except, then I was given these, you see.' He held up the brown envelope with the pictures in. 'So, I figured that from now on, you'll be treating me with a damn sight more respect than you have been lately.'

'What are you chatting about?' Jimmy asked. 'Gimme that.' He grabbed at the envelope and Paul handed it over. He folded his hands in front of him and waited.

Jimmy pulled the pictures out without caution and the girl next to him caught sight of the first one. She squealed and stood up. The other blonde looked over and gasped. She joined her friend and the two of them ran off back into the crowded club, away from their generous hosts.

Jimmy's face paled and his jaw bobbed up and down as he tried to find the words to say. Ron slid over to look and his eyes bulged so wide that Paul thought they might pop out of his head.

'Wh-what the fuck is this?' Ron cried. He grabbed the photos from Jimmy and they went through the pile. Jimmy gasped as he reached the one that looked as though he was going at it full throttle with the young man. His hands began to shake.

'No, no we didn't. That didn't happen.' He turned to Ron, his expression scared. 'These are fakes, aren't they?'

Ron was silent for a moment, staring at one of the photos where Nathan was wearing the Russian hat. He pointed at it. 'Remember Alexa? She was Russian, weren't she? I… I don't remember much, we'd been on the vodka…'

Jimmy wailed and held his head as he realised he couldn't remember the night either. 'Oh God,' he cried. 'No, fuck no. I didn't do that.' He shook his head from side to side as if trying to shake the image out.

'Well, it seems that you did. Both of you,' Paul replied, enjoying their reactions.

They looked at each other and then up to Paul fearfully. Ron swallowed hard. 'Who knows about these?'

'Oh, no one else at the moment. I mean, they were sent anonymously, so obviously whoever took the photos knows too. But I haven't shown anyone – yet.' He let the last word hang as a threat.

Ron wiped the beads of sweat that were forming off his brow. 'No one can know about these. These need to be destroyed. Are there more copies?'

'Yes, another set in my safe. I think I'll keep hold of them, just in case I ever need them,' Paul replied with a smug smile.

Jimmy groaned and closed his eyes. Ron looked down. They knew when they'd been beaten.

'What do you want?' Ron asked flatly.

'To be shown the level of respect I should be,' Paul answered. 'Who I choose to be with is nothing to do with you, nor does it affect my ability to do business. Which you already know. So, I don't ever expect to have to deal with being spoken to the way I have been lately again. Got it?'

'Of course,' Ron replied grudgingly. 'And we appreciate in return that this goes no further then, yeah?' he asked, his face anxious.

'Of course,' Paul said. 'That's what friends do for each other, right?'

'Right,' muttered the two men. Jimmy was still staring at one of the pictures in shock. Paul was pretty sure he was about to cry.

'Perfect. Well, you guys have a good night. I'd best be off. The business won't run itself.' Paul strode back out the way he came with a spring in his step and a smile of triumph on his face. That had felt good. It was true what they said: karma always caught up with you. Even if there had been a certain young man lending it a hand this time.

CHAPTER FORTY-SEVEN

The weak dawn light made its way through the window and onto the sleeping women. Tanya was curled up against Anna's back and both were fully dressed under the covers. The night before, Tanya had changed into a pair of Anna's leggings and a loose top, as they were more practical than her skirt and shirt. They wore thick socks but neither of them had access to shoes. The socks would have to do.

As she woke, Anna pulled herself into a ball, holding her stomach. Tanya awoke too, sensing the movement next to her. She looked at Anna's face and saw that it was scrunched up in pain.

'Hey, are you OK?' she whispered. 'What's up?'

'I'm not sure. It feels… achey down there. I think something's wrong.' She sat up and gave Tanya a worried look.

Tanya breathed out heavily. 'OK. Well, I'm sure it's nothing but let's just focus on getting out of here and then the first thing we'll do is head for a hospital, get you checked out.' *If we make it,* she added silently.

'Yeah, OK.' Anna nodded. She glanced up at the camera and then back to Tanya. They wouldn't know if he was watching or not. It was a risk, but as Tanya had said the day before, there was no point waiting. It was now or never.

Slipping the fork out from under the pillow where she'd stashed it the night before, Tanya made her way to the door. She pulled out the one bobby pin that had remained in her hair when she'd woken up in this place and set about using both implements to unlock the door.

Anna hovered behind her, not sure what to do. She kept glancing fearfully at the camera and strained her ears for any noises coming down the hall. There hadn't been any movement yet, so that was a good sign. She ran her hands through her thick hair and it gave her a sudden idea. She grabbed the hairbrush off the dressing table and weighed it up in her hand. It wasn't much of a weapon but it was better than having nothing.

There was a click and Tanya pulled her makeshift tools back out. She tried the handle and sure enough, the door swung open.

'Come on,' she whispered. 'We don't have much time.'

They crept through the hallway and down the stairs, trying to stay as silent as possible. The floorboards creaked loudly in some places and Anna cringed, but still no one came rushing out. She figured that if they did hear the noises, they probably all assumed that it was each other in the hallway. They had no reason to suspect it was the two women they were keeping locked away.

They made it to the kitchen and Tanya looked around. 'Wait, I need something too, just in case.' She walked over to the hearth and was about to pick up a large, cast-iron pan, when Izobel walked into the room from the pantry. She was carrying a box of eggs and some milk. She stopped dead as her eyes moved from one to the other in shock.

Anna put her finger to her mouth. 'Izobel, please,' she whispered, 'don't say anything.'

'You know I can't do that.' She placed the eggs and milk on the table and turned to walk into the hallway. 'I'm sorry, but—'

Izobel's words were cut off as Tanya swung the cast-iron pan and smacked her around the head with it as hard as she could. There was a dull clang as the metal connected with her skull, then a thud as Izobel hit the floor.

Anna gasped and ran over to Izobel. She knelt down and checked her pulse. She gave a sigh of relief when she found it. A large lump was already forming on the side of her head where

Tanya had hit her. Tanya winced and drew air in through her teeth as she saw it.

'Ouch, that's going to hurt when she wakes up.'

Anna gave her a look of disapproval and went to collect one of the cushions from the chair by the fireplace.

'What?' Tanya asked, frowning. 'It was her or us, and I wasn't about to let it be us. She'll be fine and she'll have a genuine excuse when he finds us gone. OK?' She glanced fearfully back towards the dark hallway. Her nerves were beginning to spike. They needed to move.

'I know; you're right,' Anna conceded. She gingerly picked up Izobel's head and laid the cushion under it, so that she'd be more comfortable.

Biting her lip to stop herself hurrying Anna up, Tanya's gaze landed on something interesting. 'On the plus side' – Tanya bent down and picked up the ring of keys that had fallen out of Izobel's cardigan pocket – 'we don't have to waste time picking the next lock. Come on, let's go.'

Tanya unlocked the door and they stepped outside. She paused to lock it behind her. It wouldn't stop them, but it would slow down anyone who was trying to chase them. They both paused and began scanning the ground near them. With a deep breath, Anna took the first step forward. Her heart was pounding. This could be it. At any point all they had to do was take one wrong step, just one lapse in judgement and that was it. They would be dead.

They moved as quickly as they dared, one step at a time. The ground was hard earth, packed down by years of weather and the day-to-day grind of farm life.

Tanya frowned. Wherever she looked there didn't appear to be any recent disturbances. There was no way he could have planted something like that in the ground without digging some of it up, but none of this had been touched.

'It was just a threat,' she whispered to Anna. 'Look, there's nothing here. It was just a ploy to scare us.'

Anna frowned and scanned the ground again, still not sure. This wasn't something they could afford to get wrong. Unable to find anything either, she took a deep breath and nodded. 'OK, but still be careful just in case.'

Holding hands, they began to hurry faster towards the old barn, clearing the wide open space in which they were so exposed. The sharp pebbles on the hard ground hurt their feet, the thick socks proving to be little protection, but they didn't stop. Anna glanced back over her shoulder to see if anyone had seen them, but it didn't appear so. The big old farmhouse stood still and silent in the early morning light.

The space they covered was only around fifty or so metres, but it felt like miles as their hearts hammered in their chests. Any second they could be seen – all it would take was for one of the men to catch a glimpse out of a window, or Izobel to come round and raise the alarm.

Reaching the barn they came to a stop at the side door. There was no point opening the large front until they had the means to escape. Tanya tried the door and swore as she was met with resistance. Fumbling with the keys in her hand she tried one in the lock. It wasn't the right one.

Anna stared back at the house, panic beginning to set in. They were so exposed out here. 'Come on, Tanya,' she urged.

'I'm trying,' Tanya replied. The third key turned in the lock. 'Yes,' she hissed under her breath. She opened the door and the pair bundled through, closing it quickly behind them.

Immediately a rotten stench hit them and Anna held her nose.

'Jesus, what is that?' she wondered aloud.

'They probably kept manure in here or something.' Tanya wrinkled her own nose and coughed. 'Eugh, or maybe an animal died. It's not like he would think about the running of the farm,' she added. 'God, it's really bad.'

'Tanya, look.' As their eyes adjusted to the dark, Anna saw that there was indeed a car, underneath a dust cover. 'Quick, grab the other side,' she said, her tone excited.

Tanya ran round and grabbed the heavy sheet and between them they yanked it off. Underneath was an old Corvette. It was so old that it would probably pass as antique, but neither of them cared. All that mattered was whether it would start.

Anna tried the door but it was locked. 'Keys,' she called out to Tanya. 'Look for keys.'

Tanya turned and began raiding the wall of tools that was behind her. There was a shelf with jars of nails and nuts and bolts, all carefully labelled. She rifled through each of them and in the drawers beneath.

Anna swivelled round and looked for anywhere someone might keep a set of keys. There was a pile of boxes behind the car, which she couldn't see beyond. She went to investigate. Perhaps there was a cabinet or something beyond it. There was, of course, the strong possibility that there were none in here at all, that they were kept in the house, but it was worth checking before they had to break in and hotwire it. She silently hoped Tanya would know how to do that. It wasn't exactly on her list of skills.

Anna peered around the boxes and her heart constricted. She screamed, a loud blood-curdling scream as she saw what was piled up on the floor. She took a step back and covered her mouth with her hands. She shook with horror and panic.

Tanya ran over and gasped as she saw what Anna had found. 'Oh my God. Oh shit.' She held her head in her hands trying to keep calm and not be sick. 'Not an animal then,' she said tightly.

They looked down on the mound of dead bodies. There were four of them in total, piled up one on top of the other. They were badly decomposed; nearly all the soft tissue had gone, leaving just a few patches of dead skin attached to the bones of the skeletons. Anna was pretty sure that the two lying side by side underneath were the elderly owners of the farm, by the look of their clothes. The others she wasn't sure about. One could have been their son, perhaps, but she couldn't tell for sure. He wore a suit and a bright green tie. The last she could tell was a female from the skimpy clothes on her decaying corpse. Anna's eyes filled with hot tears. How could anyone do this? He was a monster.

A hot stab of pain shot through Anna's abdomen and she doubled over with a cry.

'Anna? What is it?' Tanya asked, grabbing hold of her friend.

'The baby,' Anna said. 'I think I'm losing it.'

'Oh God, right, let's get out of here.' Tanya glanced back at the bodies one more time and pulled Anna away. 'Come on, I'll just smash the window. I'll open your door from inside, hang on.'

Tanya left Anna at the passenger door and ran round to the driver's side. She grabbed a wrench off the wall and smashed it through the glass. Throwing the wrench to the floor, she reached her hand through the jagged glass, trying to reach the lock.

The main barn doors flew open and sunlight flooded in. They winced against the sudden intrusion and Tanya shouted out to Anna as she saw who it was. 'Run, Anna, run!'

He bounded forward and grabbed Anna around the waist from behind, holding her to him. She tried to wriggle out of his grasp but he was too strong.

Tanya picked the wrench back up from the floor and with a primal roar started to run towards him, with it held up over her head.

Within a second he pulled out his gun, pointed it straight at her and pulled the trigger.

Time seemed to stand still as the bullet hit Tanya in the stomach. A look of surprise came over her face and she looked down. She dropped the wrench and fell to her knees. Her hands touched the entrance wound and she stared at the blood that quickly covered her fingers. With a last confused look at Anna she slumped backward, still clutching her stomach.

There was a moment of total silence, the world seeming to pause on its axis as Anna's shock gave way to realisation and horror. 'No!' she screamed. 'No!' Her cries were hysterical as she fought like a wildcat, bucking and twisting, scratching anything her nails could reach, trying to get out of his grip and over to her best friend. 'Get off me! Tanya! Tanya!' She screamed out her name over and over as he dragged her back towards the house.

'Get off me! Tanya!' she sobbed. 'How could you? How could you shoot her? You bastard, get off me!' Anna screamed at him as he carried on steadily without response. 'Tanya,' she wailed helplessly, tears blurring her view of the barn.

No matter how she tried to break out of his grasp, she couldn't. He was too strong and her body was weaker than usual.

Guilt washed over her as the memory of Tanya's shocked face burned into her brain. It was her fault. All of this was her fault. If it wasn't for her, Tanya wouldn't even be here. And if it wasn't for her screams when she'd seen the bodies, he wouldn't have heard them. They might have been halfway down the road by now if she hadn't done that. Tanya wouldn't have been shot. Her best friend in the world would not be dead.

'Oh God, Tanya, no!' The pain twisted through her voice as she cried in devastation. 'This can't be happening.' The world spun around her. She closed her eyes and stopped struggling as they reached the house. The life seeped out of her as what had just happened sunk in. Tanya was dead. He had killed her without hesitation, taken the shot and ended her life without a second thought. Just another body for the pile. So many bodies. So many lives cut short by this man.

'You're a monster,' she whispered through her streaming tears, her voice catching in her throat. There was no reply.

Anna felt the warm flood of blood soak through her trousers as she was dragged up the stairs, but she didn't feel the pain. The loss of Tanya was so all-consuming; the grief and the shock so overwhelming that she barely even registered that she was losing her baby.

CHAPTER FORTY-EIGHT

Fraser burst into Freddie's office at Club CoCo. 'I've got an address,' he said, catching his breath. 'That car, I followed it on the traffic cameras. Kept with it for about a mile, but then we lost it. So I ran the plates and got an address. Here.' He showed Freddie the text message that had just pinged up from his team.

Freddie scanned the address. *Heathfield Farm.* The name instantly rang a bell and he closed his eyes for a second, trying to think how he knew it.

'It's not that far from where Anna's phone signal was, Freddie. I think we've cracked it. Who do you want to take? I think we need numbers; we don't know how many of them there are,' Fraser said.

'Anna's phone… Jesus Christ!' The memory of how he knew that name and why that area had seemed so familiar before came flooding back and suddenly he knew exactly who had taken Anna.

'Freddie?' Fraser asked, confused.

'I know that place; everything makes sense now. I know who it is. Fuck.' Freddie looked to the heavens. 'I need to call Paul. Listen, can you find Bill and Sammy for me? I'm going to call round a couple of other people too. Just meet me back here in an hour.'

'On it,' Fraser answered readily. He turned to leave.

'Oh, and Fraser?' Freddie stopped him. 'Whatever weapons you have, you're going to need to bring them.'

*

Tanya opened her eyes and her breathing quickened in fright as she heard the creak of the side door. *Is he coming back to finish me off?* Tears ran down her face as she pressed the dirty rag she had managed to grab down onto her stomach.

She felt so faint. She knew she had lost a lot of blood – too much blood. She tried to hold on to consciousness, to fight to stay alive, but it was so hard. She felt so tired. *Maybe if I just close my eyes for a second…*

Someone turned on a light and she was sharply brought back round. *That's right, someone is here,* she remembered. The light harsh in her eyes after the darkness of the barn for so many hours, she squinted up at it. It was coming closer.

'No, please…' She was shocked at how faint her own voice was. It scared her.

The person walked around the car and came right up to where she lay. She cringed away, expecting the worst. He crouched down and shone the light of his torch onto his face.

It was Tom.

'Oh my God, oh thank God.' Tanya's tears of fear turned to tears of joy. They had found them. They were here to save them. She might just make it out of this alive yet. She grasped Tom to her with her free hand and sobbed into his neck. She had never been so glad to see him in her whole life.

'You came. I'm sorry, I'm so sorry for everything I said,' she croaked.

He pulled her away and stroked her face with his hands. 'It's OK, shh, don't strain yourself,' he said, looking down at the blood-soaked rag in her hands.

'Anna, oh God, she's in the house, Tom,' Tanya said fearfully. 'He has her.'

'I know. Everything is going to be OK,' Tom replied.

'Oh, Tom.' Tanya closed her eyes and breathed him in. Speaking hurt her stomach even more but she carried on anyway. 'I really am so sorry. I take back everything I said. I just want you back home. Can you forgive me?'

'I forgive you, Tanya,' Tom replied. He squeezed her hand and pushed it down off his shoulder. He lifted her head from underneath her chin and looked into her eyes. 'I forgive you for hurting me and throwing me away as if I meant nothing. I forgive you for not seeing what you had in me. I forgive you for everything, in fact. Because it helped me realise that I needed to stop messing around with people who didn't appreciate me and align myself with people who were ready to give me the opportunities I deserved. People who really see me.' Tom stood back up and looked down on her.

'What do you mean?' Tanya didn't understand. Why was he looking at her so coldly? 'Where's Freddie?' she asked, her tone uncertain.

'Ha!' Tom barked a cold laugh. 'Yes, the amazing Freddie Tyler, the kind of man you really want.'

'What are you talking about?' Tanya's face fell. 'That's not true at all.'

'Oh, but it is, isn't it? You want a hard man, one who earns shitloads and has the respect of everyone around. That's far more interesting than the likes of me, right? The stupid twat who works hard every day to make a fraction of what you piss up the wall on handbags each month,' he spat. 'You never had any respect for me. Even chucked me out when it suited you not to have me around anymore. Freddie didn't see what he had in me either,' he added. 'I offered myself up to him, to work with him, do the things that needed to be done. I just wanted a chance to get into this life. But he made me into a complete joke.' Tom's face contorted with anger.

'But that's OK,' he continued. 'Diego approached me a while back. He brought me back here to meet the main man himself, who offered me a very well-paid position with *this* firm. They'd been watching me, you see; couldn't understand why Freddie wouldn't utilise such a good man. One day, after Freddie shot me down yet again, they offered me a deal. I would give them all the information they needed to carry out their plan smoothly, and I got a seat in their firm. And when we take over Central London, there is a *big* piece of the pie waiting for me. The reward for true loyalty, for stepping up to the mark.'

He shifted his weight. 'I was only meant to help push Freddie off his golden throne at the beginning. He told me Anna would be looked after; she wouldn't be hurt. Everything was going to be OK afterwards. New management, sure, a bit of collateral damage but that's the price of progress. You were never meant to be involved.'

He looked her up and down. 'But then you had to go and treat me the same way Freddie did, didn't you? Like some worthless, expendable nobody. You crushed me, Tanya. I really thought we had a shot. But you're all the same.' He narrowed his eyes and held his arms out. 'How d'ya like me now, Tan? Just the sort of man you wanted, right? Well, you're too late. You made your bed and now you'll go down with the rest of them. Maybe you should have treated me better when you had the chance.'

'Tom, you idiot,' Tanya breathed, 'you—'

'Yeah, I'm the idiot, right? Well, I'll be the idiot in this life whilst you can be the clever bitch in the afterlife, yeah? Well done for throwing away the best man you were ever likely to get, Tanya. You brought this on yourself.'

Giving her one last look of hatred, Tom turned and left the barn.

Tanya began to shake with shock at Tom's words and the tears fell even faster. She couldn't believe it. He had betrayed them all. She'd trusted him. Despite their personal problems she'd still thought he was a good person. But all along he had just been pushing them right into the lion's den, sacrificing them to the enemy to fulfil his own agenda. How could he do this to her? To all of them? She felt sick.

As the barn fell back into darkness, so did Tanya's last hope.

'I'm so sorry, Anna. I'm so, so sorry,' she murmured through her sobs as she lay back and prepared to meet her end.

*

Two cars drove in convoy out of London and towards the rural area where the farm was located. The light was fading into the evening. Freddie knew it would be dark soon. He was glad of this. It would give them some extra cover on their approach.

In the car behind, Fraser drove Bill and Seamus, who was now out of hospital. The poison had not been a strong one. It had been easily treated and he'd released himself from hospital the following day against the doctor's wishes. He was still weak but had insisted he was well enough for work, so Freddie had brought him along for the ride. They needed all the help they could get at this point, even if Seamus was just used as the lookout.

Freddie drove the car in front, with Paul and Sammy. He had tried to contact Tom but hadn't managed to get hold of him. He didn't even know Tanya was missing. Freddie guessed he was still hurting from Tanya's rejection, but even so, he was his boss. He should be able to get hold of him.

'I still can't believe it's him, Fred. There has to be a mistake,' Paul said, shaking his head. 'He wouldn't do that to us.'

'He wouldn't do that to *you*,' Freddie corrected. 'But he wouldn't have any qualms doing this to me.'

Paul shook his head. He couldn't wrap his head around what Freddie was telling him.

'We don't know for sure it's him,' he replied.

'It's him, Paul.' Freddie's voice was ruefully confident. 'And he don't work the same way we do. He's a psychopath. And we're the enemy. It's that black and white in his mind.'

There was a long silence before Paul asked his next question. 'What are we supposed to do if it comes down to gunfire?'

There was another silence as Freddie warred with himself.

'If it comes to that, we shoot to kill. He has my family in there and nothing is more important than that now.' Family meant everything to him and sometimes that meant difficult decisions had to be made to protect them.

Paul nodded, his expression heavy. He was loyal to his big brother over anyone else in the world. He would always do what needed to be done, even when he didn't like it. Because that's what true loyalty meant.

Freddie pressed his foot down harder on the accelerator and pushed forward down the dark road. There was no going back anymore.

CHAPTER FORTY-NINE

Anna slumped down against the door she'd been banging on, her cheeks streaked with the tears that wouldn't stop falling. She covered her face with her hand, crying bitterly into them. 'Tanya…' she wailed softly, but still nobody came.

The agonising spasms started up in her abdomen again and she cried out, grasping her stomach. A fresh wave of blood flooded out around her, where she sat. She moved to the bathroom and tried to clean herself up. She had been miscarrying for hours but still it hadn't stopped. She closed her eyes and prayed that it would end soon.

She had never felt so much grief. The emotional pain engulfed her like a tidal wave. Not only had she watched the monster who was holding her captive murder her best friend, but now she was losing her precious baby – hers and Freddie's perfect creation. All the plans, all those exciting future moments that she had thought they might have together as a family, all of them were gone. They would never happen. The life that she had been growing inside of her had been snuffed out and now her body was rejecting it. And Freddie had never even known. She felt overwhelmingly guilty for all the negative thoughts she'd had when she'd first found out she was pregnant. Maybe it was her fault. Perhaps this was karma for being so ungrateful.

Anna's mind kept jumping from one to the other, the baby to Tanya. She thought back over all the memories she and Tanya had shared. The night she first met her, when Tanya had been abandoned in a petrol station and she'd caught sight of her shouting expletives at a pair of fading taillights. She'd given Anna a bed for the night, no questions asked, at a time when she had nothing.

Fresh tears washed down her face. Tanya had been the first real friend she'd found in this city. And she'd become the best, very quickly. She was like a sister, and now she was gone, shot by a psycho in some barn in the middle of nowhere.

Walking back through to the bedroom, Anna gingerly changed her leggings and laid herself down on the bed. With all the stress and the blood loss, she was feeling light-headed. She just needed to close her eyes and get some rest. But rest didn't come easy and instead she lay with all her memories continuing to play out in her head.

She must have fallen asleep, because the next thing she knew he had entered the room and was shaking her awake. She screamed and tried to back away, but he clamped a hand over her mouth.

'Shhh – be quiet,' he ordered. She obeyed, too exhausted and grief-stricken to do anything else. He slowly removed his hand. 'Get up,' he ordered.

Anna stood, holding her aching stomach. For the first time since she had been here, he sounded stressed. There was a note of panic in his tone.

'Walk. Go,' he barked, pushing her towards the hallway.

Anna felt more blood leave her body and the ache intensified into deep pain. 'I can't. Wait,' she muttered through gritted teeth as she braced herself against it.

'Move,' he yelled, grabbing her around the waist and pushing her along in front of him.

'Argh!' Anna cried out, slumping back into him as another wave of agony took hold. 'Where are we going?' she asked.

'To another room. What's wrong with you?' he asked, irritated. They had moved into the light of the hallway. He turned her round and looked down to see why his leg felt wet. He touched his dark trousers and his fingers turned red with blood. His eyes moved to Anna and he realised what was happening.

'Oh,' he said. 'Well, it's for the best,' he reasoned calmly. 'We can start anew with no ties to the past.'

'Oh my God,' Anna cried. 'What the *fuck* are you talking about? In what world do you think I could ever see you as anything but the monster you are?' The anger she had held inside bubbled to the fore. His callous words on top of everything that had already happened triggered a snap in her brain. 'You *murdered* my best friend. The stress you've put me under has killed my *child.* You stand against *everything* that I care about and you think I won't turn on you the second I get a chance?' She barked a bitter, high-pitched laugh. 'Because I will. If I live through this, even if you win your fucked-up crusade, I will kill you the second I get a chance. The second you turn your back, I'll be ready and I will *fucking* kill you.'

Anna bent over in pain as she came to the end of her rant. She didn't care anymore. Nothing mattered except for the burning hate running through her veins. If she achieved nothing else she would put an end to the psycho who had taken so much from her and she no longer cared if she burned in the fires of hell for it.

His eyes glinted with cold amusement. 'Well, well, well. I didn't think you had it in you, Anna,' he said. 'You've always been such a good girl, such a straight player.' He tilted his head, studying her.

'Even good girls have their limits,' she said, staring back at him with blind hatred.

Diego stepped out of his room behind them, rubbing his eyes. 'What's going on?' he asked.

'Tool up. Someone triggered the motion sensors down the bottom of the lane. I saw two cars coming this way. They'll be here any second,' he replied.

Anna felt a spark of hope. It had to be Freddie. She saw worry flit across his face and a manic smile began to form on her own. She laughed out loud.

'He's here, isn't he?' she asked, hope and wonder colouring her tone. 'Freddie's found you.' She shook her head with glee. 'Everything you've worked for has been for nothing,' she spat, taking a further step towards him.

Anger flashing in his eyes, he grabbed her and turned her round, forcing her further down the hallway. 'Get in there,' he shouted, shoving her into his office. 'I'll be back soon and then we'll finish this business together.' Slamming the door behind her, he locked it from the outside.

Anna tried to open it, but it wouldn't budge. 'Shit,' she cursed. Ignoring the pain in her stomach, she spun around wildly and looked for anything that might help her. The monitors on the desk caught her attention and she sat in the chair to look at them more closely. There were five screens in total. One of them showed her bedroom, empty now. The other four were angled around the outside of the house and down the long, winding lane leading up to it. Her eyes scanned these quickly and she made a noise of excitement as she saw the two cars pulling up just outside.

With renewed hope she looked around for a weapon of any kind. She opened the top drawer of the desk and her eyebrows shot up. There was a handgun in there, the one she had seen him use earlier. He must have forgotten to take it in his haste to move her.

Picking it up she checked the magazine. It was empty. Her heart dropped. Rifling through the rest of the drawer, she paused as a movement on the screen caught her attention. They were here. Her heart skipped a beat and she leaned in closer to watch.

CHAPTER FIFTY

Freddie stopped the car at the front of the old farmhouse and Fraser pulled up nearby. They had turned their lights off a mile away, but even so he was pretty certain that Anna's kidnapper would know they were here by now. The house was in darkness, not a sound to be heard. It didn't fool Freddie one bit.

He indicated to the others to fan out around the house. There were six of them, but he didn't know how many men they were up against. Every one of them was armed with a gun. Freddie wasn't taking any chances.

Keeping the car door between him and the house, he called out. 'I know you're in there. I know it's you. Come out here, now.'

Freddie saw the window open and the gleam of gun metal. He froze momentarily as he caught sight of the naked hatred in the face just beyond it. The pause was all the other man needed and he cocked his gun.

'Freddie!' Fraser yelled. Freddie didn't move. 'Shit.' He started running towards him, closing the short gap between them. The other man took aim and Freddie stepped back, looking around for cover. 'Move,' Fraser yelled, his police training coming to the fore.

He reached Freddie and shoulder-barged him as hard as he could to the ground just as they heard the shot ring out.

Paul cocked his gun and pointed it up at the window, but the shadow disappeared. Freddie swore as he stopped rolling and sat up.

'Fred, you OK?' Paul ran over to his brother.

'Yeah, just,' Freddie replied, checking himself over. 'Bastard,' he seethed, looking up at the empty window. 'That was no warning shot. He was shooting to kill.' His lips formed a hard line as Paul helped him up.

'Thanks for the shove, Fraser.' Freddie turned to the other man gratefully. Fraser was still lying on the ground a couple of feet away. Freddie walked over to help him up. 'Come on, we've got to move. We're sitting ducks out here.'

He paused as Fraser didn't respond.

'Fraser?' He lay on his side, facing away.

Freddie crouched and pulled him onto his back. Fraser's eyes stared up into the sky, unseeing. Blood trickled out of the small bullet wound in his skull. He was dead. The bullet hadn't missed them – he had just taken Freddie's place.

'Shit,' he muttered, closing his eyes and groaning. Paul joined him and let out a long breath as he saw Fraser.

'It's not your fault, Fred.' He knew Freddie would be beating himself up. 'He knew what he was doing. There are always risks in this game. Things just didn't work out this time,' Paul said soberly. He stared down at the dead man's face. At least it had been quick.

Freddie growled in anger. Fraser had been on his payroll for years and although he didn't usually have much respect for two-sided plods, Fraser had always been the exception to the rule. He trusted Fraser and liked the guy. Fraser had always come up trumps and had never been afraid to actually earn his money. Men like that were hard to find. Freddie shook his head and glanced back at the house darkly.

'We need to move.' Freddie looked around at the others' faces. Shock, grim determination, sorrow, but no one's face showed fear. He nodded. They were ready to move forward. 'We're going to make him pay for that,' Freddie vowed. 'No one shoots one of my men and gets away with it.'

'Paul, Bill, you go round the back and do a sweep of that barn. Seamus, Sammy, come with me.'

Paul and Bill slipped off into the darkness and Seamus and Sammy fell into line behind Freddie.

'You sure you're up to this?' Freddie asked Seamus. The boy still looked peaky.

Seamus nodded. 'You already got the bastard that poisoned me. I need *someone* to take my frustrations out on,' he replied. Freddie tilted his head in acceptance.

Taking one last look at Fraser's body, he turned away and moved towards the house. He tried the front door. It was locked. They crept silently around the side to see if they could find another way in.

*

Paul and Bill reached the barn and entered through the side door. The stench from the bodies hit them and each of them knew straight away what it was. They exchanged a knowing look. Turning on the light on his phone, Paul headed straight to the back of the barn – the most logical place to dump them, he figured – beyond the abandoned Corvette with its smashed side window. He made a sound of disgust as the light revealed the four bodies.

'Jesus…' He moved aside so Bill could see. Bill looked down and shook his head.

'He could have at least disposed of them. What a mess. It's not like this place is short on fields; we're surrounded—' A noise made him pause and turn around. 'Did you hear that?' he whispered.

'What?' Paul replied quietly. He cocked his head and listened.

In the silence they could just make out the sound of someone breathing nearby. Their breath came out with a strange rattle, sounding laboured. There was someone in here with them.

Bill signalled for Paul to go down one side, whilst he took the other. They silently crept forward, keeping their guns cocked and their senses alert.

As Paul trod carefully around the junk that was strewn around the barn, the breathing got louder. He was close to whoever it was. He shone his light forward, expecting to be met with a fight, but as he turned past the boot of the old car his mouth opened in surprise at what he found.

'Shit, it's Tanya! Bill, get over here,' he yelled. He dropped to his knees next to Tanya's inert body and pushed her hair out of her face. She was grey and unconscious but still just about breathing. He shone the light down on the rest of her body and grimaced. Tanya was holding an old rag against her stomach. It was drenched in blood. He guessed she had been trying to stem the bleeding. She was leaning up against a stack of sandbags and there were bloody drag marks for a few feet. Paul calculated that she must have pulled herself over before she passed out.

Bill bent down and looked her over. He tapped her face, trying to get her to wake up. 'Hey, Tanya, can you hear me? Tanya?' There was no response.

'We need to get her to a hospital – quickly,' Paul said. 'Help me get her to the car.' He slipped his arm under her back and started to lift her.

'Try not to scrunch her up; it'll make the bleeding worse,' Bill replied as he grabbed her legs. Paul slipped his second arm underneath her as they lifted her from the ground, trying to keep her as flat as possible as they walked.

They moved as fast as they could without jogging Tanya around too much until they reached the cars. Bill glanced up at the dark house. It was eerily silent.

'Take Fraser's car,' Paul whispered, glancing over at the dead man's body. 'He's not going to need it now and you can dump it after. No trace.'

Bill nodded. They gently lifted Tanya into the back seat and laid her down. With a nod, Bill set off and Paul turned back to find Freddie. He marched off towards the back of the house, praying to God that he didn't stumble across Anna next.

*

Freddie, Sammy and Seamus walked through the back door of the property with caution. It was the only door that had been unlocked and they made their way inside down the long hallway. Freddie moved forward, keeping to the front. All his senses were on high alert. He had no idea what to expect. The house was large and rooms went off in every direction.

Suddenly, in front of them a young man came running out with a baseball bat above his head. He ran towards them with a yell and Seamus pushed Freddie out of the way. Without hesitation he aimed at the head and shot him dead. The man dropped the bat and fell backward, blood seeping out onto the floor from the small hole in his forehead.

Seamus blinked and lowered the gun, looking at it in shock. It was the first time he had ever shot at a real person. It was the first time he had killed a man. He looked to Freddie, unsure what to do next. Freddie gripped his arm and nodded at him, his expression silently indicating that he knew how Seamus felt. The first time always felt surreal, no matter how hard you were, and it would be something Seamus would have to come to terms with in his own time.

'No!' There was a high-pitched scream as Izobel launched herself out of the kitchen onto the man's body. 'No, no,' she moaned. She looked up at them with hatred. 'You killed him! He had no choice and you killed him.'

Before anyone could answer, Izobel screamed with hot rage and launched herself down the hallway. There was a glint of metal as the moonlight shone on the carving knife she wielded. Freddie tried to stop her, grabbing her arms and turning her round. There was a struggle as he realised in shock that she was a lot stronger than she looked.

'He had no choice, *we* had no choice, you bastards!' she cried. Freddie tried to restrain her, but Izobel kicked out at his shin and he lost his balance. The pair went down like a pile of bricks, Freddie landing on top of her. He quickly rolled off and braced himself to stop her again, but she didn't move.

'Izobel?' he said. 'Get up. Where's Anna?'

He paused and looked closer, pulling her over onto her back. The carving knife stuck out at an odd angle just below her chest. She had fallen on it in the struggle. Izobel was dead. He blew out heavily and looked up at his companions with a grim expression.

'Fuck,' he breathed.

'You tried to stop her, Fred,' Sammy whispered.

Freddie nodded. It couldn't have been helped. He had only been trying to restrain her, to get some information. He hadn't meant for her to die. So many wasted lives littered their path towards Anna. He had to put an end to this – now.

Freddie stood up and they continued slowly down the hallway, checking each room as they went.

*

He unlocked the door and Anna threw herself at him.

'Easy, Anna,' he said through gritted teeth as he grabbed her arm and steadied himself. He held a knife up to her neck. 'Did you really think I wouldn't come prepared? Now stay still,' he snarled.

He was starting to get worried. Things weren't going as planned. He hadn't intended for Freddie to find out it was him yet, not until he was safely behind bars, out of the way for good. But somehow he had worked it out. *How?* he wondered.

Now it seemed that two of the three people he had working for him had gone and screwed things up. It was down to him and Tom and they had no way of contacting each other. He didn't even know where Tom was right now. But he had one last game up his sleeve, one that he knew Freddie wouldn't be able to get out of. He dragged Anna through the hallway to the top of the stairs and called out.

'Oh, Freddie,' his voice was mocking, a sing-song tone to cover his fear. 'I've got your favourite toy up here. Aren't you going to come and get it? Now, now,' he said as Freddie ran into view. 'Not a step closer or I'll slit her throat right here.'

Freddie stopped and held his hands up, his heart momentarily lifting at the sight of Anna still alive. His eyes flicked over to the man holding her and his gaze burned with anger. The two men stared at each other for a moment, a myriad of dark emotions radiating out from them, through the hallway. He stared back at Freddie with naked hatred and Freddie wondered how on earth it had come to this.

'Michael,' he growled. 'Let her go.'

*

Tom walked into the hallway behind them, breaking the thick tension. Seeing the three men in the hallway he immediately tried to turn and run. He tripped over Izobel's body and sprawled to the floor. Sammy grabbed him and pulled him upright.

'Tom? What are you doing here?' Freddie asked. Tom stayed very quiet, all his earlier bravado disintegrating now that he was faced with Freddie for real.

'Oh, haven't you worked that out yet? Tom works for me,' Michael said. 'How do you think I've been getting my information? He was under your nose this whole time. And the funny thing is, if you had just taken him seriously, his loyalty would have been to you. But you didn't.'

Freddie turned to Tom, shocked and disgusted. 'How could you?' he said.

Tom jutted his jaw out in defiance. 'You treated me like a joke. You all did. Even my bitch of an ex-girlfriend.'

Freddie's eyes flashed at his words. Sammy clamped a hand over Tom's mouth, sick of hearing him speak already.

'That bitch of an ex-girlfriend is worth ten of you, you piece of shit. You don't get to bad-mouth her, and you certainly don't get a chance to do this to anyone else ever again.' Freddie curled his lip in disgust. 'When we get out of here, your life is over.' He turned away.

Sammy relaxed his grip a little as everyone turned their attention back to Michael and Anna. Feeling the slack in his hold and realising Sammy was distracted, Tom swiftly twisted his body around. Sammy's hold broke and Tom ducked before Sammy could grab him again.

'Hey!' Sammy shouted. In one fast movement, Tom turned and punched Sammy in the face. No one had been expecting the move and Sammy fell back against the wall. Tom turned and ran, this time jumping over the bodies in his way.

Sammy recovered and set off after him at lightning speed. Seamus fought the natural urge to join him and help. He knew his boss needed him here. The sound of the two men faded away into the distance.

Freddie pursed his lips. He would deal with Tom later. Right now he needed to get Anna away from his psycho of a brother.

'Let her go, Michael. Now,' he ordered.

'Oh, I don't think so. At least not yet. I want something from you first. A few things, actually,' Michael responded.

'What do you want?' Freddie asked.

'Well…' Michael began to walk Anna down the stairs slowly, the knife still tight against her throat. Her breathing was fast and ragged as adrenaline coursed through her. She looked around, trying to calculate how to get away from him. 'The first thing I want is for you to get out of my way, so Anna and I can go for a little drive.'

'Not going to happen,' Freddie replied firmly.

Michael ignored him. 'Then I want you to call up the local police station and admit to all of your crimes. I want to hear that you've made a full statement and that you'll be relocating at Her Majesty's pleasure for the rest of your miserable life. And then,' Michael said, smiling, 'then I'll bring Anna home, safe and sound. And don't worry.' His dark eyes were eerily blank in the shadowy light. 'Both she and the business will thrive under my management.'

'You're fucking mad!' Freddie exclaimed.

'Oh, no one's challenging that. But in this life you have to embrace a bit of madness if you want to survive.' He cocked his head. 'I'm curious. What gave me away? I wasn't expecting you here just yet.'

'The farm. The car was registered here. I remembered the address,' Freddie replied.

A few years before, Michael had taken Freddie out to the farm to ask the owners if they were interested in selling. He had come across it by chance one day and had taken a liking to it. He'd told Freddie it was the perfect safe house, hidden from general view with lots of barns and no neighbours for miles. Finding a gem like that so close to London was rare; it would have been a good addition to the Tyler portfolio. But the elderly owners had not wanted to sell, even for a price way above the odds. They had a son who they wanted to pass it down to one day. Michael had not taken kindly to this and had brooded over it for days.

When the address came up in Fraser's search, he had known at once that it was Michael. The profiler's words had crept back into his head. *Humans are creatures of habit. Psychopaths are drawn back to places they know and that logically assist their needs.* Michael was a fully fledged psychopath – this much they knew from the last mess they'd had to clean up. Freddie kicked himself for not allowing him to be locked away then. He'd sent him off under a new identity to South America with a new name and passport for a fresh start. He'd thought Michael could start again, that maybe the change would help him get better. But this had just been wishful thinking. This wasn't an illness; this was just who he was. Dark, angry and empty to his very core.

Michael growled and shook his head as though trying to get something out of it. 'No, no, I told them to stay off the cameras. Idiots!' he shouted. 'You have to do everything yourself.' He pressed the knife harder against Anna's throat and a trickle of blood made its way down her neck as the tip pierced her flesh. She whimpered and bit her lip.

'Michael…' Freddie's eyes darted wildly from Anna to his brother and he stepped forward slightly, his hands rising up in the air. 'You don't want to hurt her. She's your family.'

'Pah! Family!' Michael laughed without humour. 'You didn't think much of your *family* the night you faked my death and shipped me off in disgrace, did you? No pride for your family then, was there? Oh no, you let the world think I was dead. No longer a Tyler. Ousted from the family business. Well, it's *my* business too – you don't get to do that.'

'He was saving your life, Michael.' Paul walked into the middle of the open hallway where Freddie and Seamus stood staring up at Michael and Anna on the stairs. Misery was etched on his face as he looked up to his little brother. 'You fucked up. Freddie was just trying to keep you alive. Hargreaves wanted you dead.'

'Then we should have killed him,' Michael yelled, his voice shaking with emotion. 'You should have taken him out like you take out every other threat to the Tylers.'

'He's the Secretary of State for Justice, Michael – you can't just take him out,' Freddie exclaimed. 'And aside from that, you kidnapped and tortured his daughter, an innocent girl who had nothing to do with anything. There are rules in this life that have to be adhered to and you broke them. I did the best I could, gave you a chance to start again.'

'Start again?' Michael narrowed his eyes. 'I went from being a baron of the underworld to some nobody in a country I didn't want to be in. Stop acting like you were being a brother and just admit the truth. You wanted me gone so you could have this all to yourself. And you, Paul' – Michael turned to his other brother – 'you could have stepped in but you didn't. You just blindly follow him like some fucking sheep,' he spat.

Paul shook his head and fought back a wave of grief. He had loved his little brother all his life. Losing him last year had been like losing a limb, but like Freddie he had known it was the best they could do for him in the circumstances. His voice wavered as he replied. 'We wanted you back here more than you can ever know. What we did, we did for you. To find out now that this, all this' – he held his arms out helplessly – 'is you… How *could* you, Michael? How could you do this to us? We're your family.'

'You ain't my family. But this is my business and I'm here to take it back. You're going to live the rest of your days in a fucking cell, whilst I take back what you took from me. And I'll take a little more to boot.' Michael turned to look at Anna and a manic smile crept across his face. He leaned into her hair and took a long, loud sniff, his eyes on Freddie, daring him to protest. 'We've got a bright future ahead of us. Isn't that right— Argh!'

As he reached the last three steps Anna faked a fall, slipping down and back against Michael rather than pulling away against the knife. Her ploy worked and he pulled the knife away for just a second, long enough for her to turn around and pull the gun out of the waistband of her leggings.

She cocked the trigger and pressed it against Michael's forehead at the same time that he grabbed her arm and pressed the knife back to her throat.

*

Tom peered out from the side of the hedge and watched as Sammy raised his hands to his head in despair. He held his breath and tensed his body, ready to run to the next hiding place. He had been moving from spot to spot as silently as he could. It was the one advantage he had, that he knew the site inside out and Sammy didn't. Tom knew he couldn't outrun Sammy and that he had a gun, so he decided to lay low and keep moving until the other man gave up. It looked as though Sammy had reached that point now, as with a slump of the shoulders he marched off back into the house.

Waiting another couple of minutes in case it was just a ruse to flush him out, Tom squinted at the dark doorway, trying to see if Sammy was still there. He didn't appear to be.

As quietly as he could and keeping low to the ground, Tom ran around the back of the house to the stables. Skirting round the side he made his way into the small space between the rear wall and the overgrown boundary fence, then glanced over his shoulder one more time to make sure he was still alone.

He crouched down by a wooden panel in the back wall and pulled up one of the slats. It moved easily and silently. He reached in with his arm and rooted around. After a couple of seconds he made contact with the rough material of the gym bag.

'Bingo,' he whispered. He pulled it out and unzipped it for a quick look. There was still a decent amount of money left in there: Freddie's money that Michael had taken from the bank. The keys for the bike were there too, attached to the ring on the zip. He pulled these off.

Michael didn't know that Tom had seen him sneak behind here a couple of times. He'd decided to check it out and had found the little hidey-hole and the motorbike. It was clearly Michael's getaway should things go wrong, his Plan B. Except he hadn't had time to utilise this, it seemed.

Not one to pass on an opportunity, Tom figured he might as well take it for himself. It wasn't like Michael was going to need it. He shrugged the bag onto his shoulder and pushed the motorbike out from behind the stables. Warily checking that Sammy hadn't come back out, Tom rolled it forward onto the track and mounted the sleek vehicle. He pushed in the keys, twisted them and the bike roared to life.

With one last fearful glance at the house he pushed down on the throttle and set off as fast as he dared on the rocky ground. He shot around the side of the house and straightened up as he set off down the long drive.

He prayed that no one was behind him about to shoot. He crouched down and pressed harder on the accelerator. Beads of sweat formed on his lip. Anxiety pierced his heart and sent it hammering against his chest. He waited for the shot to come, to knock him off his bike, but it never came. He reached the end of the driveway and veered out onto the main road.

He'd done it – he'd got out! Tom celebrated in his head as his heart began to slow back down. His joy was swiftly dampened though as he thought about what this now meant. He was now on the run. He would have no choice but to live in exile. There would be no returning to his life. His home, all his friends, his family… he couldn't go near any of them anymore.

Tom sped down the country roads, a million thoughts running through his head. It was all Freddie and Tanya's fault. If they had just treated him with a little respect, he would never have gone to work for Michael in the first place.

Now what was he going to do? He had to do something to change this situation; he couldn't live like an escaped convict forever. His lips formed a hard line. For now he had his freedom. He had freedom and money and as much time as he needed to come up with a plan to sort this all out. And he *would* sort this out. He refused to lose this time, no matter what it took to win.

His eyes glinted in the dark as a sudden idea hit him. As the smile slowly curled across his face, Tom slowed down and changed course. *The enemy of my enemy is my friend,* he thought darkly. *And it's definitely time to make a new friend.*

*

Michael laughed in Anna's face, a loud, manic laugh, but Anna stayed deadly still. Freddie didn't move, scared he might tip Michael over the edge. 'Oh, you found my gun, did you? Nice try, sweetheart,' he mocked, 'but I don't keep it loaded. First rule of firearm safety.'

'I know you don't. I checked,' Anna replied, her voice shaking slightly.

'So what, you thought I'd just forget and I'd hold my hands up and let you ride off into the sunset?' Michael snorted. 'Not much of a plan.'

'No, that wouldn't be much of a plan, I agree. Which is why I searched until I found the bullets. Third drawer down in the dresser, opposite the desk,' Anna said, her voice growing stronger. She pushed the gun harder into Michael's head and he blinked, hesitating. 'My plan was a little different. You see, I probably would have just walked away, left you to the police to rot in some mental asylum, but we're beyond that now. You finally pushed me over the edge this morning when you shot my best friend and caused me to miscarry my child. Mine and Freddie's. Our blood,' she shouted.

'Oh my God…' Freddie gasped, looking down at the blood around Anna's feet for the first time. Fury and pain filled his face and he started forward. 'You son of a bitch!'

'Not another step,' Michael growled, tightening his hold on Anna's arm.

Freddie stopped and gave a roar of frustration. He looked up at the two people in front of him and for a minute the crazed madman holding Anna at knifepoint transformed into the happy little boy Freddie had known and loved. An image of Michael at six years of age flashed into his head. He was laughing and running round the garden, innocence and happiness radiating from his smile. A wasp stung his hand and he ran to Freddie, crying.

It's OK, mate. Come here – let me take a look. Freddie had sucked out the sting and wiped the tears from his eyes. *Such a brave boy. Do you want an ice cream?*

Yes, please, Freddie! You're the best!

The little voice echoed off back into the dark corner of his most treasured memories. He felt his heart die a little as he realised that the man in front of him now was no longer the boy he'd helped his mother raise. He wasn't even the man Freddie had loved a year ago. He was nothing but a monster, wearing his brother's skin. Because the brother he had known and loved would never have done any of this.

'You broke into our home, you stole from us and tried to set your own brother up with the police. You kidnapped me and shot my best friend. You've killed our baby,' Anna's voice broke, 'spilt our blood without a second thought. Now I want nothing more than to return the favour,' she said with naked hatred in her eyes. 'But that's not my call to make.' She tilted her head towards Freddie but didn't take her eyes off Michael. 'It has to be yours, Freddie.'

Freddie took a deep breath and looked at Paul. He could see the grief on his brother's face but as he asked the silent question, Paul nodded his agreement. They both knew this could only end one way now. No matter how they felt, Michael had crossed too many lines for even blood to save him.

'Finish him,' Freddie said, his voice ragged, but resolute. 'Pull the fucking trigger.'

'You'd kill your own brother, Freddie? You couldn't manage it last time, could you? No, you know she hasn't got it in her,' Michael taunted. 'She's no killer. She's not built like you and me.' He laughed.

Anna narrowed her eyes, coldly 'Some women burn in the fire, Michael, and some women are born from it.' She saw fear in his eyes as he suddenly realised that she did have it in her. He opened his mouth to try and stop her but he was too late.

The sound of the gunshot reverberated around the house and Michael's body crumpled to the ground, lifeless.

'Anna,' Freddie cried out as she fell to the floor. He ran over and grasped at her neck, terrified that Michael might have still managed to slice it. He nearly cried in relief when he found it still intact. 'Thank God.' He held her shaking body to him as she wept in shock and relief. Sammy and Seamus quickly ran upstairs past Michael's body to check that there was nobody else in the house.

'Freddie, the baby…' Anna's face crumpled as she tried to tell him.

'I know. It's OK…' He looked down and felt anguish spear his heart. He'd wanted this baby from the second Tanya had told him. But it wasn't meant to be. 'It's going to be OK,' he soothed.

'It's not – the baby's gone,' she replied, her cries bitter.

'I know.' He held her, knowing that nothing he could say would make it better. 'Listen, we need to get you to a hospital. Come on, can you walk?'

'Yes,' she replied, letting him help her up. She stared down at what was left of Michael. 'I'm so sorry, Freddie…'

'It was the only way,' Freddie admitted. He swallowed down the grief that threatened to spill over. Right now he had to look after Anna. He would mourn Michael later. 'We'll deal with all this together, don't worry.'

Anna grabbed Freddie's hand as he looped his arm around her waist and they walked slowly out to the car.

EPILOGUE

Anna walked through the hospital hallway holding a bunch of pretty peach roses. They were Tanya's favourite.

Tanya had been in a bad way when Bill had dropped her off at the hospital and although she had been stabilised, she was still in a coma. The doctors had said there was a fifty-fifty chance she would wake from it and if she did there was a chance she would have to learn to use some of her motor functions all over again. Anna vowed to be with her every day until she came back to them again. So far it had been three weeks and there was still no sign of her coming round. No one dared to suggest to Anna that Tanya might not wake up. It wasn't something she was prepared to hear.

After a brief hospital stay to make sure no further damage had come of her miscarriage, Anna was home and back to looking after the businesses – although with much more help from Carl. He had insisted on taking on more responsibility after watching Tanya drive herself into the ground trying to run things without Anna.

Placing the wilted flowers that had adorned the vase before in the bin, Anna arranged the new ones and filled it up with fresh water. She placed it on the table beside Tanya and sat in the chair next to it. She picked up her friend's limp hand and held it between both of her own. Reaching up she pushed a loose strand of Tanya's thick wavy hair off her peaceful pale face.

Anna swallowed. 'Carl's got some new cocktails for you to try.' She tried to lift her voice to sound positive, but it sounded forced even to her own ears. 'He says I'm no good as a taster as I only like certain things, whereas you' – she forced a laugh – 'well, we all know you'll drink anything.'

The slow constant beeps of the heart monitor filled the silence as Anna continued to squeeze Tanya's hand.

'And you know, Drew has been asking about you. He's been quite helpful, actually, in assisting with the comedy club. You know, when he's not doing his acts.'

Anna stared at the tubes that seemed to run in and out of her friend at every possible point and tears filled her eyes.

'Come on, Tanya. I need you to wake up. I need you here with me. Please.' She laid her head down on her friend's chest and cried.

*

After getting the girls the medical care they needed, Freddie and his men had gone back to the farm and spent some time arranging the fresh bodies into a position that looked as though they'd had an internal disagreement and all killed each other. They were careful with Fraser's body, to show that he had been trying to help, the hero of the hour. It may have looked suspicious to a trained eye, but they left it with no trace that any of the rest of them had been there.

It had hit the news a couple of days later after Freddie had given the police an anonymous tip-off. Michael had been reported as Steven Munroe rather than Michael Tyler, after the police found his passport. They had no reason to suspect it was a fake. Freddie was glad, as they had decided as a family to keep the truth from Mollie and allow her to carry on thinking he was living a good life in South America. There was no point hurting her any more than was necessary.

Tom had not been seen since he had escaped from the farmhouse. Freddie had sent out searches but so far he hadn't come up on any radar. He was certain that it would only be a matter of time though and when Tom was found, he was going to be made to pay for what he'd done.

Freddie sat at his desk in Club CoCo and stared sadly at the picture of himself with his two brothers when they were younger. Even though there had been no other way, Michael's death would always weigh heavily on his heart.

There was a brief knock and the door opened. He slipped the photo away into the top drawer of his desk. Paul walked in and sat down opposite Freddie with a tired half-smile.

'Alright, mate?' Freddie greeted his brother fondly.

'Yeah, I'm OK. Just got back from seeing Sammy.' He rubbed the bridge of his nose. 'We may have a problem.'

'What sort of problem?' Freddie asked with a frown.

'Well, apparently one of his contacts has called to give us a heads-up. The Five Families want to know what happened to Frank Gambino. All they know so far is that he came to London, met with a few people – ourselves included – and then he disappeared. Joe Luciano is coming over with a bunch of his men. They want answers and apparently they're starting with us.'

Freddie took a long deep breath. 'Well, let's get to work then brother. There's a lot to be done.'

A LETTER FROM EMMA

Dear Readers,

Thank you so much for reading my book, whether this is the first one you've picked up or whether you've joined me through the Tyler series from the beginning.

I want to say a huge thank you for choosing to read my book. If you did enjoy it and want to keep in touch, you can sign up to hear about my next book. Your email address will never be shared and you can unsubscribe at any time:

www.bookouture.com/emma-tallon

This series has been a real journey for me, both professionally and personally. When I began the first book, *Runaway Girl*, I had no idea I would ever come to actually have it published. It was just a way for me to vent about some things that had been going on in my personal life at the time. When that moved on into a series and I was able to develop the characters I had created, it opened up a whole new exciting world of possibilities.

Watching Anna, Freddie and Tanya evolve under my fingertips has been like watching real people. Over the three books so far, they've taken on huge personalities of their own. Sometimes even I don't know what they're going to do or come out with next! I feel like the struggles they face in *Boss Girl* have really drawn out deeper parts of their personalities that are very raw and real. The simultaneous weakness and strength that Tanya displays throughout this book is something I have particularly enjoyed uncovering. I've had a great number of you contact me in different ways over the last two books to tell me she's your favourite character and I can really see why.

I'm looking forward to developing this world and these amazing, colourful, flawed characters even further in book four, so watch this space! To keep up with all the updates on the series, please follow my author page here – *www.facebook.com/emmatallonofficial* – and if you could spare the time, I would be so grateful for your review.

As an author who spends months and months writing these books and creating every scene with loving and critical care, it means so much to see what readers think and feel about the story; who you hated, who you loved, what you want to see more of. I read every comment, every review and every message, so please keep them coming! Reading your comments makes all my hard work worthwhile.

Thanks again for all your support. None of this would be possible without you.

Best wishes,
Emma X

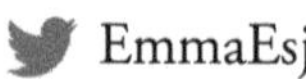

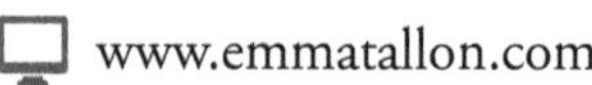

ACKNOWLEDGEMENTS

I just want to say a huge thank you to my amazing editor, Helen, who I'm sure I've driven to drink on many occasions over the course of our edits. She's truly fantastic at what she does and without her support and dedication these books wouldn't be what they are today.

My next big thanks goes to all my incredible author friends who are always there to offer support, guidance, a shoulder to lean on or a joke to brighten my day. The Bookouture lounge, where most of you reside, keeps me sane and I am so glad to have you guys in my life.

In particular, I want to thank Casey Kelleher, Angela Marsons and Dreda Say Mitchell for all of your incredible encouragement and your friendship. I value that more than you know and it spurs me on even through the toughest of days. Thank you. So much. You are true Boss Girls.

And lastly, a big thank you to my readers. I couldn't do this without you and your support is priceless. So, here's to you! Keep smiling and keep reading.

Lightning Source UK Ltd.
Milton Keynes UK
UKHW020755130219
337246UK00010B/264/P